The Service of Clouds

The Service of Clouds

DELIA FALCONER

FARRAR   STRAUS   GIROUX

NEW YORK

Farrar, Straus and Giroux
19 Union Square West, New York 10003

Copyright © 1997 by Delia Falconer
All rights reserved
Distributed in Canada by Douglas & McIntyre Ltd.
Printed in the United States of America
Library of Congress catalog card number 98-71019
First published in Australia in 1997 by Picador /
Pan Macmillan Australia, Sydney
First Farrar, Straus and Giroux edition, 1998

For my mother and father,
and Richard Harling.

'What causes this blueness, the depth and intensity of which is often quite remarkable? In 1955 the Town Clerk of the City of the Blue Mountains . . . sought an explanation from the Department of Physics at the University of Sydney . . . Professor Harry Messel, replied . . . that light is scattered most effectively off very small droplets of oil . . . from such indigenous oil bearing trees as the eucalypts . . . [But he] qualified his explanation with a word of caution . . . "I must emphasise that this is merely a guess and . . . has to my knowledge not been investigated".'

—John Low, *Pictorial Memories: Blue Mountains* (1991)

'. . . it may be said that so endless are the possible varieties of the clouds, and so bewildering their changes of form, that no classification which was based upon form alone could ever hope to be complete.'

—George Aubourne Clarke, *Clouds: A Descriptive Illustrated Guidebook to the Observation and Classification of Clouds* (1920)

'. . . if a general and characteristic name were needed for modern landscape art, none better could be invented than "the service of clouds".'

—John Ruskin, 'Of Modern Landscape', *Modern Painters* (1856)

The year the Hydro Majestic Hotel failed as a hydropathic institute Harry Kitchings fell in love with the air and stayed. Les Curtain began to feel the dusk in his lungs. It was a romantic year. Men carried thermometers and dreamed of women struck by lightning. Postmen hauled packets filled with love and human hair. Women carried notebooks and pressed storms in them like flowers. You could feel our love rising from the mountain tops like steam. At least that is how Harry Kitchings might tell it.

What were we in love with? That is an awkward question. If I were to reply that we loved each other it would be for the sake of expediency and politeness. But it is only a half-truth unsuited to this time in that Blue Mountains town when the clouds at the end of every street were filled with the grand dreams of elsewhere. It is more accurate to say that our lives were lived in the service of these clouds which took the forms of our desires. We loved them with a passion that expanded and filled the sky. It was our clouds, for example, which boys carried in photographs to the trenches. The sight comforted them for they knew that these were different from German clouds which were full of dead men's souls. It was among our clouds that consumptives learned to chew mist instead of words, to grasp love or be smothered by it. Their bodies mapped the symptoms of our strange yearnings: our thirst to hear voices in the air, to feel the liquid tremors of the earth. If you place your head on a consumptive's chest you can hear waterfalls. I know. I have done it.

To live in that high land is to lose familiarity with the shapes of things. You cannot trust your eyes. In a single day I have witnessed the tremulous birth of the world. I have seen canyons boil. I have watched rain fall upwards from the foot of Mount Solitary. Before my eyes, beneath sliding veils of vapour, trees have formed soft oceans in the depths of valleys dappled by cold blue shadows in which parrots swam like tropical fish. When the mists come the edges of cliffs blur, rocks melt, chasms close over and streets drop into precipices. Your feet are shod in lichen. Your hair breathes vapour at the roots. You are walking on clouds. There were days when I have flung coins into the valleys and they have skipped across the billows.

Who can say precisely where love starts? I could tell you that my passion for Harry Kitchings had its origin thousands of years ago when that mighty ridge broke off from the Penrith plains and rose into the air. Yet it may have begun later when the explorers, who could only think of the clouds as clumps of wool waiting to be baled, had already passed over these inconvenient mountains to settle the grassy

Bathurst valleys, and other, more leisured, travellers began to notice the graceful definition of their peaks. Or perhaps it started when Governor Macquarie sat in a swaying carriage and saw through his homesick tears that the Blue Mountains resembled the Scottish Highlands.

As I write, another beginning presents itself. I imagine that a French artist looked out into the purple distance of Govett's Leap as the sun dried out his brushes and the flies drowned in his jar of turpentine, and dreamed of the dark blue shadows of the Simplon Pass—and from his pocket a tube of azure paint fell into the waterfall and the oily tumbling water stained the valleys blue. Or I could tell you that our story began fifty years before Harry Kitchings' arrival, when the wealthy cut paths and lookouts in the cliffs and named them after well-born women, cleared the scrub away from waterfalls, and built the frames of back doors and verandahs to make the landscape match the paintings in their eyes. All these beginnings are true.

I can only tell you this with certainty: I had not noticed the colour of the mountains until Harry Kitchings arrived in Katoomba, felt his spine fill with air, and gave himself up to the madness of photography. Of course I had seen Mount Solitary and the dark spur of Narrow Neck, forming a valley beyond the steep length of Cascade Street, as I climbed each day from my house to Mr Medlicott's Dispensing Pharmacy. But I had not yet learned to see them as expressions on the face of nature. From the moment I met Harry Kitchings, and began to see through the frames of his sight, I became aware of their magnificence.

For the next nine years I was to study him as keenly as the weather. I could chart his movements and moods. Without looking I could feel him climbing back to us from his excursions in the valleys with a soul as tender as an opal when it is freshly dug up from the earth and fingernails can break it. As I worked I could feel him balancing on the top of cliffs, using his faith as an axis while my thoughts also buoyed him like a breeze. His oceanic dreams carved caves and valleys in my heart, just as the spite of the councillors left stalactites in his.

That clouds contain the precipitated yearning with which we clothe the nakedness of the world is a lesson I learned when I grew used to the thought that I could never be that still point which Harry Kitchings sought. Then I met with another cloudy man and learned that on a misty path one is most likely to encounter oneself. I lived to see Harry Kitchings give up breathing when he realised that the air was no longer treated with respect. At last I embarked upon my own cloud study and heard in the sky a multitude of human voices which, as the years passed, stopped seeking out echoes in the distance and took less ambitious shapes. Indeed, I have realised that in such an insubstantial place it requires courage to trace the shape of history. It is easier to see clouds than rocks, and it requires less effort to describe the grandeur of mountains than the contours of a life.

But that is all geology now. All I have left are Harry Kitchings' photographs which sit among the clothes in my trunk like silver fossils. Back then the mountains were an entirely different shade of blue which was never caught by any camera and has thus been lost in the passage of time. They shone with the brilliance of stained glass and formed glowing chalices for clouds. Now that Harry Kitchings is gone from me the colour exists only in my head. For by the time new photographic processes arrived in the mountains, seeking to capture their colour, it had faded, in part as a result of this boldness.

Listen, I will make the clouds rain stories for you.

The shifting character of our passions can be read in the history of the air.

To understand this story you must put yourself in the place of those earnest young men who visited us then with guide-books in their hands and tried to imagine these valleys in the childhood of the world; who, when they looked hard enough, could see the ephemerality of mountains, rising, trembling, and melting like jelly. I will try to revive for you this time of liquid possibility when the valleys were brimful with our love of elsewhere, a love stronger than any atmospheric process, a love which turned the mountains sapphire blue.

Back in 1907, however, as the Swiss doctors coiled their stethoscopes in their trunks at the Hydro Majestic and returned to Sydney, when its centrifugal douches and bowel kneaders were spirited away by the Chinese waiters to water their vegetable gardens, and when young lovers on winding paths felt the frail explosion of health-giving lightbulbs under-foot, we were smug. We felt that our world was beyond measure and our love could not be cured.

CUMULUS

$$=\ 1\ =$$

I first saw Harry Kitchings leaning from a basket which had been lowered over the Katoomba Falls. I saw a small, angular body in a dark suit with its back turned away from the sheer sandstone wall which rained waterspray and yellow flowers. I saw two men in the acacia scrub at the top of the cliff struggle to keep the basket steady, placing their feet against the base of a tree as the slipping rope burned the soft bark and dislodged the wattle blossom. Below I watched a smooth hand take a folded handkerchief and gently wipe the moisture and powder from the camera lens. I saw a tripod, miraculously still, pointed at the water.

He had come here to test his faith.

He had already heard of the power of mountains, their capacity to produce strange passions like the hairy fruit which grew upon the alpine trees.

He had been told the air was too thin to support any certainties.

He knew that it was possible to become mad from living too close to the face of God.

I stood on a high cliff path already chilled by the afternoon shadow. Even from there I would see that Harry Kitchings had been touched by photographic madness.

I could not help it. During the course of my work as a pharmacist's assistant I had learned to recognise epidemics of the soul. I was already familiar with the town's secret boils and rashes. In my head I could consult a map fragrant with the scents of neuralgic powders, shaving lotions and resolvent pills. When Katoomba itched, I knew.

I knew, for example, that when the temperance speakers came to town there would be a quiet demand for Gin Pills, their packets printed with that frightful command, 'Take them in Time'. I had come to expect those young men from the Bohemia Apartments who came to us to purchase thermometers with the hope of detecting exotic ailments, or bought phosphorous pills to relieve the guilty habits of self-pleasure. I dispensed Rexona to salve burns from electrical experiments and dealt with the fern lovers' scratches. If the programs featured by Baker's Cronojector caused Brain-Fag, it could be eased with Clements Tonic. Two years later, when King Edward's tennis instructor visited the Blue Mountains, I would sell Dr Sheldon's Magnetic Liniment to both men and women to relieve the pains of unrequited love.

That is the lighter side of it. Others sought out cures for nameless illnesses for which our stocks proved painfully inadequate. We sold nerve tonics to wives who could not bear the indignity of the marriage bed and to English visitors reduced to tears by the climate's foreignness. A sick headache back then masked a multitude of failures. Children were sent to us while their fathers were at work to purchase mustard baths to still the life of a brother or sister in the womb. Mr Medlicott, whose possession of an eligible son attracted as many customers as his talents in the dispensary, sold gallons of his Toilet Cream. Spinsters applied great gouts of hope to faded cheeks each night and cried themselves to sleep, the fear of long years of visiting other people's hearths spinning out around them in the night. It broke my heart, the weakness of our remedies. It was like applying a corn plaster to history.

Mr Medlicott was unconcerned. He smiled at the full cash register and said, 'Each age contracts the diseases it deserves.' Yet he was contemptuous of these ailments of the soul. He favoured recent scientific theories which presented illness, old age and death as failures of the will. He took great pleasure from industrial disasters. If he heard news of a child run down by a motor carriage or an accident in one of the factories at the edge of town he would leave me to mind the store, snatching up his notebook and pencil, eager to record the precise capacity of the body to withstand the effects of impacting metal and burning tallow.

I was born with historical eyes. Inherited from my mother, they are clear and grey and prominent in my face, recording symptoms, focusing on the seams and pockets of the world.

As a child I quickly began to scan bodies for signs of the unspoken, catching knees and elbows in attitudes of abandon or disarray. I observed my godmother raise herself on the arms of her commode chair to pass wind and watched my father grab at the maid's hidden ankles. When he smiled I saw a knot in the wood of his upper denture. My mother saw these things too, but had the grace to turn away. She devoted herself to the science of hygiene, ensuring that the grates were clean of ashes or, in moments of leisure, pursuing pests in the rhododendrons. In the lantern slides of my memory her recording presence is registered as a blur at the edges of rooms; a sharp sweep of long skirts preceding a swift withdrawal down corridors, the shadow of her dishonour caught in the merciless shutter of my sight. I said to Harry, years later, when the war had just started across the sea: 'I am familiar with the spirit of your bare-faced mechanism. The world is full of symptoms which stick to light and gelatine.' These words made him miserable, until he lost himself in the next unpeopled landscape. How could I tell him, then, of the day I caught my mother in a moment of despair, returning from the garden, and the sight of a strange gift, tied up with my father's favourite ribbon, left for someone else beneath the oleander? That day she explained to me that other people blinked in unison. Only she and I had eyes which closed, indiscreetly, out of time. This was our curse. She told me that I must learn to lower my lashes or I would never find a husband. I stared past her into the pale haze around the Irish strawberry trees where I watched our gardener, a small man with an unpronounceable name, stooped in the sweat of his invisible labour.

There were other things my eyes noted. The accidental manner in which my father had jumped ship in Australia—his dread of clinging to rigging as the wind knocked small boys' skulls against each other like conkers coinciding with the announcement that gold had been found beneath the earth near Ballarat. The possibility that if my mother had not worn a velvet bow in her hair during their first meeting, my father might not have found her beautiful, or, indeed, have embarked upon the career of his life. My mother's collusion in the matter of my father's illiteracy, which led her to read documents aloud while, having misplaced his spectacles or muddied his hands, he dug his shoulders into the parlour chair with the meekness of a child. The rapidity with which my mother, worried that he would not find the way to heaven without her, followed my father into death in my sixteenth year.

My father's great passion was ribbons. In any other form, that emotion frightened him. Perhaps this affection had something to do with memories of the harshness of rope, stiffened by sea salt into corded knots which refused to yield to the touch. Or an association, below decks, with the unforgiving company of men. Disowned by his family for the abandonment of his apprenticeship, he continued each year of my childhood to send packages to England filled with yards of samples from our factory which his mother neither acknowledged nor returned but which, perhaps, tied the plaits and trimmed the camisoles of unknown sisters and nieces. My mother, for her part, wrote the polite letters which accompanied them to a family which ignored her existence, the difficulty of address imparting to her accounts of our lives a strange and timeless formality. She fingered the slippery smoothness of the ribbons and thought about their unsuitability to the fugitive nature of human hair, about the daily task of binding and untying. Hair, like the heart, required endless discipline to achieve the semblance of stability. The knots in ribbon constricted into permanence or dissolved.

She did not understand how my father loved that factory: the regularity of machinery, the tautness of spools, the intestinal unwinding of fabric—the thought of his ribbons, snaking across oceans, tying us firmly to Greenwich time. While he could not read letters, the steady increase of figures across a page affected him like poetry. At Federation, as a reward for his workers' diligent completion of special orders for bunting and thick red tapes, my father hired a coach to convey them to the parades, where they viewed the work of their Sundays split crisply by the sharp new blades of ceremonial scissors. That was three years before the collapse of the business and four years before his death.

My mother's sharp eyes had foreseen our family's misfortune. From the moment they had focused on him, she knew that my father's new partner was unworthy of his trust. She noticed the careless way he buttoned his fly returning from his frequent journeys to our outhouse. She stiffened with disgust when she noticed the stench of his urine, thickened with hops, clinging to the hem of her skirts. She instructed the maid to sprinkle the floor with lime after his visits, but did not remark on the way that cupboard doors had the habit of swinging open, mysteriously, in his wake. I also noticed the way he attacked a slice of roast at table like a dog, taking it straight down his throat unchewed, resentful of the knife and fork and the intrusion of women's voices. As the men talked behind closed doors, my mother sponged the ring of gravy stencilled on the table by his plate. He was never forgiven for suggesting to her, one afternoon, as he spat in the herbaceous border, that she might replace a bed of roses, freshly trimmed in their summer bed of straw, with the more productive silverbeet.

It was useless to warn my father since he laughed fondly at my mother's observations. 'One cannot conduct business,' he told her, 'on the basis of a man's disrespect for Koch's bacillus.' For my father was like a man possessed by opium, consumed by the visions his partner had conjured of our family business spread across the world: of his ribbons tied across the mighty bosoms of the suffragettes; trimming the parasols of dowagers in India; supporting the pendulous medals pinned to the heroes of colonial rebellions. Chief among the visions which swam before his eyes were his own crimson tapes around the laws and briefs of Westminster and the Inns of Court. His partner unfurled these dreams like protoplasm while his gaze promiscuously caressed the possessions on my father's mantelpiece. As he spoke he twisted a spool of my father's best Scotch thread around his thumb. In love with the thought of his ribbons stitching together the pink pieces of the British Commonwealth, my father agreed reluctantly to economise. He acquiesced to the purchase of cheaper materials and the extension of the working day. He acknowledged his excessive generosity in the matter of lighting and spoke soothingly to his employees of the glow of future profit as they bent their heads closer to their work. He explained patiently to my mother that the durability of ribbon was a miscalculated indulgence, for it deprived women of the pleasures of regular change. My mother saw him sign bills of lading in mysterious languages while she was not consulted.

My father recognised the ribbon tying the bailiff's documents. He accepted the package in the rain and by the time he reached home his hands were stained red by his own cheap dyes. No one from the factory acknowledged him in the street.

When he was laid out on the kitchen table my father's mouth and internal cavities were plugged with a bright confetti of offcuts. I could not help noticing a frayed pink edge which had slipped like a feather between his stitched-up lips. A large tartan bow was fastened beneath his chin, for, minutes after he died, my mother had bound his jaw tight to hide his expression of surprise. She was thankful, as she gathered the silky loops like a child's shoelace, that he had died first and spared himself the sight of her decay. She lathered and shaved him and passed a warm washcloth over his face. I helped her flatten his legs and tie them to the mattress. He lay as he had desired to live, a gift wrapped by the gentleness of women. Outside, the sky was cloudless and the afternoon resolved itself, briefly, into a still bright point.

The truth we told to no one: that my father had spent the last year of his life attached to the bedhead by a silken harness. Out of the attic my mother had chosen a wide band of watered silk, the type he had sold to drape along the aisles at weddings, as pale and creamy and light as moths' wings. She tied it around my father's waist and ran it over his shoulders, as if dressing a pale toy soldier. She let out twelve feet of material, cut the bolt, and bound the other end to the bed. My father walked to the new circumference of his world and stood suspended at the edge. He let the bedhead take his weight. He leaned forward, a foot raised in the air, as if considering a precipitous leap. My mother closed her eyes and left the room.

In this way my father was protected from wandering to a factory he no longer owned. Sometimes he fretted the knots around his waist and begged to be taken to kiss the blisters on the working women's hands. At these times I would search the drawers of my room for ribbons and pile them on his lap until he laughed and gave orders for the maintenance of invisible machinery. Or I would feed him scrambled egg while he cried and ground his gums and called me by his mother's name. Once, when he had been left alone for an afternoon, my mother and I returned to find a room filled with coloured bows. At other times he feared he was at sea and lashed himself to the washstand as if it were a mast; or thought that he had drowned, and had to be gently delivered, by tuggings on his leash, from the ocean floor beneath the bed, clutching the chamberpot as if it were a giant shell. His life unwound from its spool and spilled softly to the corners of the room, too slippery now for tape measures or for brooms. To my father, my mother and I appeared like delicate flotsam, floating across the room, fringed with lace: he feared that we would break against the walls. Finally the whisper of satin waves filled his ears. Death, a high velvet tide, smothered him.

A shameful secret, the frailty of men—and the sly hinge of my adult desires.

After my father died there was little to be packed. My mother watered her plants a final time. She gave a potted geranium and a case of ribbons to the maid. She was overcome by weariness. The house, after her years of imagining it as a home for my father, seemed to disintegrate before her brick by brick. She was no longer anchored by my father's love.

Now, she said, I want to go as the clouds go.

That wish would bring us to the Blue Mountains.

A local newspaper at the turn of the century records the dramatic effect on singers of the mountain air. It was thought to rapidly expand the throat, producing notes of elastic strength and clarity. Yet, the paper warns, a voice coaxed by the clouds to sudden maturity might also constrict, falter and lose its sweetness. Under such circumstances it was hard not to take the weather personally. In this first decade of the new century faith was essential in dealings with clouds. They had to be propitiated.

My mother, being possessed of a practical temperament, did not use metaphors lightly: she expected them to do a full day's work. She could not sit still. Her spine no longer fitted stiff-backed chairs. Instead she draped her limbs over my father's armchair. She closed her eyes and imagined herself drifting lightly on cushions of air, soft and unlaced from the corset of household hours. Without self-consciousness she began to hum unfamiliar melodies with notes as shiny as sequins in the dim light of the mourning house. So when she spoke of going as the clouds went her mind turned to higher landscapes. She wanted to study the clouds with her own keen eyes and learn how to live from her observations. She would stretch the lining of her heart across the broadest valleys until it was so thin it floated on the updraughts like a silver haze. She would see her life spread out far below her gaze until she could make out its bright topography at last.

She had read about this place; where kitchens were built at such high altitudes that the clouds drifted into bread through open windows and made it rise without the use of yeast; where the clouds were always white; where the mountains were so blue that bowerbirds, stunned by concupiscence, dashed their brains against the sapphire cliffs.

My mother and I sat inside the Steamed Fish as it made its slow ascent from Penrith. Around us serpentine purple crests rolled to the horizon, softly rounded, as if the motion of an ancient wave had been arrested on its way out to the sea. Closer to Katoomba, the train moved through tunnels and passages cut into mountains, allowing us to trace in the synclines and anticlines the tidal motions at the heart of the rocks, and in the cracked strata the remains of a crevasse where the broad shelves of the ocean floor once dropped to greater depths. The sides of the valleys grew more sheer; they were steep and blue; huge orange cliffs split the vegetation. Thin trees stuck out, sideways, from their seams.

In 1906 the Blue Mountains line was like the fine silver anchor of a spider's web, a dream cast out from Sydney which

at Mount Victoria. It was vulnerable to a multi-
rruptions: from horns and hooves, the curiosity of
children and irresolvable grief. Cattle stumbled out of the fog
into the pistons with blank faces. Suicides leapt to embrace a
cold steel force and a thunder which dulled their final
thoughts. Three days before our journey Gertie and Will
Emmerton had placed stones on the track and giggled as the
front carriage reared up from the rails.

In the face of such contingencies, each of us took a heroic
role, bracing our feet against the floor, rehearsing with the
weight of our trunks and bags the explorers' wilful ascent
nearly a hundred years before. We pitied those empty corners
of the world in which the native imagination could not
encompass the possibility of mechanised disaster. For a mind
which could not leap along the fixed tracks of polished ideas,
regardlesss of the risk, would never appreciate the view from
mountains. Now that they no longer stood in the way of the
Bathurst plains, the Blue Mountains were suddenly beautiful.
Harnessed by sleepers, they could be indulged. In the cities
we calculated the girths of our souls with imperial measures.
Sometimes they grew soft and slack. Then we took them for
exercise in the clouds.

In my mother's lap the *Mountaineer Complete Pocket Tourist
Guide to the Blue Mountains and Jenolan Caves* rested beneath
her folded hands. Like the other travellers who crowded the
carriage we were lured by its description of the mountain air
outside as a healthful elixir of sunshine and gas. According to
Dr Phillip E. Muskett, whose work was extracted in the
Guide, this gaseous cocktail was both a stimulus and a

soporific. It was highly charged with the antiseptic qualities of ozone while its diathermancy caused it to be richly saturated with ultraviolet, which in turn encouraged the production of haemoglobin in the blood. We marvelled at the beneficence of clouds. They would encourage us to eat and sleep. They would soak into the pores of our skin, improving its texture and the quality of our blood. They provided a soft refuge for the nervous and chased old-age cells from ancient veins. Rarefied like the air, we would thus escape the dullness which weighed upon the denser lowlands of the nation. Professional and literary men, Dr Muskett claimed, would benefit most from such absolution. Nevertheless, the metabolism— that agent of change which worked within all of us—was certain to be stimulated, for better or for worse.

Following behind us in the luggage compartment was a heavy trunk filled with ribbons which had been ironed and tightly rolled. For my mother had conceived of a fitting tribute to my father's memory which we were to execute at Echo Point. She described the details now with girlish excitement: we would stand at the jutting lip of the platform at the lookout; the vertiginous drop would trick our minds into imagining the movement and depth of a vast blue sea; we would hurl ribbons like streamers into the abyss below, as if we stood at the rail of a cruising liner. She described the flight of colour from our hands—rainbows arching and quivering through the air—each band choosing its own course according to its destiny and weight—the startled lyrebirds far below treading in nests of fallen spectrums.

Although we could scarcely afford the fare we hired a cab

from the queue outside the station at Katoomba. As the driver urged the horse into a trot, we looked up at the Carrington Hotel along the length of its two wide driveways. We passed houses with names like Aircourt and Balmoral. Then the road began to drop away from the guesthouses and shops. For a moment, every way we looked we saw sky. Far ahead, the road appeared to open into a valley shored up by plunging honey-coloured walls. Thin traces of cirrus cloud were drawn up around the rim. Past the paddocks and dairies, we turned off this road, and drove among the larger estates where tall radiata pines cut dark green lines of demarcation through the bush. The driver pointed out a mansion which had been built for a girl with weak lungs who had died before she could be brought here to endure the exquisite cruelty of taking each breath on the edge of an abyss. Beyond the sloping orchard where the hazelnut trees were in bloom a tennis court balanced on the valley's edge. With our long sight my mother and I saw a ball hesitate over the void before dropping out of sight, belted into the valley with a wooden racquet by a rich young man bored with keeping score. Approaching the point, the air was chilly, charged with that coldness which rises at dusk from the interiors of rocks.

We hauled the trunk to the edge of the lookout and unlocked it. The chimes of bellbirds filled the valley with a delicate pulse as if the river below were powered by some clockwork mechanism. Above us a flock of black cockatoos pushed their blunt heads through the breeze in clumsy flight. Like the women in dark narrow-waisted skirts who walked below us on the steeply winding tracks, they seemed to propel themselves purely by the force of will. My mother and I took a deep breath and faced one another. We each held a handle and began to swing the case. The balls of cloth flinched higher with each swing, beginning to unfurl, testing themselves for flight as the case arched over the safety rail at the limit of our strength. Achieving momentum they leapt out into the air, diving towards the scraps of trees hundreds of feet below.

Yet my mother's calculations on the train had not allowed for the strong updraught at this point. Beneath the platform where we stood breathless the winds which gathered in the valley met the sheer wall of the cliff, veering upwards with a mighty force. A writhing web of streamers was hurled back at us from the gorge. Tangled strips of cloth lashed our faces and wrapped around the dampness of our hands and necks.

Thinking back now I am stunned by the ironies of history.

My mother and I stood shackled in velvet and cotton, staring at Mount Solitary, framed by the Three Sisters and Orphan Rock.

$=\ 2\ =$

If it had not happened so soon after his conversion, Harry
Kitchings might have thought that he suffered from some
strange physical disorder. He had begun to see straight dark
lines framing the landscapes in his sight. He had started to
regard space and distance as uncertain. He was painfully sensitive to variations in the light. He was aware that the appearance of everyday objects could shift as quickly as the weather.

To Harry all this was proof of the existence of God.

To his mother it was evidence that he had succumbed to
the thirst for images in his blood.

Harry was born in the winter of 1873 with a silver umbil-
icus wrapped around his neck. Before he drew his first breath
and began to cry his skin had a strange metallic sheen. His
hair was so fine and short that it appeared like a dusting of
gold upon his head. His mother wondered if accumulated
years spent hunching in fuming cupboards had caused toners
and nitrates to seep into the family veins. She had once seen
an etching of spermatozoa with long tails magnified under a

microscope. She thought of them wriggling into her womb like little balls of overheated mercury seeking some predestined alchemy.

From her first husband, who was to become Harry's uncle, she had learned that Harry's paternal grandfather once worked in Melbourne as a daguerreotypist. A photograph was something slow and tidal then, like shadows settling on a silver pool. Plates were fumed gently with the vapours of mercury until they were as sensitive as the palms of hands. Images sank into them until their descent was stopped by salty water and they hung suspended forever beneath the metallic surface. Then they were toned with gold and slipped into leather pouches or bound in heavy metal frames. These were gestures suited to their preciousness. Unable to be reproduced, no single image was the same. The grandfather's customers swiftly expressed a preference for being photographed standing side-on to the camera in silhouette, regarding an imposing view. If taken from the front they had a tendency to look like furtive moths pinned by sharp shafts of sunlight to the canvas backdrops, for few faces could endure the harsh interrogation of unfiltered light or compose themselves under the scrutiny of long exposures.

Harry's grandfather liked watching the lines of spectators form along the stairs to his rooftop studio. Faced with this new technology, his subjects did not know how to stand. Their limbs threatened to float as awkwardly as water-weed across the slippery surface of a plate. The catcalls of the crowd did not calm them. Harry's grandfather particularly enjoyed strapping the trembling ladies to the metal frames, adjusting the angle of their necks, and telling them to keep quite still.

It was not easy work. The new city was a place of fickle and parsimonious sunlight. It was a town of thefts and potholes and mean bars where a man might lose his soul. Harry's grandfather was once chased into the thick scrub at the top of Bourke Street by an evil-tempered goat and lost his way for several hours. When he was asked to photograph his customers by the Yarra Falls, offal from the abattoirs would often drift through a long exposure, creating unsavoury distortions in the turbid waters. The streets were full of black faces too difficultly dark to capture on a silver plate, so that ten years later no one, not even he, remembered they had been there. Yet trade was lucrative. The new settlers queued to be photographed so they could prove to themselves they did indeed live in this town so new that the streets were full of the smell of builders' dust and houses and children appeared faster than they could be named. It was a strange time when men were prepared to pay more for a picture of a naked woman than it would cost to see one in the flesh. In another decade these townsmen took their potholes to the goldfields and churned the soil until motes of gold dust floated in the air. It seemed to blow gold in the streets of Melbourne too, as each council built its own town hall, trumping its rivals with ornate columns and thick-cut stones. The miners came back and turned their gold into gold coin and their gold coin into the record of their gold-toned faces, polished and refined. Sometimes a fleck of gold dust would fall from their clothes and settle on the daguerreotypist's plates: then an odd hernial bulge would grow in the image around the aggravation like an oyster's pearl.

Harry's grandmother had been a whore. In a moonlit room in Little Bourke Street she had lain on a bed with her skirts lifted above her waist and the daguerreotypist had fallen in love with her silvered flanks. When he lay with her she was smooth and slippery beneath his hands. He walked back to his studio through the muddy streets feeling as if his body had been fumed with her breath and steeped in the salty juices of kelp until it had been revealed in some new way even to itself. He bought her a ring and wrapped her in fine clothes and gently clipped her into his frames, teaching her to emulate the posture of a lady. She bore two sons and a daughter and held that pose until her death.

He would not investigate the new process imported from abroad. He refused to dignify a passing fad which amused French sailors, but grossly underestimated the tastes and judgment of his race. Who would pay, he asked his wife, for portraits as indistinguishable from one another as dinner scraps—printed on the paper in which one ought to wrap them? The images were thinner than butter, spread over the surface of the paper. They were grainier than coarse bread. They could be reduced to pulp by a sunshower and blown along Swanston Street by the slightest breeze. He waited a year for customers until three young graziers stole his sign as a souvenir. He punished his elder son when he found a calotype of a woman wearing a corset hidden in his room. He no longer walked onto the roof because his eyes were bothered by the sun. Bats had nested in the canopies and drapes and soaked them in acrid urine, confused by the steeples which sprouted from the city each day and pierced their old paths in the sky. One moonlit night Harry's grandfather hired a carriage and stood at the edge of Port Phillip Bay. He reached out to touch the sea's shifting silver flanks, longing to steep himself in the juices of kelp and put a stop to the sorrow which had etched into his bones. His shoes remained where he had leaped from them. When he was found the fish had eaten out his eyes. His smallest son could never forget the implacable blankness of his eyeless face.

The elder son set out to avenge his father's sight. His mother began to notice that his personal habits were strange, his movements mysterious. He spent nights on the rooftop, tinkering with his father's cameras and pausing on occasion to pleasure himself by the roof's edge, aiming juddering arcs of silver fluid over the street below. By day he joined the crowd at the window of the new talbotype studio in Spring Street, his clothes emitting the sharp stink of bat. When he placed his bag on the floor it rattled like a skeleton. At other times, as he climbed the stairs to the studio, his little brother could hear sounds like the sea coming from the large bundles in his arms and hid under his bed, pursued by the floating vision of his father's eyeless corpse. Once the house jumped on its foundations as a series of explosions sounded on the roof, as if someone had ignited a chain of firecrackers. That night the elder brother sat at the dinner table with a face like thunder and would not speak, even when one of his eyebrows fell into his plate.

Yet, slowly, he was learning. From his experiments he

found that light was something which could be softened: in this way he could erase the lines of judgment from a face. He learned what his father had not, that people would not thank an honest cameraman. Soon he could cut a glass plate to size without gashing his fingertips. He could calculate the precise time needed to coax an image onto a glass negative while the collodion coating was still wet. He developed a lens fast enough to catch the movement of a bat's wing and was startled by the mathematical beauty and suppleness of its motion. From this moment he thought of the flight of his own ejaculate as a series of secret articulations with the air. He could hold his breath for long periods of time while preparing nitric, sulphuric and cyanide gases in the fuming cupboard. He thought of the strange nature of this new process, which poisoned the image in order to grant it eternal life. As he coated his plates with gun cotton he took a savage delight in photography as a kind of war upon the world. While the picture on the glass was as delicate as breath, this solution he painted on it was strong enough to blow off a hand and leave shards inside a heart.

Once he had finished Harry's uncle could not stay put. He burned the rotten draperies of the studio and set a small terrier loose among the panicked mice. He packed his glass plates into ten slotted wooden boxes and collected together the cameras he had bought and invented, whose internal spaces corresponded to the different sizes of the glass. He poured his chemicals into heavy glass bottles, fitted them with thick stoppers, and wrapped their bases in his father's old trousers. He made neat stacks of developing dishes. He conveyed them all to a small custom-fitted cart with the words 'Photographic Van' stencilled on the side. He washed his hair and combed it and went out looking for a wife.

It was an odd honeymoon, conducted without sheets and bedheads. Inside the van on a road near Healesville, the new wife undressed and lay on a mattress on the floor. In the darkness outside she could hear the horse moving and thought fearfully of the hugeness of its sex. She had abandoned her religion for this oddly handsome man and the inside of the van, with its curtained door and its smell of wax candles, felt as guilty and close as the confessional. Her back was stiff from sitting all day beside him on the wooden driver's seat. When he undid his flies his swollen organ stood out in the air, balanced at a strange angle as if its head were held up by a string, as improbable as the lenses on tripods lined up behind him against the wall. She saw a drop of moisture suspended at its tip and shrank at the thought that it might fall. He said nothing, but squatted down before her and surveyed her thoughtfully. Like developing a plate, he had heard, the best results were achieved when the working surface was wet. He spat upon his hands and annointed himself carefully, as if greasing the folds and creases of a camera case. He worked another foamy gob between her legs, testing the precise strength of her external membrane, and pushing past it with his fingertips to gauge her internal dimensions. Before he lowered himself over her, she braced her feet against the wall as he commanded. Her trembling transferred itself to the boxes of glass which shivered and set up a soft vibrating wail inside their slots.

She was surprised by a sensation of heat. She thought with panic that he had miscalculated. Yet the resistance ended and she felt, through the burning, an uncomfortable fullness. She watched with detached pity as he jerked above her with his eyes closed, sweating, and oblivious. Around her, as the van rocked, the large bottles moved closer to the edges of their shelves like fat men, the empty trouser legs swinging backwards and forwards beneath them in the air, the explosive and poisonous contents washing against their glassy sides. This caused her more terror than the pains of love. It was only when her husband had finished and she felt a strange chemical substance run out of her, independent of her will, that she felt any pity for herself. 'Don't cry,' he said to her, as he rolled over. 'Tomorrow I'll teach you how to cut up glass.'

It seemed to her that they travelled through every frozen town in Victoria. Even the desert in the west was as cold as a plate-glass negative at night, the dry grasses white on a pale soil beneath a darkened sky. When she went to relieve herself strange rat-like creatures with large ears hopped about on silent feet and regarded her with the haggard faces of ghosts. Once, after a racing carnival, they camped the van near a riverbed. She woke to see a large goanna crouched beside her as the last of the photographs from that day disappeared down its bulging neck. Her husband chased after it but it ran up a tree, its stomach full of carnival hat and horse. Another time, in a treacherous storm, he whipped the horse up the steep roads of the Dandenongs and ignored her screams as the cart swayed until, in anger, she threw a bottle of collodion down over the rocky edge, and the forest canopy below lit up like a circus tent.

When they arrived at a town, they would set up a makeshift studio in the open air. He placed Doric columns and vases of dried flowers on a chequered rug. Or he nailed together a staggered row of wooden waves with foam painted on their crests. He arranged curtains of gauze and mirrors to catch the light at flattering angles. Each different region required special vigilance: against specks of red dust which imbedded themselves in the gelatine surface of the photographs, or the cloudy bloom of northern dampness. After he had sold the pictures of women with worn faces who had squeezed themselves back into their wedding dresses, and of wiry children in their Sunday best, his wife would wash and scrape each negative clean upon her knees, as if she were scaling a fish.

When she was angry, which occurred with increasing frequency, she would perform this job with little care. In the next town his photographs would turn into strange montages: a matron and a cat-faced boy were joined at the waist like Siamese twins; the body of a dead man lay upon a christening rug, a bride stood next to the hanging carcass of a bull, a rosette pinned to a naked, amputated limb.

To make matters worse, his sister had begun to send letters from abroad which tracked them down out of sequence, spilling from their pages sand from Luxor and folded paper animals from Japan. Envelopes from China held the pressed leaves of strange plants which perfumed the chill chemical interior of the van. Unlike her little brother, Harry's aunt had, as a girl, tiptoed up the steps to their father's studio. With the sharp, attentive face of a bat she had observed her brother's experiments and his violent movements at the rooftop's edge. By the time she reached her majority she was no stranger to the mysteries of science or of men. Having purchased her own cameras, she travelled over distant mountain passes carrying a sun parasol and commanding the men who conveyed her equipment with the same determination with which she wrote to London to badger the Royal Society to recognise her work. She would survive a typhoon in India and cholera in South America to choke many years later while being force-fed in an English gaol, the doctor's report recording that she had suffered from a seizure brought about by the intemperate insistence with which she had demanded the women's vote.

Even now, years before her ignominious death, her brother could not forgive her. He stared at the images of two great Egyptian giants as high as a cliff-face seated in thrones carved into the rock until he could no longer bear it and tossed them into a dam. He crushed the incommunicative faces of sphinxes and native porters in his hands. He looked with envy at her pictures of roads strewn with cannonballs: stroking them with his fingertips he could feel the correctness of it, the equilibrium between the gun-metal coating of the negative and its registration of the weight of death.

His restlessness increased. Sometimes he stayed in a town only for an afternoon and whipped the horse on to the next before he had finished making up his prints. One day his wife looked down at her hands after an evening cleaning up the plates and saw a whole family staring at her in reproach, their unprinted faces shining like snail tracks on the red flesh of her hands. The next day her husband announced that he would only take photographs of important and historical events. He spent afternoons in hotels listening for news of captured high-waymen and grisly murders. He returned in the evening and cursed the horse as it stumbled in potholes on the dark roads which stood between them and a corpse. If there was no news, he used her in a violent manner, concentrating only on the moment when his tensions would find a release and his mind would be cleared with the brevity and brightness of a collodion explosion. His wife's skin started at his approach the way the horse's hide twitched over its spine at the sound of a march fly. For his part, he felt a perpetual hunger which neither food nor drink could satisfy. Everything tasted of camera. He could not bear to think of the important moments happening without him all around the world.

The morning he heard of a great war in America he made up his mind. He installed his wife in a small cottage in Hawthorn. He bought himself a berth on a ship from Melbourne in which he was to share a cabin with young Australian men eager to fight for the Confederates. He signed the bill of lading for his photographic van and shouted instructions from the wharf as it was lowered on ropes and pulleys into the hold. For two years he was happy. He drove his van into valleys where smoke was still heavy in the air. He set up his tripods on hillsides where corpses lay as swollen and pale as mush-rooms on the ground. He paid desperate men in tattered grey uniforms with rags tied around their feet to arrange these bodies in the configurations which best fitted the dimensions of his lens. He captured the surprise in their sightless eyes. In a carriage on a steam train he met a man with a goatee and long golden hair who offered him a card and showed him a machine for displaying stereoscopic views. He committed the process to memory and sailed for home to make his fortune.

He did not return. His ship foundered on the Melbourne heads. Although his body was never found his boxes of negatives were washed up unharmed onto a beach on the Bellarine Peninsula. His wife unpacked the first and shuddered at the small shipwreck of bodies it contained. She stored the rest of the boxes unopened beneath her bed.

At the funeral a small, fair man averted his eyes from the empty casket. He introduced himself as her husband's brother. Like him, this younger man was strangely handsome, with high cheekbones and heavy-lidded eyes. His gloved fingers beneath her elbow were long and gentle and his quiet attention a comfort. He told her that he was a clerk in an emporium in Sydney. After a long and tentative courtship conducted by post she accepted him as her husband and they settled into the peace of a second marriage.

Harry's mother was happy to keep a house in which experimental flash powders did not sit next to the baking soda and make their way into damper which exploded in the fire. Her new husband did not lift the hem of her nightdress like a camera cloth. Harry, a late baby, delighted them both. Yet, very quickly, she noticed with anxiety her son's tendency to wander as he grew. When he was still a baby she would sometimes find him asleep on the floor some distance from his crib. Later he would stand at the bottom of her bed with open eyes although he was asleep. She thought about the elemental nature of photographic processes, their dependence on substances like eggs and gelatine. If an image could attach itself to glass or metal, she wondered, could it move through the thinner surface of the skin and leave its residue upon the heart? Had these things made their way into the blood of her strange observant child?

She would take no chances. She swore her second husband to secrecy. She cleared her first husband's possessions from beneath the bed: those boxes with their ghastly harvest of bodies which sent a cold chill through the mattress; a chipped Grecian column on its side; the collapsed wooden waves of painted seas which seemed to bear the crates eternally towards a distant shore; his fast lenses for photographing children and the wings of bats. She placed them in the shed, locked it with a chain and padlock, and threw away the key.

You might wonder how I know this.

Once, in his studio, while he stooped over the sink in the kitchen and made me tea, I opened Harry Kitchings' family album. It is amazing what you can see around the corners of photographs with historical eyes.

= 3 =

I could not master the art of spirit drawing. In my aunts' view I was ineducable. After my mother's death they banished me from the Fresh Air League. With tight mouths they took me to Mr Medlicott, who shared my indelicate interest in diagnosis and my fascination with the human form.

We had come to live with my aunts in Cascade Street because my mother's urge for a floating life had been frustrated by a lack of money; after several months she had not been able to make the rent on our small cottage on the Bathurst road. As office bearers of the Fresh Air League, she knew, her sisters could not resist a supplicant. 'No day without a deed to crown it' was the motto of the League. My mother's eldest sister recited it, twice, as she showed us to our room. She examined my mother's face which she had not seen for thirty years and could not forgive it for manifesting the signs of age. She told her that a good dose of mountain air would soon restore her bloom. It was a tonic for anyone, she said, who desired to be useful. She glanced at me and flinched as she met the unswerving judgment of my gaze. 'Except,' she added, 'for morbidly disposed young girls.'

The younger of my mother's two eldest sisters followed us into the room and stood breathing quietly, reaching out a hand to attach herself to the grey muslin which bound her big sister's arm. It was the first time I had laid eyes on either of them. Yet, with this single gesture, I understood at once why, in spite of my father's many young siblings, my mother had always referred to the second-eldest sister as my 'Youngest Aunt'.

For sixty years my aunts' lives had grown together like the ropy trunk of a coppiced tree. Between her two eldest sisters and my mother seven children had died in infancy. Those first two sisters grew up in a house full of names which hung like withered fruit from the vines of descent in the family Bible. Sometimes they remembered other small bodies sharing the nursery or leaving squashy purple tracks beneath the hanging branches of the mulberry tree. They could not recall faces. Instead, they felt a series of presences which clung to their childhood like phantom limbs. They remembered Father telling them not to upset Mother with any noise or distress. She sat often with a cold rag on her head in a darkened room after the clatter of cutlery or a disturbance in the light had brought about another seizure of despair. On the bedside table bowls of liquid gathered dust. The baby, my mother, cried in some distant section of the house, until she was silenced by the wet-nurse, who had bared her dark nipples to my grand-father during her interview in the drawing room and told him how she had toughened them each night with the application of a nailbrush. A retired jockey, who was more comfortable tightening girths on horses' bellies, he had leaned forward at her invitation to feel their texture and blushed when a pale blue bead of milk had sprung forth at his touch. My aunts claimed that they could not remember this incident although my mother, strangely, could.

My mother's sisters touched each other's faces in bed and in their whisperings had invented fifty secret names for death. They agreed: if they did not lie with their feet or fingers outside the blankets and if they tapped the bedhead ten times each Jesus would not take them as they slept. They lay in bed, each willing the rhythm of the other's breath until they came to believe that they breathed for one another. Their father encouraged them in their odd behaviour. He laughed and gave them pennies when they ran home from their Sunday lessons at the church hall to check that the stout house still stood at the same address. He consented to their requests at Christmas for mourning brooches and rings made from the pumice of Pompeii. After their mother died, when he sat them on his knees and brushed their hair, they had felt his tears falling on their hands. He told them, perhaps with a smile in his voice, that each drop of salty water stole a year from his life. 'You will never marry and leave me a lonely, sad old man?' he asked. And they did not. Years later, they sat on the front verandah and watched my mother go out walking with the ribbon-maker. Their shuttles worked at the same pace at each end of the tatting which hung suspended between their laps. The lace was as soft and white as the whiskers on their father's cheeks. They noted the roughness of the ribbon-maker's hands. They detected the slight instability in his walk, as if his legs had never acclimatised to the certainty of land. There was a relief in his eyes when he looked at my mother which suggested that he would not be averse to the luxury of death. They had known then that one day she would come to them like this.

After their father's death my aunts had sold that house full of pauses and unfinished sentences and moved to Katoomba. It was said that the air there was so dedicated to the preservation of life that people only died from boredom and disdain; that five generations lived together under the same roof; that the streets were so close to the floor of heaven that the voices of the dead murmured comfort in your ears when it rained. They bought this last cottage before the bush began which extended to the falls and, over the years, as if each surface was as vulnerable as skin, they had clothed the mantelpieces and tables and even the candlesticks with tatted lambrequins and mats. The fire was rarely lit. On crisp nights it comforted them to watch the tendrils of their breath entwine beneath the bedroom ceiling.

'Father always allowed you to be laced too tightly for your age,' my eldest aunt said to my mother, as if that explained our troubles now.

Lady Harding, the patroness of the Fresh Air League, had settled in Katoomba because the tree ferns in the area made her think of vases full of peacock feathers. It amused her to build a grand house here and imagine that the valleys were as tame as drawing rooms stretching from her verandah. Inside the house, to extend the joke, Sir Wilfrid Harding had overseen the construction of a frondescent arbour. He filled large glass cases with honeyeaters and emerald bowerbirds which had been stuffed and rendered lifelike by the taxidermist's art. He purchased thick green wallpaper on which a pattern of furry leaves rose up to the touch. Blank spaces in the emerald glass around the door admitted milky patches of frond-shaped light. The house was built among the dark radiata pines through which my mother and I had travelled when we first saw Echo Point.

On the afternoon when my aunts took me to my first meeting of the League, the birds stared at us from their parched branches and bowers with open beaks and glassy eyes. Their stillness threw into contrast the rare New Guinean plumage which bobbed upon the women's hats. Lady Harding welcomed us to the Cathedral of Ferns, as this room was known among the members of her circle. She invited us to enjoy the 'picnic' she had prepared. Mayonnaise of salmon and fancy cakes and a silver bowl of champagne cup had been laid out on a table which was covered with a chequered cloth. Sir Wilfrid was nowhere to be seen, having disappeared with the English newspapers into the foliage of the house.

I had been brought to this meeting by my aunts in my mother's place. I was under strict instructions not to disclose the circumstances of my father's bankruptcy. In particular, I was not to reveal that my mother had spited their wishes by finding paid employment. Instead, I was to say that she was in delicate health and indisposed to make the trip. Soon enough, to my aunts' relief, I would not have to lie.

Through her talents for household management and horticulture my mother had secured a position supervising the Ladies Home Page of the *Blue Mountain Echo*. Mr Thornelow, the newspaper's chief of staff, had known for some time that he required a lady editor. The newspaper offices received a large number of unsolicited contributions of household hints and feminine gossip which caused him as much confusion as if they had been postmarked from the moon. Yet he was not eager to pay for such assistance. It was an insult to nature, he said, to presume to remunerate a woman's skills. My mother replied that she only responded to a slight if she felt it was intended and that she had too much faith in Mr Thornelow's good character to take offence from such behaviour. He began to sweat as she assessed him with her cool grey eyes. He felt them take in his dusty spats and a melting clot of wax in the hairs of his moustache. In addition, he was moved by the graceful angle of her neck to a heightened emotion which he understood as chivalry. He was at last persuaded by her suggestion that an honorarium would guarantee discretion. In this way my mother negotiated a small weekly sum which was sufficient to cover our expenses in my aunts' household management. Her career as 'The Wasp' began.

The regularity of this work suited my mother. The necessity of remaining indoors did not. While I accompanied my aunts on visits to the Masonic Hall where worn women and delicate children waited in the corridors, she prepared her columns in my aunts' stuffy rooms. Under Mr Thornelow's instruction she divided them into small sections and paragraphs so that they could be cut and squeezed around the large oblong advertisements of Nurse M Coan, the high-class corsetiere. She learned quickly so that she would no longer have to feel his moist sausage breath against her neck. As The Wasp she wrote advice on the discipline of maids, the maintenance of linen, and the polishing of shirt-fronts. With her sharp eyes she could turn a walk down Main Street into a commentary on the unfortunate combination of green silk and amethyst. She specialised in the use of ribbons in the trimming of parasols and hats. She lectured on preparing dainty meals for invalids. She warned women against the false economy of a hurried convalescence. She stood over the kitchen table at my aunts' house testing recipes for Turkish Skin Balm and Imperial Cream.

Before this meeting of the League began the members were anxious to discuss The Wasp's latest column. It was clear that it was Mrs Grudge's new bonnet which had been described as 'an erection rather than a hat; an architectural wonder in which flying buttresses of ostrich feather met gutters of tulle, and dahlias perched like eager gargoyles on the rim'. Veronica Grudge, the town's elocutionist, had taken to her bed in an attack of rage which had developed into neuralgia. According to Lady Harding, who had visited her that morning, her face was puffed up beyond recognition and it was unlikely that she would recover in time for her pupils at the girls' school to perform their pieces at the next Eisteddfod. Unable to insert her plate into her swollen mouth, she had lost her ability to roll her *r*'s. A single note played on the piano was like an ivory needle plunged into Mrs Grudge's head. There was doubt whether her voice would ever regain its full emotive range, which had once moved a room to tears when she had recited the 'Death of Queen Victoria' in the voice of little Edward.

According to Lady Harding, Mrs Grudge was convinced that the writer was a friend of Miss Memory, the new elo-cutionist who had moved recently to Leura. Already Mrs Grudge's more ambitious students were driving to the next town for private lessons, lured by the newcomer's liking for show. Someone recalled that Miss Memory's performance in a recent Musicale had included some gestures which were rather 'Vaudeville'; these had been cheered with enthusiasm by the gentlemen—especially those young men who slouched about the corner of Main and Katoomba streets with evil on their minds, who had caused this spot to be known locally as Expectoration Corner. It was rumoured, another said, that Miss Memory had once played the pianoforte in Sydney in a hotel near the Quay. 'All forte and no piano,' Lady Harding said now, describing her technique.

There was also the possibility, which remained unspoken, that The Wasp might be someone from this very circle: a cuckoo in Lady Harding's ferny bower. The edge of suspicion in the room seemed to sharpen the tines of forks. The women felt them pricking at their lips as they conveyed pieces of tennis cake into their mouths. Hard fragments of nut clung to their vocal cords, causing them to clear their throats. With my keen nose I recognised, beneath the scents of liniment and gardenia, the leaking stench of Epsom Salts.

After luncheon the meeting was called to order. For seven years it had been the mission of the Fresh Air League to prevent and arrest disease. Over that time, with the funds collected from costume balls and private donations, the women had purchased farm homes at Springwood and Blackheath where sickly children and anaemic mothers were sponsored for a month. My aunts had told us how they were plucked from Surry Hills and The Rocks, where the skyless lanes were thick with hanging washing; where rats ran like ink in the gutters at night; where white children were exposed to profanities in several different tongues. The pamphlets produced by the League recounted the stories of their transformations. At the farm homes infants who were strangers to the bathtub played in streams full of sunbeams. They picked apples and ate milk puddings as soft and thick as clouds. They performed exercises in the mornings with hoops and clubs. All meals were served with generous lashings of mountain air. Then, as the ladies from the League wept, the children were driven back to the train platform and returned to the squalor of their daily lives in Sydney, with the taste of beef tea still lingering on their tongues.

I was also under strict instructions from my mother this day. I was not to divulge that she regarded the activities of the League as a form of unwitting torture. She said, 'They need to import the children to the mountains in order to convince themselves that the air is fresh.'

It had been Miss Moss's duty to choose the inspiration. She adjusted her pince-nez on her nose and read to the room with a shaking voice:

'Let me today do something that shall take
A little sadness from the world's vast store,
And may I be so forward as to make
Of joy's too scanty sum a little more.'

There was an appreciative murmur and nodding. She handed the text to my eldest aunt who entered it in the minutes book.

Apologies were tendered, the minutes of the last meeting were read, and the League's finances were reviewed by the treasurer. Then Lady Harding made an announcement: 'Ladies, I have a box of children and a box of women. Where shall we begin?' The vote for children was unanimous. From a black box with a lacquered lid she poured onto the floor a large number of letters which had been written by ministers, charitable institutions, lady volunteers and the poor themselves. The tops of the envelopes had been slit already with a paper opener. She read the letters to the group as my aunt summarised their contents for later voting. One letter, reporting child prostitution in the city, enclosed an advertisement cut from a newspaper in which the children for sale were referred to by code as sweet broccoli and corn. The author had rescued a small whore who swore like a parrot and had to be fastened with safety pins into her clothes. Having isolated her from the other children at the orphanage, the writer wondered if a month in the country away from temptation might restore the childhood which had been stolen so cruelly from her. There were other cases no less shocking: an abandoned baby had been found in a grain cart at the Darling Harbour railyards, with pigeon droppings and chaff stuck like

a halo around his head and thin green stalks of wheat ger-
minating in his ears. A little crippled girl, whose nose had
been bitten off by rats as she sat in an empty house all day
strapped with a belt to a kitchen chair. Or, more simply, there
were poorly spelled letters from women whose breasts had
run dry and could not feed their babies. As these letters were
read I felt my youngest aunt's fingers creep into my hand and
confide their sadness to my palm. I looked the other way and
kept my own hand slack.

The League voted on which of the children who had been
recommended should be conveyed to the farm homes without
delay, and scheduled a number of self-nominated applicants
for further interviews the next week at the Masonic Hall.
There was a good deal of argument about the little prostitute.
Lady Harding said that while the air was restorative of the
health its powers did not extend to spoiled virtue. It was also
doubtful, she mused, whether the girl could be thought of as
a child, given that she had acquired knowledge and experi-
ences beyond the imagination of a married woman. My eldest
aunt replied with passion that all sins could be remedied
through education and repentance. However, it was agreed,
on the vote, that the League must continue to support the
proprieties and not admit this precocious child. Then the box
of women was opened and the consumptive, battered and
exhausted were graded and assessed, to be granted or denied
their moment in the clouds.

After a short break, during which the women sorted out
the details of their rostered duties, the speaker arrived to
address the group on the possibility of setting up a boys'

brigade of the Fresh Air League. A retired officer of the colonial police, he emphasised the importance of learning to
protect the Blue Mountains' precious assets. He displayed a
sketch of the uniform which he had designed, of long shorts
and a belted jacket, and proposed to give lessons in drill,
meteorology and semaphore on the estate's expansive lawns.
The mastery of each task would be rewarded with a 'cloud',
a white patch which could be sewn by each boy to the sleeves
of his uniform with blanket stitch.

He spoke with enthusiasm as the shadows of the pines slid
like hatpins through the house. Outside I watched the Hardings' cat, General Gordon, patrolling the perimeters of the
flower beds, with his tail held in the air.

I had no philosophical argument with spirit drawing. Nor did
I have any difficulty holding a charcoal pencil deftly between
two fingers and a thumb. I simply could not draw with my
eyes closed or dimly focused on the far side of a room. Sooner
or later the sights before me would creep across the page. In
some of my sketches my mother rests her cheek against the
frame of a window, the weak mist of her breath separated
from the fog outside by the thinness of a windowpane. In
others, my aunts wait for the air to guide their hands, necks
stretched back in attentive rictus, legs slightly apart, paper pads
upon their knees. Or they move tight agitated fists across their
laps, feeling the whisper of charcoal through the grain. Their
mouths are slightly open. The faces of young spirit men
materialise at their fingertips: framed by fine curling hair, they

have the intense eyes of hypnotists. Unlike Lady Harding my aunts could not talk and draw at once.

My mother did not see how any current could enter this house which was nailed and shuttered against even the most determined gust. Draught excluders were crammed in every doorway. The fireplace struggled to draw breath. Yet in spite of my mother's insistence that stifling rooms incubated influenza and catarrh, my aunts were determined to keep the windows tightly sealed. They said it was essential to maintain a harmonious balance between the gases in the house. For there were other spirits here, like shy marsupials, which required a familiar habitat. They curled themselves inside the pouches of the air and suspended soft nocturnal hammocks from the picture rails. Their large round eyes were troubled by the light. They reached out velvet fingers with spatulate ends to climb up the walls in the dark. They had been lured indoors gently, following the smoky trails of candles, and had been domesticated with the scent of lavender. If they were startled they would rush back out onto some unknown heath, hungering for the taste of flannel flowers.

In particular, my aunts did not want to disturb the spirit babies nestled in the fuggy air. Ten years before our arrival, they had invited a famous medium to the house who specialised in full-form materialisations. For an extra fee she offered trance speaking and would call on Shakespeare as her spirit guide. The large cabinet she brought wore a decoupage of labels from great ocean liners. She had left England gladly, tired of being on guard against those sceptical men who had recently begun to leap up and snatch the curtains from her cabinet during seances and who wrote scathing letters regularly to the *Times*. There had also been a sudden influx into her trade of sharp nubile girls who ran about in calico shifts and invited the gentlemen to wander freely with their hands. She liked Australia, where the spirits were less plentiful than sheep. In the old country they were headstrong; here, in this new country, they needed to be coaxed rather than appeased, since they were shy and uncertain in the ways of ghosts. Yet sometimes, if she was not careful, she felt an angry droning at the edges of her skull, as older presences demanded her attention; the concentration needed to tune them out left her with a migraine headache which persisted for several days. When that happened she had to take a rest cure at Manly and give herself over to the soothing lapping of the waves.

My aunts had assembled a large group on the heavy furniture of the drawing room. A creaking of whalebone registered the widows' agitation at the thought of hearing their husbands issue marital demands from beyond the grave. Victoria Douglass had asked my eldest aunt if Mr Douglass would appear wearing mutton-chop whiskers now that they were no longer the fashion, and blushed at the thought of seeing his cheeks for the first time smooth and bare. Outside, on the other side of the curtains, the sun and the cicadas hurled themselves against the glass. The room was so hot that the women's feet swelled against the laces and eyelets of their boots. The medium sat between my aunts. Her still hands made damp patches on the beeswax polish of the tabletop. She explained that she conducted her business on the principles of science. Death was merely the transformation of the soul. She asked them to imagine the spirits in the air as fluctuating lightning looking for a conductor and showed them the scars of fire down her arms.

The medium had walked into her cabinet. She asked my aunts to tie calico bandages around her neck and hands and secure them to a pole. Then she bade them to bind her ankles and give the other end to Mrs Douglass. At her command they closed the curtains and waited in the darkness.

After a couple of minutes a breeze had begun to stir the room and the portraits hanging from the picture rail began to quiver. A quick, repetitive rapping was heard against the ceilings and the walls. The table began to rock and rose into the air without spilling a drop of water from the vase of cornflowers which slid about upon its top. Antimacassars and doilies flew around them like snowflakes in a storm. Suddenly three small coffins appeared and spirit children jumped out and ran about the room. Their cheeks were as pale as plaster and their white-lashed eyelids were marked with delicate purple veins. Yet they were most definitely children, for they smelled of soil and the lettuce at the bottom of silkworm boxes and the urine of white mice. They pinched the women and pulled the earrings from their ears. They reached out and stroked their cheeks with small indecent hands. Two widows fainted but my aunts sat straight and did not move. The cord attached to the medium's cabinet was as still and limp as death. At last, when the yellowed knucklebones of sheep tumbled from the ceiling by the hundreds, the children played jacks with them and used them as tors to hopscotch across the floor.

Then their bodies appeared to elongate and they slid behind the fire screen. When my aunts pulled back the curtain of the cabinet the medium lay in a faint upon the floor. A frothy substance bubbled from her lips, as if she had vomited a cloud.

From this moment the house was filled with babies too delicate to appear on my aunts' drawing paper. Sometimes they could be coaxed to leave an outline on the finest tissue paper, but usually the only signs of their presence were small depressions on the counterpanes and chairs. If you found them soon enough, their nests smelt of milk and were warm beneath your hands. When my youngest aunt told me this story she said that even as she spoke she could still feel the touch of the spirit children's fingers on her cheek. From the way her hand rested on her breast I knew that she also heard an intermittent cry this autumn afternoon, as some part of her hardened in response to a hunger in the air.

Strange that my aunts could see spirits but passed without a glance by dark faces in the streets around the Family Hotel.

Odd, too, that they refused to see the shadow of death move across my mother's face.

My mother particularly disliked those letters which arrived at the newspaper offices each week and were delivered with the others to my aunts' house in a laundry basket; unsigned, and full of insinuation, as if they had been scrawled by malicious spirit hands. It was in this way that we learned of Mr Medlicott's collection of pessaries, glass syringes and prophylactics and his pamphets full of Latin words on the perfection of the British race. We read the names of visitors who moved about us unchecked, coughing into handkerchiefs, spreading the tuberculosis bacillus. One week, five anonymous letters announced that Miss Clerkenwell had contracted a private complaint from her weekly appointment with the vegetable cart, although no one could recall the driver's face. My mother could see where angry pens had split the ends of their nibs in the formation of emphatic periods. She could trace the trembling of anger in the spindly violet hand which claimed her as a friend. From the slant of the copperplate and the choice of stationery my mother could tell that most letters were written by women. That winter, she began to fear that the inks released poisons into her blood and dulled the beating of her heart.

She had little time to go outdoors and seek a cure. With her left hand she massaged the pins and needles in her shoulders. She told me that those airy youths with spaniels' curls, whose portraits were pinned up above the mantelpiece, were more eager to inspire the workings of my aunts' pens than her own. Even spirit men, she laughed, were quick to disdain the domestic workings of the house. When she kissed me at night she smelled of nutmeg and rosewater and boracic acid. Sometimes she thought the spirit babies hung heavily from her skirts, attracted by the scent of eucalyptus.

On the few occasions when my mother walked with me along the mountain paths, I saw a blueness around her lips as if each crack in their surface revealed the heart of a little glacier. Her fingers were cold. When we reached the lookout she was short of breath. As she bent her head forward I noticed a white frost along the valley of her part and her voice when she spoke was as thin as ice. She said she could only see a landscape marred by stains. The valleys were creased. The paths were dusty. The cliffs were dull and needed polishing. She wondered how she had ever thought them stunning.

For the last month of my mother's life Katoomba was wrapped in winter mists. In the mornings the valleys were like giant kettles slowly filling up with steam. From their surfaces veils of cloud unfurled and sluggishly detached themselves. The wet branches of the trees were wound in vapour and thick and pale with moss. Biscuits softened in their tins. Spiderwebs broke under the weight of clouds. When we stood at the Witch's Leap we could only sense infinite voids hidden behind walls of bulging whiteness while we heard waterfalls falling forever against invisible cliffs. My mother whispered that she could not breathe and undid the buttons at her throat. The mist in the valleys made her think of ink. It spilt over the safety barriers and ran into her thoughts. She thought of my father, alone, wandering in the clouds, lured to the edges of cliffs by the bright parrots which dived laughing at his head. Three days later she was dead. Heedless of my aunts' protests I threw open every window in the house until the dew settled on the tables.

Among the photographs in my trunk there is a portrait taken by one of Harry Kitchings' competitors on an autumn afternoon. My mother and my aunts, dressed in dark skirts, are standing in profile at Echo Point. Their hands rest light as lichen on the guard rail. At the right of the photograph, level with their heads, the Three Sisters stand in outline, underexposed against a sky streaked with cirrus cloud. Each woman stares out across the void as if waiting for a message from the clouds. The dark cliff curves in and severs the air beneath their feet. The sight of these three sisters—the ill one standing in the middle; their proximity to those careworn rocks— aroused in the photographer a strange excitement. There was something stirring about the association of women and vertigo and death. With a trembling voice he had asked them to keep still. He arranged them against the view and locked them in his frame. He depressed the shutter and extinguished time.

In the photograph my mother and aunts loom at the cliff's edge like a beautiful accident caught in the lens of the photographer's desire. But I cannot quite believe its symmetry. For I was there that day, standing behind him as he bent beneath his velvet cape in poetic agitation. Being a fourth and inconvenient body, and not a sister, I was not allowed to pose.

Let me tell you what really happened. In the relentless shutter of my sight my aunts are caught doing household calculations in their heads. My mother scans the horizon for stains. Only the thought of the next deadline stills her urge to climb over the railed edge and leap with arms thrown open out into the air—to let her filling skirt carry her, bobbing and luminous, across the currents like a jellyfish, trailing lazy tentacles of vapour, following the clouds.

$$=== 4 ===$$

Perhaps Harry Kitchings' conversion was as sudden as he
claimed. Maybe it is true that he woke one morning,
as his mother disinfected his sickroom floor with carbolic acid,
to find his eyes watering; that he saw the scales fall from them
and drift onto the counterpane like dandruff; that he became
aware of the presence of God filling the room like the shadow
of a mountain. It was a good account, as Harry told it. We
appreciated its symmetry and neatness, for this has always been
a town which thrives on storytelling.

Yet I find it difficult to believe. It is not the strength of his
faith that I doubt, for I witnessed him step off cliffs with his
eyes closed many times to land on rocky ledges, while, just
as trusting, I squandered the gifts of my youth on him. Instead,
it is the suddenness which disturbs me. I think it is unlikely
that one day Harry Kitchings was drinking beer from a bottle
bearing the same brown label which, still damp, was reproduced all around him in piles as high as the ceiling while he
worked the treadle of the press with his foot—and that the

next he was in pain but sober, and planning from his sickbed to send every man, woman and child home from Katoomba with their pockets filled with clouds.

I'll wager that Harry's mother, with her boxes of secrets which clattered like windchimes in the shed at night, shared my disquiet.

She knew that since the moment of his birth each cell in her son's body had been quietly growing towards the light.

Now in 1906 the thick bandages around his left hand had put an end to that career which had so far thwarted the family madness. She wondered, as he muttered strange feverish things in his sleep in this house among the jacaranda trees in Neutral Bay, if it had only been deferred. When she rested the mop against the wall she noticed that her heart was beating fast inside her head. She thought that she could smell the brine in the old cases she had hidden near the outhouse. She realised, for the first time in sixty-eight years, that she felt her age.

'Ask the doctor,' Harry had begged her, 'to open up the stitches and tell me what is written on my bones.'

Training Harry to be a printer had seemed a good means of defying the directives in his blood. Harry's mother was familiar with the principles of homoeopathy. She knew that small doses of poisons which reproduced the symptoms of an illness could be administered in order to prevent it. It occurred to her that this science might be extended to the treatment of photographic manias. While a number of skills required by their trade were similar, printers, she knew, could not lure young girls to their offices, as photographers did, by offering to catch the light reflected off their bodies in the hollows of their hands. The press could not be strapped to a body like a ridiculous appendage. Its untreated papers did not encourage habits of peering into things, trying to unlayer them, lifting light at the edges, desiring always to force some revelation.

When Harry was five she had given him a set of little rubber stamps which, inked and pressed onto butcher's paper, formed the firm, unambiguous outlines of zoo animals and centurions and Eskimos. He had, in addition, a number of blocks painted with the letters of the alphabet, and another set of wooden squares, with which it was possible to reconstruct, by turning them, six colourful illustrations of stories from the Bible; in these pictures the baby Moses smiled among the rushes, while Jesus, his hair cut neatly in a page-boy, stood on a box to preach at the temple as a child. Harry was also kept at a safe distance from the harbour where reflections slid on the glassy water as if they were looking for a frame, and tall ships filled with explorers and adulterers sailed for foreign lands. Yet, in order to stop him craving for the sea, he was sometimes allowed to walk among the bubbling crab-holes with his mother at noon when their shrunken shadows skipped like footballs near their feet. Each night, as a countermeasure, a teaspoon of salt was stirred into his tea.

By the time he was eight, Harry could write in perfect copperplate, and make fair copies of the illustrations of piano-fortes and iron knockers in the catalogue of Lassetters' Universal Providers in Pitt Street where his father worked. When he showed a talent for mathematics, his father gave him a wooden case on which they burned his initials carefully with heated pins. It contained a compass, two carpenter's pencils and a ruler which folded into three, with which they tried to calculate the speed of light. With squared graph paper his mother set him to copy the shiny black and silver etchings in her *Commonwealth Book of Cakes*. She was not to know that as her son traced the glacial smoothness of their slopes and the rosettes stuck like crampons in their sides, he dreamed that he scaled the crevasses of the Matterhorn. She did not know that the first time he tasted wedding cake he was disappointed that it did not taste of silver.

Nor could Harry's mother protect him from the packages sent by his aunt which turned up in the hallway unannounced and for which no one appeared to have signed. Harry's father was not alarmed. He smiled mildly when he saw her familiar capitals scrawled into the brown paper so hard that they had torn it. 'She is the only person on this earth,' he said, 'who has the capacity to bellow by post.' But Harry's mother was disturbed by those packages which bore suspicious scents of stout and gin and gunpowder, and a less tangible odour which she identified as sex. Inside, there were gifts for Harry: a brass telescope given to his grandmother by her last lover, a squinting sea captain who had been obliged, after their first encounter, when the bedhead had bucked against the wall and a gale blew the sheets around his head, to fix an old anchor to each bedknob to keep the bed from sliding from the room; dark jungle night-moths and pale desert insects pinned to boards through abdomens as large as eggs; the opaque and calcareous thumbnail of a Chinese scribe, stained by ink and opium, a substance which, given her own thick visions, she did not recommend to Harry until he was 'at least sixteen'; a collection of Keats' poems, the stiff pages stinking of sailcloth, which she claimed had been found in Shelley's pocket on the day he was pulled dead from the variegated waters off the Italian coast. In other packages, he found a whale's tooth, a shrunken head, and a ring woven from the twiny hairs of an elephant's tail. She sent him Whymper's *Scrambles Amongst the Alps*, all the volumes of Ruskin's *Modern Painters*, and the journal of an adventurer who had transcribed the sounds made by Niagara Falls onto musical staves. 'Having never clapped eyes on you,' his aunt wrote, 'I do not know if you are a namby-pamby, a bully, or a nincompoop. Therefore, I have taken the liberty of choosing the presents that a chap like myself would want.'

Yet, apart from a brief passion for collecting shells on his harbourside walks—which were arranged along his windowsill and filled the house from time to time with the pungent smell of baking marine animals—and a tendency to peer for prolonged periods of time through doors, Harry displayed none of the ill effects anticipated by his mother. He went to school each day but his language was not coarsened. He returned promptly each evening. His mother could detect no evidence of an unhealthy desire for the company of other children and their corrupting games.

Thus, at fourteen, having never developed a craving for opium or photography, Harry left school, and was apprenticed to a printing works in the city across the bay. His first job was to stand in the dark dock where the basement met the street and take delivery of the large rolls of india papers and bonds and book woves which the paper merchants, silent men with blind men's hands, collected from the different mills. Each night Harry's mother painted his paper cuts with a swab soaked in mercurichrome. The marks along the insides of his arms lasted for weeks before they faded, strange purple idiographs which were crossed and amended by each day's work and revealed by each evening's application, so that Harry's workmates soon christened him 'Tattoo'. His mother found this nickname, bearing connotations of flesh and savagery, so distasteful that she discontinued the practice but by this time the older men had forgotten the name of their shy apprentice and the nickname stuck faster than dye. It was even used by Harry's father when he sat on the damp bench of the steam ferry next to his son and read to him about the fluctuations in the prices of glass and iron, as the pages of the newspaper writhed and filled like sails in the salty wind.

Harry's mother had also noticed below her son's rolled shirtsleeves the tautness of his forearms. He had a bird's skeleton, light and hollow-boned like his father's, but there were knots and striations in the long bands of muscle that ran along the bones and up to the hollows of his shoulders, which corresponded to the work of cutting and counting and wrapping the supple piles of printed paper on the workroom tables. Soon he could tell by its weight the number of pages in a bundle. In each sheet he could feel with his fingertips the thickness and direction of the grain. He learned to sweat only at lunchtimes, in order not to stain the expensive laid papers with his hands. On his mother's advice, he carried a clean shirt to change into after he had eaten, seated among the barrels and offcuts in the inky shade of the loading bay, chewing and listening to the laughter of the older men. Sometimes it was directed, gently, at this light boy whose body was too thin to crush the paper scraps and seemed, instead, to float upon them. His features had not thickened yet. His lips, which always settled into the hint of a smile, had not set, like theirs, into a straight, grim line. He seemed, beneath fleshy eyelids, half closed, to be turning dreams, as regular as a printing press, over and over inside his head. When he stood, the offcuts trailed from his damp body like seaweed off a dead man's arms. But he returned from the dunny, wearing his fresh shirt, as dry and golden as if someone had thrown a handful of talcum powder over him.

A year later Harry was allowed to spread inks onto the rollers and learned how to slow the huge machines so that not a trace of pigment passed as set-off onto the backs of the pages which were piled on one another. When he had mastered that task he was trained to watch out for monks and friars, those rogue smudges and ghostly spaces caused by the slip of a roller or the bite of a frisket which disturbed the secular order of the print. As he worked, he watched the other apprentices on their hands and knees, becoming faster at filling the type cases which the foreman had emptied on the floor, until they could reach into them without looking to fill the compositors' blocks. He saw how they adjusted the spaces between the words so that no widows lingered at the tops of pages, or orphans at their bases, stray words which discomforted the readers' eyes. Much later he learned to adjust the weight of the inks so that the letters penetrated so far, but no further, into the surface of the page. One day he found that he could tell by a difference in the percussive notes of the machinery if the tones of a page had changed. Then, without pausing, he felt for the aberrant sheet with his fingers as it came damp off the rollers, and threw it, without looking, on the floor. That day, he realised, surprised, that he was eighteen and a man.

For the next month Harry rarely caught the ferry with his father. Instead he went with the other men to hotels near the Quay. He drank beer and felt his tongue come loose and words wash golden through his mouth. He took long stairways cut through the night and leaned his head on the coldness of stone walls. The sawdust from the bar-room floors caught between his socks and shoes and made his footsteps slippery. He saw women in the doorways of tenements whose faces glowed as pale and milky as the moon. The back lanes behind the hotels were soft and sweet with phlegm and rags, stools and figs, and the discarded legs of crabs. Once he bent over and saw splashed on the cobbles his own hot intestinal gush. He walked into another public house and drank more, as if he filled one of those dark corridors he passed with light, as if his chest were also an indistinct architecture of shadows open to the street. When his mother boiled his clothes in the copper she could hear the faint bubbling of curses and saw, rising from his pockets, the grey steam of ocean liners.

She knew that he must travel in carefully measured doses or be lost to her forever.

She sent him out into the world as a journeyman, trusting in the press to serve him as a great, dark anchor.

For the next fourteen years, I am guessing, no dreams troubled Harry Kitchings' sleep. His nights must have looked like flat black landscapes. He would wake in the morning and never wonder, like other sleepers, where he was, or feel that dim nostalgic sense of returning to himself. His soul was packed as tight as a compositor's letters in their case. Only when he was on a drunk might he feel it begin to dissolve and drift, as soft as candle smoke, brushing its own edges.

During this time he travelled around the country, following his trade to stilted wooden offices in Queensland, so small that the editors composed the papers' stories straight onto the plates with their hands in the letter cases and their braces hanging loose around their waists. He stood in sheds in the goldfields around Kalgoorlie where the printing works grew fat on spoiled hopes, setting and printing auction handbills and foreclosure notices. There, in an iron shed in the middle of the hot pumpkin-coloured desert, Harry had seen a French etcher die, mad with fumes and loneliness, having swallowed a pitcher of nitric acid in order, he said, to cleanse the orange from his blood. In Gippsland, Harry had helped a bankrupt editor force the door of his flooded workshop. The man had laughed when he saw the Brevier and Bourgeois letters poking from the muddy floor spelling out the failure of his life. 'Damn! I never saw type lifted so fast,' he roared, before he sat on a birdcage and wept.

At a sheet music house in Hobart Harry worked for six months printing love songs and Federation Waltzes. Each evening he walked to work through a lemon-and-violet dusk when the air was as chill and sweet as a meringue and the whole island seemed to drift south towards the Pole. Each night he and Wish-Bone Sam drank whisky and read the copy out to one another, checking the galley proofs for dirty words snuck in by the typesetters during the day, before they oiled and started up the presses. They mixed the gold and purple inks with their fingers and spread them smooth across the rollers. They adjusted the weight of the black ink so that the fat notes did not bend the tight lines of the staves. The loud machines slapped down gilded love words by the thousands. Towards dawn Wish-Bone Sam walked down the hill in the direction of the harbour while his heartbeat echoed off the sandstone walls. In a cold yard behind the customs house a salesman sucked the colours from his fingers, turning them like pianola rolls, until his head was filled with sentimental tunes. An hour later Wish-Bone Sam returned and wiped his groin with discarded copies from the press and threw them on the floor so that it looked as if the damp black quavers had issued from his sex. As Harry rested, Wish-Bone Sam cleaned the office for the morning shift, waking him when he had finished, and they stood together in the doorway, squinting, until their eyes grew accustomed to the light. Then Wish-Bone Sam walked back up the hill, quickly, before his heart snapped, towards the woman in his life.

One summer Harry Kitchings worked for a type company in Broome. Each morning the orders were collected and delivered by a limping Malay boy with air bubbles in his head. He told Harry how he had nearly drowned, far beneath the sea, his foot trapped inside a giant shellfish. He said he had been rescued by a woman who brought him lifeless to the surface and pillowed his head on the warm ocean and breathed into his mouth. As he gulped the air her beauty had closed like a bright starfish around his heart. When he woke up on the beach with three of his toes gone there was something lodged inside his skull. He said it was the pearl which he had felt buried in the flesh beneath her tongue.

It is hardly surprising, then, that once he had heard this story Harry scarcely glanced at the women who moved heavily through the humid streets of Broome, their chests encased in bodices as stiff as coral, as he walked home towards his dreamless sleep. Through the slatted wall, as he lay on his bed, he could hear a temperance lecture taking place, in the tent which had been erected on the bare expanse of red soil behind the church next door. He heard the speaker say, 'May God wither the hand which reaches to befriend the demon drink,' before his lantern slides melted in the heat; an event which only those who were drunk witnessed as a miracle. As the crowd left, the first gusts of a tropical storm whipped the guy ropes from their pegs. Harry lay beneath his mosquito net, listening to the creaking walls and the flapping canvas, feeling the cold beer bubbles rolling through his veins.

I cannot remember how much of this Harry Kitchings told me and how much I have made up, as women do, stitching together the scraps a man offers of himself. There are certain details which he surely did not mention, which I must have deduced later, based on my bitter knowledge of the ways of men. It has occurred to me since that perhaps his whole past was my invention; that I recited these events against his silence over and over in my head until they became real, in order to convince myself that we were close; that he may have worked deliberately at vagueness, keeping himself as distant and insubstantial as a cloud, flinching from my feelings, watching with pity as I tried to give his words a shape. Even now I am unable to bear this thought—that he may have told me nothing of his life.

On the other hand, I have also wondered if most women, faced with putting together worlds from the few words granted us by men, are not, by necessity, the great and unacknowledged storytellers of this country.

I can only tell you this. Our love was not the kind that could be marked in history and maps. We did not speak of it ourselves but instead deduced the landscape of our feelings from looks and gestures and the grandeur of his metaphors. It was a soft cartography which we inhabited. When my disappointment came, no one would believe that our love had existed and there was no language to describe it. Then, at last, as my heart shrank, I began to doubt it myself.

Yet I must stop here before I anticipate too much. I am aware that my sadness has drifted into this account and insinuated itself between the lines of every page, while history does not work like this, recognising its own symptoms, heading always towards one end.

At this time, like a thin band of cloud on the horizon, my betrayal was very far away.

Harry Kitchings returned to Sydney in 1905 two months after his father's death. One lunchtime, troubled by a persistent headache, his father had finished checking his columns of figures and closed the three bottles on his accountant's inkstand. For the first time he did not take the stairs, but used the gilded customer elevator, smiling and nodding each time its doors opened onto vast bright floors filled with French-shape bedpans and piano-box buggies and steel ceilings and electroplated wares. The mirrors around him made him dizzy. He marvelled to feel the floor, at each twitch of the great steel cables, tremble and lurch beneath his feet. In the courtyard he found that he had no appetite, but began regardless to eat his sandwich because his wife had made it for him, pressing it flat with her sensible hands. It surprised him when he noticed that there were tears springing from the thick flesh around his eyes. Two storemen found him lying sideways on a bench with his legs curled up beside him. They wrapped him in a dust sheet and lugged him through the trades entrance, up the back stairs, and into a stock room, where they laid him on a pile of Persian carpets. When a trickle of eggy blood ran from the corner of his mouth the manager put a plug into an enamel bathtub and ordered them to lift him into it. A doctor, shopping for lamp fittings on the first floor, consented to examine him and pronounced him dead.

Harry's mother ran down the hill to meet the ferry, filled with a presentiment of this disaster, her feet sliding on the thick jacaranda blossoms. All through January and February, until Harry Kitchings could come home, the purple tracks of her grief would linger on Kurraba Road in spite of the heavy rains.

As the ferry berthed, and the delivery boys struggled to lift the bathtub by its clawed legs over the gangplank, she saw her husband's head nodding on the frail stem of his neck. At the house she instructed the boys to lay Harry's father on the dining table. When they were gone she kissed him softly on the lips and tasted the dried blood in his moustache. She held his thin knuckles to her face and felt how his polite fingers had been made strangely weightless by death. He looked younger than he had when they were married. It was only when she saw the breadcrumbs that she cried. Nobody at the store where he had worked for thirty years had thought to brush them from his chin.

For three days, until her husband was put in the ground, the grim unprinted faces from a hundred towns and deserts appeared again on her palms, weeping silver tears.

Two months later, Harry Kitchings put down his travelling kit, opened the door of his old bedroom, with its smells of leather bindings and firecrackers and scented woods, and felt his childhood dreams press around him like the smooth familiar contours of a shell. It was as if the last fourteen years of empty nights had not taken place. He had left no traces of himself out there: no phosphorescent trails of dream or nightmare to connect him to those landscapes. When he sat on the edge of his bed he felt a dull ache at the base of his spine. He realised that since the last time he had sat there a stiffness had crept into his bones, as if, in spite of the repetition of his days, they had still filled with the sorrow of time passing. After eighteen years of lifting type he no longer made the quick, cartilaginous movements of a boy. His skin had set upon his flesh and become tough and brown from passing between so many time zones. The collar of his shirt itched. His lungs were tight, even with the window open. His throat hurt. 'I'm going out for a wet,' he told his mother, kissing her cheek in the hallway, before he walked to the nearest hotel.

He found work quickly in a small printery owned by a mission society in a lane off Goulburn Street. At nightfall when he walked home past the cramped back quarters of the leaning tenements, where the sun reached only as a faint colour and never as heat, the cool air set and glowed around him. The strange flat scents of dried jasmine and star anise gilded the skin of the waxy orange twilight. Inside a draughty wooden shed, Harry printed hymnals and Bibles and the mission's journal, the *Trumpeteer*. When the society was short of funds he printed beer labels for a brewery at the Argyle Cut.

The type was set by Bolter O'Grady, a short bald man with trembling fingers which ended in fat pink buds of flesh where he had bitten the nails back deep below the tips. He had worked as a cook for the society on a steamy island in the Coral Sea where he had seen the brown men who had been moved there from the mainland absorb that strange humidity in the air into their skins which prevented cuts from healing; he had seen the red splits in the soles of their feet as they knelt in the chapel praying for forgiveness. One day Bolter had cut his own arm with a boning knife. The wound swelled up and a week later, when he squeezed the hot pus out of it, a mass of wriggling larvae exploded onto the tabletop. The missionary had found him screaming and holding his arm over the open fire. They had had to tie him up and lock him in the men's dormitory but he raved and howled until the men refused to stay in the camp and picked the locks and swam over to another island. Bolter stripped naked and ran out of the open door to show the missionary's wife his stomach, as pale and segmented as a maggot's, as proof of what he had become. He would eat no meat. He could only be kept alive with communion wafers dipped in gin.

The mission society had shipped Bolter back to Sydney and trained him to lift type. On most days he sat hunched on a high bench at the linotype-machine and worked swiftly with his tongue between his lips. Sometimes, as he worked, he would tell Harry Kitchings about the mission: about the time, when the society had sent more books than food, that he had to soak the thick pages of hymnals and layer them with custard to make his puddings; how the bloated musical notes had tasted like currants; how the mission would let nobody into its church in George Street unless they brought threepence for the offertory plate. At other times, when large cockroaches flew into the rollers and were squashed onto the maps of Africa, or when he found their brittle egg cases floating in the open tins of ink, or when he saw too many foreign faces in the streets, Bolter would think that he was up north again, and drink gin and mutter prayers and bite his knuckles until they bled.

On the day that Harry's hand was crushed between the platen and the type, Bolter heard the bones break and saw his fingers burst open like sausages on a fire. He leaned back and pressed the keys of the linotype-machine as if it were a huge church organ until Harry had stopped moaning and then he shuffled out into the lane singing hymn tunes softly to himself. Some time later an old man wearing slippers on his feet came in through the open door. He held Harry by the chin and shook his head from side to side until he woke. He frowned at Harry's hand which was already as swollen as a pig's trotter. Wrapping it tightly with Harry's handkerchief, he helped him to the tram. 'Do not eat fish or the wound will become infected,' he shouted in his ear, as he pushed him roughly up the steps.

For a month Harry Kitchings lay in bed and when he rose he had turned into the man whom, one year later, I would begin to love. At least, that is a simple way of putting it, if you do not believe, as I do, that this feeling had already started in the multiplication of cells, in my father's jumping ship, in the cutting of roads and lookouts in the Blue Mountains—that we simply began to inhabit these stories because we could not do anything else, mistaking all these other people's histories for our own.

Whatever the truth of that may be, I can tell you this much. For those two months Harry Kitchings' condition showed almost no improvement. It may have been because his mother had fed him scalloped oysters in spite of the warning he had received in George Street that seafood increased the heat of wounds and left a person vulnerable to ghosts. Perhaps it was because the press had broken Harry's concentration so that now his skin could no longer resist the strong contours of his childhood dreams as they forced themselves around his flesh. It may have been due to the insanitary nature of the workshop or the leakage of red map inks into his blood. For Harry's hand remained inflamed and resisted the application of iodine and fomentations. When he woke from a turbulent sleep he re-read the books stacked upon the shelves until the print seemed to move about before his eyes, and kept moving in his dreams. When he slept, his moustache was stuck to his upper lip with sweat. His mother wiped it with a cloth as if the blond hairs were pale pencil marks which she tried gently to erase. She observed that he slept with his face pointed at the ceiling, his neck arched back, so that the soft boy's skin around his Adam's apple was exposed. He held his good arm tight against his side. She laid a hand across his forehead. His expression did not change. His body lay straight along the cool length of the bed.

His mother stepped back. She thought, surprised, *He has never had a woman.*

When the swelling lessened and the bandages were removed Harry's left hand had set into the gesture of a cricket player about to make a catch, the three middle fingers bent back, a deep depression where his knuckles had once been. Printed into the flesh around the stitches there was a broken line of text, the letters set in Gothic type. It was from one of the mission's Bibles, yet neither Harry nor his mother could decipher it.

Harry had been drinking as he worked the press, so he

dictated a letter to his mother which she posted to the mission society, requesting a conference with Bolter, who had set the type, and might recall the passage. The chairman replied that there had never, to his knowledge, been a George O'Grady in his employ; indeed there were no records of his existence. As far as the society knew, he wrote, Harry Kitchings had been working on his own, and had failed in his duty when he had left the print shop unattended. As a consequence, thieves had stolen a crate of Bibles, and an entire month's issue of the *Trumpeteer*. For weeks their pages had appeared around the city wrapped around legs of ham and lining the insides of newly polished cabinets. The thin india papers of the Bibles had been folded into little envelopes for dried plants which weighed less than air on the herbalists' scales. Young ruffians had been sighted in The Rocks rolling psalms around tobacco.

Harry Kitchings knew now that he had been sent a message from God and that it would be his life's work to find out what it meant.

As he peered and squinted at his damaged hand his condition began to worsen. He lay for hours watching the sunlight thrown by the water into his room and thought that the motes of dust which floated in it were angels with bright transparent bellies; in his dreams they turned into pink schools of prawns and chased him through the night. His bones ached. His face burned. His hand began to swell again, oozing a silver fluid, as if mercury were forming beneath his skin. That was when the lines appeared around the edges of his vision. He watched the shadows around him stretching and contracting, slug-like, as they felt out the limits of these new frames. He saw each object in his room detach itself from the next as if it no longer shared the common element of air. He observed that his white sheets were made up of particles of light, bunching and unbunching into clumps and billows. He was almost weightless now. He recognised his body as a coincidence of light. His eyes were as sensitive as photographic plates.

When Harry told his mother these things she called for the doctor, who examined him, and said he had infected his hand by reading it too much. 'There is little more I can recommend for your son,' he told her, 'except a change of air.' As she saw the doctor out she realised that Harry would become a photographer or die, and knew then what she must do. She used a jemmy to retrieve the cameras and the glass plates with their blooms of mould from the shed and took them to his room. Then, when she had cried all her tears, she made arrangements to send him to the Blue Mountains.

These were the symptoms of summer which I had come to recognise: sunstroke, dizziness, and gravel rash; thrush, bee stings, and apoplexy; a nostalgia for unremembered things. Everywhere I looked I saw skins grown pale and tight from eating too much cucumber. I sold purgatives to relieve torsion of the intestines induced by eating tennis cake and riding in hot air balloons. I observed people with bandaged limbs who had forgotten the continuous proximity of death in that high place and stepped over the railings to walk too near the edges of the valleys. I saw rope burns on their arms which had occurred during rescues as they were winched up moonlit cliffs.

To this list I added the dull sadness which clung to me like the blue sweat of eucalyptus that hung over the valley at the far end of the town.

It had been seven months since my mother's death and I was still haunted by the smell of calla lilies.

In spite of her wish to slip into the ground as quietly as a letter sliding into its envelope, my aunts had walked to Chandler's in Main Street and purchased a coffin with ornate silver handles for my mother. They shook their heads as if her death was the final example of her wilfulness. They found her request to be buried without her undergarments too scandalous to consider. After we had laid her out, the women of the Fresh Air League came to view my mother's body, offering scented posies as tickets of admission to the spectacle of death. They also offered their company at my aunts' house to revenge themselves on my mother's disdain. They inspected her face and compared the other flowers around the coffin with their own. They dabbed their eyes and ate cinnamon cakes and whispered loudly to my aunts that I did not cry. My mother lay with her eyes resolutely closed, a small frown-line between them, as if she concentrated hard on staying dead. She had told me once that her wedding bouquet had been filled with lilies purchased by my father, who found comfort in their firm white flesh. Not wanting to offend him, my mother had caused a murmur as she walked up the aisle carrying those waxy flowers of death. The hard orange stamens, when she touched them, had left a greasy substance on her fingers. My aunts had dismissed her distaste for these flowers, when I told them, and arranged the long stalks around her in the coffin.

In the months which followed I had little appetite for anything except lemon drops and sherbet which brought a rush of saliva to my mouth. I was plagued by the sensation that the dry tips of gum leaves pricked the insides of my veins. I suffered continually from a tightness of the throat, as if I had swallowed china, its cold weight settling on my voice. I was a hollow thing, afflicted by lightness, unable to stand still. My bones itched and my wrists were full of air. At night, if I could sleep at all, it was only with my hands tied with a ribbon by my sides beneath the counterpane: for if this precaution was not taken I would wake with my fingers chafed and sore from drifting from my body to feel for some hidden hinge in wood or cloth or air.

It had something to do, in addition, with the repeated shock of crossing doorsteps. In the cardamom stillness of Medlicott's Dispensing Pharmacy the customers moved slowly. They stood back on their heels to regard the coloured powders arranged in long rows along the wall behind the counter as if they chose embroidery silks. They felt the weight of cold glass stoppers in their footsteps and the hush of gentian violet on their tongues. Yet when I stepped outside to sweep the doorway or to take the cashbox to the bank, the light leaped down to slap me in the face. Cicadas shrieked as if they were squeezed between fingers of brightness and calibrated the rising electricity in the air.

After work, in order to put off returning to my aunts' house, where the windows were nailed shut and the air smelled of warm cushions, I walked to Echo Point. Since the day my mother died, when I threw the house open to the mist, the spirit babies had disappeared. They would not be lured back with bowls of milk or teething rusks. Even the bottles of eucalyptus oil which I brought back from the shop and placed in saucers with lit wicks did not attract them. Only the mosquitoes cried around our heads at night. My aunts consulted newspapers from the city and wrote to the clairvoyants who advertised in their columns. Most did not reply, although some wrote back to ask my aunts how many months they had been troubled by the spirits, and informed them of the price of exorcism. It was Mr Medlicott who made sense of this strange correspondence at last; their notices bore a family relation, he said, to those advertisements for Madam Krutz's Reliable Pills, which promised to cure female irregularities by removing any obstructions. 'By that, of course,' he said, 'they mean unwanted infants.' From this time on my aunts had worn black and sipped their tea like invalids with trembling lips. Their skins grew dry and thin and often bore purple marks as if the air itself had thorns which punctured. They locked the piano and draped the mirrors as if they expected an electrical storm. They hung heavy curtains over the doors, in the faint hope that any remaining spirits which clung to our shoulders in order to escape would be brushed back by the cloth. To my aunts' credit they did not mention that I had been the cause of this disaster, and to my shame, preoccupied as I was by my own loss, I would not admit it.

On the hottest afternoons of that summer, when I reached the lookout at Echo Point, the light was thick and golden, as if it had passed all day through a butterfly's dusty wing. The leaves crackled like pale brown moustaches beneath my feet. I did not walk so much as swim through the currentless air, mouth open, pores gilling, moving towards the promise of an icy pool which might snap the skin back taut around my ankles. Yet even on these days, in the clefts where the ladders made their way through the sandstone cliffs and the mountains fell asleep in their own shadows, I could feel a faint chill rising from the green veins marking out the snaking courses of the creeks, in which there lurked the promise of curling up in the cold wet hearts of stones.

And sometimes, as I returned to the viewing platform in the twilight with my clothes sticking to my back, the air pilled into restless, dirty clouds which rolled over the cliffs and lay brooding across the valley. Rapidly, the sky grew quiet and black. The length of Narrow Neck turned purple as if it rubbed against the darkness. At last, sudden fists of wind shook the clouds by their corners until light rushed out of their folds, shivering and racing between the cliffs at the far end of the valley at quickening intervals, until, drawing closer, it struck wood and stone and revealed itself as brilliant veins of silver lightning. At each strike the whole valley jumped with light, as if it had been caught by a photographer and startled by his flash. When this happened I did not move to join the others who had snatched at parasols and children and flown towards the kiosk. Instead, anchored by a sense of closeness to my mother, I stood still in the wind and watched as the bushes drew themselves up flat against the cliffs. I saw leaves and tufted blossoms tossed into the air. At last, as I leant over the railing, the first cold raindrops, as heavy and erratic as bumblebees, flew up into my face.

I thought, *This must signify something*, and yet, when I looked down into that great space, my loneliness returned.

Perhaps it was this—the sight of clouds raining upwards—which also caused the strange imbalance in my blood.

'I proposed to my wife in an aquarium,' said Mr Medlicott. 'In Melbourne. At the Royal Exhibition Building. She was the daughter of a Spring Street hotelier. I had travelled there to view the patent medicines imported from America. There were sixty large sample cases in that exhibition. Bile Beans for Biliousness, Ayer's Cherry Pectoral, Dr Collis Browne's Chlorodyne. Pink Pills for Pale People—inspired, that. In pharmaceutical terms they were all quite ordinary. Opium sometimes, a syrup, an alcohol content of around thirty per cent. But that was not the point, you see. It was the names which acted like digitalis on the heart.'

Later, he said, they had walked under stalactites of Spanish cork and viewed penguins and a sea elephant. The aquarium had been built at a distance from the sea, like a great dry diving bell, in the middle of a landlocked suburb. In order to keep the creatures there alive the attendants had to truck in water from St Kilda beach. 'But that was the beauty of it,' Mr Medlicott told me. 'Those hundred-gallon tanks, four of them, hauled to Carlton on carts across the city. Three underground tanks to store it. An air compressor, powered by a steam engine, to oxygenate the water.' He had paid threepence for each of them to see that it was possible. They had stood in front of a tank full of blinded carp which butted at the glass sides with their heads. The fishes' eyes were veined and opaque, like white opals, the result of a brief experiment with an artificial salt solution which failed before the deliveries of sea water had resumed. It was a shame, Mr Medlicott said, that they had not persisted. The boldness of it had given him the courage to propose, right there in the fishy darkness, while the aquarium orchestra played; and Mrs Medlicott, a sensible woman, had accepted without qualms. When they had walked outside they were engaged. Giant turtles grazed on the lawns around them, tethered by their necks to small stakes in the grass.

In this way Mr Medlicott had greeted me and begun to introduce me to my duties. I was to present myself at the pharmacy at eight o'clock each morning and begin by polishing the mirrors and the display cabinets and rubbing linseed oil into the carved acanthus leaves which wound themselves around the pillars in the centre of the shop. Next I was to wash the bottles and sweep the rainbows of science which accumulated on the floor of the dispensary beneath the pill compressor. Mr Medlicott said, 'You are to think of yourself, Miss Jones, as the enemy of dust.' There, behind a curtain, he devised his own patent medicines, which at this time included Medlicott's Digestive Friend, Medlicott's Toilet Cream, and Medlicott's Invigorator. Later that afternoon, he told me, he would do something about ordering me a white smock from Mullaney's Universal Providers further down the Main Street. Once I had proved myself, he said, I could stand behind the cash register while he worked on his experiments.

'That is a strange greenhouse you work in,' Les Curtain said in the winter that followed, as I sat beside him in his carriage, and he stamped his gardener's boots on the floor against the cold. That was the only thing he said for the rest of the journey west along the dark ridge from Katoomba towards the pink snow clouds which covered Medlow Bath.

Too shy and too excited by the icicles which hung from the soft mouths of the horses, I had not asked him what he meant; and later that afternoon, when I met Harry Kitchings for the first time, and heard him describe the characters of the clouds, I forgot everything which had been said before. I did not see Les Curtain for more than a decade. Then, when I listened to the waterfalls in his chest and heard his thoughts, I did not have to ask. He was thinking of orange rind and camomile, rhubarb powder and male fern suspended in bottles behind the counter like the ghosts of plants. He referred to the leafy columns and the vases of bird of paradise pointing their dark tongues at the ceiling; the thick leadlight windows in which the light was punctuated by the red, abstracted silhouettes of tulips; and the wooden pansies with gilded edges which ran above the picture rails.

Mr Medlicott did not like these decorations. Looking at the carvings gave him hayfever. Sometimes he sneezed gold leaf or found rosewood splinters in the viscous fluids in his handkerchief. Indeed, as he told me now, he had little tolerance for the cacophony of flowers. I was to take the *Papaver somniferum* as an example. Once the whole plant had to be steeped in wine or honey in order to manufacture sleeping draughts. The resulting liquids were impure, their effects were difficult to predict until, at last, scientists had remedied this imperfection in design. 'Today, from that jumble which we call a poppy,' my employer told me 'it is possible to isolate twenty-seven different alkaloids.' He promised that one day he would show me morphine crystals, finer than needles, beneath the microscope, which took the shape of rhombic prisms. 'Now *that* has the beauty of mathematics,' Mr Medlicott said. '*That* is floral poesy.'

It was his private hope that his customers would one day outgrow their urge for botany and insects. The Mountaineers, he thought, had too much leisure, and as a result over-extended their cerebral muscles. They could not enjoy an afternoon stroll, he said, without first stopping for a handful of camphor for their killing jars. There were houses where you could not open a book without half a desiccated forest falling onto your lap. It appalled him that when they pur-chased medicines his customers did not ask him how they acted. Instead they asked what country the plants had come from; whether they had smooth or jagged veins upon their leaves; how many seas they had crossed upon their way. 'They are like spoiled children,' he told me, 'who want you to indulge their questions. You will learn this soon enough.'

Mr Medlicott's eyes moved quickly as if they followed the passage of slim silver bullets slicing through the air.

Since that morning in the Exhibition Building his dreams had run on metal sleepers. When his son was a little boy he had amused him at bedtime by calculating the current market value of all the useful substances stored inside his body if it was rendered down for sale. Few things moved him like an accident, where he could see steel or rubber bonded onto flesh. Yet he acknowledged the necessity of the floral deco-rations. 'As things stand,' he said, 'we are witnessing an evo-lution. We are coaxing the Mountaineers from the trees. For the time being'—when he made a sudden gesture with a small hand around the shop I saw that his knuckles were as pale and white as salmon bones—'for the time being we must offer them a few twigs and branches to cling on to.

'Do you understand? Never mind. In good time,' Mr Medlicott said. In their china jar, beside him, the leeches moved with luxurious slowness up the inclining sides, waiting to tap reservoirs of blood beneath a patient's skin. With twitching fingers Mr Medlicott encouraged a tuft of hair back onto the smoothness of his skull. He dabbed his forehead with his cuff protector. He adjusted his glasses for the fifteenth time upon his nose and fixed on me so that I saw myself reflected briefly in the dark liquid of his eyes.

'Did you know,' he asked me, 'that the first chemist in this colony murdered his wife with prussic acid?'

I could not help smiling. I thought again of that tank in an aquarium where quick fish darted forward to nip at something on the glass.

'From now until autumn,' said Mr Medlicott, 'we will see nothing but sprains from turning chocolate wheels and scratches from needle-threading races. The Bazaar Bacillus is upon us.' He retreated, gloomy, to the dispensary where Alderman Bronger waited to discuss the chemistry of soft drinks with him. There they tasted the samples from the alderman's factory, adding tartaric acid to the bottles to make them fizz, and combining the syrups with cocaine. They offered the latter as health tonics to the men and women who came in sweating from the fairs, after balancing eggs on spoons or jumping about in sacks.

Each weekend after that, waltzes drifted from the phonograph in the kiosk and hung in the air over Echo Point. It was impossible not to move in three-four time. The boys' division of the Fresh Air League dropped their rifles and stopped marching on the Hardings' field. Further up the hill, on Saturdays as I worked, I heard the undertakers' hammers at Chandler's Funeral Parlour hit the coffin planks with one sharp blow and two soft taps like heels upon the floorboards of a ballroom. Across the road a train took up the rhythm as it left the platform, until the great silver elbows of its pistons loosened and forced it faster down the track. Young men practised dance steps secretly inside their shoes and used pins to pop the blisters. They squatted in the new rotunda in the park and carved girls' names with penknives deep into the wood. The metronomic light beat into the darkened rooms where women pulled underslips through sewing machines and practised at their pianos. I heard Mr Medlicott tell Alderman Bronger that treading the pedals *appassionato* gave them rashes between their legs. When a girl asked me for camomile lotion Mr Medlicott stepped out to serve her, rubbing his hands and bobbing gently on his toes.

Rich heiresses came to stay at the Carrington Hotel in Katoomba Street, were wooed by Globe Trotters, and forgot to take their pianos home. All that summer their instruments were arranged in a grim conga line along the terrace. The curves of their great black bellies were like twilight cliffs butting one another. No messengers were sent to take them back. Eventually children prised the keys and hurled them at the wedding parties stopped in open automobiles at the level crossing. When they struck the chrome, Harry Kitchings later told me, the metal had vibrated. As if each car was a tuning fork, he said, and the long silver strings of railway track needed to be tightened.

Groups on their way to masquerade balls at the Carrington often stopped in at the shop, the women dressed as wood nymphs with long folds of pale green silk floating from their arms. They coughed as the cold night air touched the whiteness of their throats. One had pinned into her hair a dozen yellow butterflies which her beau had netted in the valley. Others, dressed as scullery maids, tickled each other with their dusters, and scattered new feathers around them on the floor. Mr Medlicott sold them little metal contraptions of his own devising which, when screwed onto the fingertips at night, forced the nails into a perfect filbert shape.

Every evening I watched the young men who lived in the Bohemia Apartments in Park Street turn the corner in a group. They moved up Main Street, pausing at the windows of Bartle's Men's Emporium, and engaged in certain conversations with the rough youths at Expectoration Corner. I saw Mayor Gordon, who had bought this corner allotment at a bargain, leave his plans and waxy seals on his table and rush out of his real estate office to send them on their way. He stood and watched their backs until they turned into Lurline Street and walked into the park with the stone arch high above its gate.

Toward the end of summer, the Mutoscope and Biograph Company had erected a large tent behind the mission, forcing the Aboriginal encampment further down the grassy slope into

West Katoomba. On hot still afternoons on Main Street it was possible to smell the canvas, as violent as a sailor's dream. As the sun set the dynamo groaned reluctantly to life; the Refined Entertainers who performed throughout the program could be heard gargling 'The Rose of Tralee' and other sonnets through a mixture of raw egg and tar. The company carried 20,000 feet of the latest French and American films which their advertisement claimed required a separate cart to themselves. During a recent run in Penrith a bushfire had claimed the edges of the town and the metal canisters had to be lowered into the Nepean River. For, as Mr Medlicott told me, the slick ribbons of nitrate film could be ignited by the smallest spark. By arrangement with the company he kept the box plan on the counter, where couples stood to choose their seats and discussed those airships, lady doctors, and tramp hypnotists featured by the cinematograph with a casualness which only increased my agony to go.

When I went walking on the mountain paths there were amateur photographers poised like preying mantises over every view. They wore dark suits. Their shoulders were stooped. Their hands clutched at cameras which grew like shiny eyes out of their waists. Mr Medlicott thought that they looked as if they were peering into keyholes in the air. He had recently installed a high glass cabinet in the centre of the shop displaying rolls of film and stop baths, developing fluids and tweezers. He passed off the footbaths from the Hydro Majestic as developing trays.

Even the professionals sought Mr Medlicott's chemical advice. This particular afternoon Mr Fowler drank Alderman

Bronger's sodas with him. He was unnaturally tall with double-jointed knees so that his boots poked through the curtains and bruised my ankles each time I moved behind the counter. Visitors often remarked that when he met them at the Three Sisters to take their photographs they had heard him approaching for half a mile, humming, his long flat feet slapping the sandstone paths. This morning he had come to purchase smelling salts. The previous Sunday five amateurs using his darkroom had fainted as they developed their films, overcome by vertigo when they saw their views. He also told Mr Medlicott about a recent client, a man from Sydney, who had posed each weekend of the summer at the railing of the lookout with a different schoolgirl by his side. 'The remorseless way he squeezes their hands,' said Mr Fowler. 'It makes my blood run cold. He orders three prints of every photograph. I believe he has some kind of peculiar collection.'

I heard a familiar vibrato in his voice. When I stepped behind the curtain I recognised the self-righteous angle of his chin and those ginger fingers, which each seemed endowed with an extra joint, reaching for another bottle from the sink. It was Mr Fowler, I realised, who had photographed my mother, trembling with excitement, as she stood on the dark lip of her death.

As I had then, I stood behind his shoulder and said nothing, and he did not recall me.

It is hard now to recall myself.

I will try, nevertheless, to describe my younger self for you, before I became a faded spinster, before I was finally invisible.

My limbs had a fluidity then which I only appreciated or noticed once it had been lost. My youth produced on Mr Medlicott's face an expression of hopeful respect. If his hand brushed mine at the till there was a tensing in his stomach, as his muscles stiffly recalled the posture of his romantic years before they relaxed again upon his belt. I had attracted the attention of several boys, who bought me summer drinks at the Niagara and ices at the Coffee Palace. Yet they soon discovered that I was full of large feelings which would not be squeezed between a main course and dessert. As I spoke about that odd dissatisfaction which I had felt at Echo Point during the rain, and sought to understand it, they stroked their thin whiskers, or blushed and looked down at the spoons, or glanced with embarrassed eyes toward the nearby tables where other girls simpered and asked flattering questions over toast. Before they could try to kiss me, their mothers, unimpressed by my knowledge of distempers and my ignorance of charmeuse, ordered them away.

I did not know that I was beautiful. My aunts had not mentioned it. Instead they encouraged me to disguise my insolent looks so that some kind man might ask me to be his wife. It was only many years later, when I saw myself in the photograph taken in 1916 of the Katoomba War Workers, sitting in the front row on the ground with a pair of knitted socks upon my lap, that I noticed it with surprise.

In the photograph I am the only woman in the group who is not wearing spectacles. About their pupils my eyes have the lunar whiteness of a hypnotist's. They look past the camera, and into the distance, since the photographer is not Harry

Kitchings. There is, as well, in this photograph, when I look at it today, something too composed about my face. I can see it now, that gravity which was unlikely to appeal to men. My mouth, full and sceptical, turns down a little at the corners. My neck is long and unlined and ends in a slick curve at my collarbone. I still have what my aunts referred to as a bloom. The only concession I have made to pinning back my hair is to catch the two front pieces loosely in a clip behind my head. It is thick and dark and falls down to my waist. This I imagine as the last year of my youth, although I had been told already that I was too old to think of marriage.

One detail catches at my heart.

I am wearing the stiff uniform of the Katoomba Red Cross Society with dark stockings and thick black shoes as if rebelling against its whiteness.

Back in 1907, however, I only understood myself in terms of what I had not done: I had never caught a boat; I had not viewed a cinematograph; I had not once engaged in what I imagined as the conversation of adults. No man had called for me; I had never danced, or received a stiff cardboard invitation in the post. I had not found a friend with whom I could share, without translation, the dark language of my thoughts. And, if my memory plays me false, or I am now too bitter to admit it, and I did have a sense of my beauty, back then, when I worked for Mr Medlicott, I was yet to learn that this alone is not enough for men, in spite of what they say.

By the time that photograph was taken, nine years later, I had seen my name printed on the belly of a cloud. I had developed habits of forgiveness. I had learned the difference between melancholy and despair. And, having watched Harry Kitchings' love take new shapes, I was eventually to move to a place of illness and taste a man's own blood upon his tongue.

I was irritated by my aunts' misdirected mourning. When they were asked to help with the catering for the Chrysanthemum Ball, and chose instead to stay at home, I was furious that this cost me my first opportunity to attend a dance. I was ashamed by the manner in which they carried obituaries and abortionists' advertisements from the *Echo* in their bags and unfolded them to read to strangers in the street. I shrugged off their admonitions to take care each time I went out for a walk. Whenever they mentioned the spirit babies, I headed to the kitchen and washed the plates so roughly that the sound of clashing porcelain would frighten any ghost.

At that age I felt their sadness only as a random visitation which might be borne and cured like any other illness. I did not understand yet that it formed the very element through which we moved, like Mr Medlicott's fish, our eyes blinded by salt water. No waltz could quite mask the strange echoes of the valleys or make familiar the hollow caves and cold stone forests which stretched beneath our feet. And it may be for this reason that it was not just I, but so many of us, faced with too much sky to bear, who could not believe in other people's sadness. We dressed up as tramps and natives to eat cake at costume balls and read books to discover what we thought was real despair pressed flat between the pages.

Halfway through that summer, as I continued to despise

my aunts, a plague of bicycle enthusiasts from the city arrived and sped along the roads in a vicious quest for ozone. They raced each other down the steep length of Cascade Street. They rode between the mountain towns wearing fancy dress to some new costume pageant or another. One Saturday evening after work I stepped without looking from the kerb at Expectoration Corner onto the road where Main and Katoomba streets met. I ignored the shouts of the young men who loitered there and cleared their throats regularly on the pavement. 'Just recently,' Mr Medlicott had told me, 'Alderman Bronger slipped upon a sputum and nearly broke his arm. He brought it to the pharmacy. We examined it beneath the microscope. There were traces of mercury in the phlegm. We both agreed. It belonged to a man with a venereal disease.'

I was engulfed by the ringing of angry bells. My elbows scraped along the gravel. A pedal gouged my leg. I felt something glutinous beneath the palm of my left hand. A large group of bicyclists dressed as explorers and Hawaiian princesses careered down Main Street in the direction of Leura, scattering the crowds. Behind them, a tall geisha and a skinny demon pedalled hard in pursuit of the pack. When I opened my right fist I saw that I still held the sharp felt point of the devil's tail which I had caught at as I fell.

As I sat in the gutter, passed by carriages filled with ball gowns and lobsters and heavy trunks, those vehicles appeared to move with a supernatural precision, as if the air opened up before them, and cords of light drew them on. Some years later, when I saw the cinematograph at last, in which bodies started through the doorways of high buildings as if they had been pulled from them by magnets, I would experience this sensation again. It seemed to me, as I watched the traffic now, that this was how it always was for the other Mountaineers. In spite of their melancholy, or perhaps because of it, their feet moved firmly, as if they traced the lines of longitude on some invisible map. They did not doubt their feelings. They did not pause or look from side to side. I remembered something my mother had said, as she read those poisonous letters: that such confidence, given the defective nature of our vision, was something we would never share.

A small hand tilted back my head. Mr Medlicott, squatted before me, breathing heavily and staring deep into my pupils, hoping for evidence of concussion.

I had begun to wonder whether the stunning blueness of the mountains had in addition something to do with the milky liquids sold by Mr Medlicott. The babies whose mothers purchased soothing syrups looked at us with a strange calmness and moved their lips as if they held the round buds of poppies in their mouths. My aunts stooped to touch their tiny fists which were coiled as tight and red as flowers which have yet to open and unwrinkle in the air. There were young men with peppermint breath whose eyelids were as heavy and sleek as petals in the sun. And, next door, behind the sign saying 'Tailoresses', the Misses Moon sucked our throat pastilles and felt the air as layers of chiffon as the afternoons slowed and the whole sky seemed to catch upon their needles.

Sometimes, when people's breath rattled beneath their collarbones, we lit and gave them Cigars de Joy or strapped glass nebulisers to their faces. Afterwards drifts of marijuana smoke and eucalyptus steam curled through the leadlight stillness of the store.

In Mr Medlicott's Acclimatising Tababules there were plants from all corners of the Empire. We sold them to those residents who were not native born to help them bear the heat. In the dispensary I helped him make his little landscapes. He ground roots and resins with his pestle and placed them in the pill compressor. He coated them with shells made out of sugar.

When they took them our customers felt layers of cool moss growing beneath their skins. Flowers opened like water-lilies in their veins. They imagined their own hearts growing as pale and transparent as orchids, behind the ivory branches of their ribs.

They said it was like swallowing Kew Gardens.

So it is no coincidence that Harry Kitchings should come here, with his cameras and his new belief in God, searching for that particular shade of mauve which grew in a mountain distance.

It was a colour, Ruskin had written, that only the civilised could recognise.

We were all looking for it one way or another.

$$= 6 =$$

E ach winter, in the first years of the new century, thick
snowfalls of a depth not since recorded attracted girls
with ice skates and troops of Tyrolean dancers to the Blue
Mountains. In the valleys waterfalls stilled into pale tableaus
of falling, as if the ancient choreography of stalactites had
broken, cold and limy, through the surface of the earth. On
Lady Harding's estate, snow clotted the needles of the ornamental pines, making her think of paintbrushes with their tips
pointed at the sky. Having discarded the last of the hoarded
keys of pianos by throwing them at walkers from the lookouts,
the children now stole oranges instead, so that they could
bowl them along the corridors in the mornings, heavier than
crystal, glazed with ice. In parlours the skidding needles of
Victrolas scratched figure eights on frozen records. On the
roads horses' shins snapped like the frail stems of wineglasses.
And sometimes, as the steam from the chimney turned to
sleet, a train driver leaned out of his cabin, was struck by snow
blindness, and drove his engine off the rails.

It was because we were all thinking of Shackleton, at the Pole, about to drive his dog sled again past pyramids of ice.

This winter, in 1907, the famous champagne air at Medlow Bath had turned to sorbet. Wrapped in a pink boa of snow-clouds, the Hydro Majestic Hotel sprawled on the long cliff ledge as if it were a chaise longue. Globe Trotters passing through Katoomba said that they had become drunk there simply by letting the snowflakes sizzle on their tongues. They had not seen snow like it, they claimed, since they left Old England, a fact which had only increased their intoxication.

In the hotel grounds, even if you were sober, it was impossible to walk in a straight line through the snow. Workmen tried to clear it from the paths but their spades would not follow the concrete edges, and instead meandered to and fro across the gardens as if they followed the tracks of snails. At night visitors lost the way from the casino to their carriages and wandered through the gardens, catching their toes on the shapes of discarded Neptune's Belts, the water turned to ice inside them. The coins flew from their pockets and were lost until the snows melted and the lawns shone gold with guineas. Wombats lumbered across the tennis court each morning searching for their hidden burrows. Lovers' snowmen, once built, quickly listed sideways. Each dawn a patrol of waiters with chisels was ordered out into the cold to chip away any distasteful features. Years later, when the heavy snows no longer fell, Les Curtain told me that the matter of disposal had never been discussed; whether by accident or the waiters' mischief, the disembodied organs appeared in ice chests or reared up from the first hole of the golf course. Odd, Les

Curtain said, to reach into a flower bed and find your hand upon a frosty nipple.

I believe it was the opening of this hotel, on a site chosen because it looked like somewhere else, which also caused the strange disturbance in the weather.

The Hydro Majestic was as turreted and turbanned as an elephant house. It was longer than the Gare d'Orsay in Paris and on these grey winter afternoons when the clouds gathered it was not difficult to imagine that its cavernous halls harboured some great smoking train which might burst forth to rush towards the pale clockface of the sun. Or, on brighter days, you might think it a vast Brighton dancehall on a pier pillared with rock and skirted by foamy mauve and violet. The verandahs, of Italian marble, hung over the Megalong Valley so that it was impossible to stand there and look out, dizzy, towards Sensation Point, without catching in the wind the pink scent of Ferrara. The casino, purchased in Chicago, had been carried here on the deck of a boat, which had passed, as it drifted out of New York Harbour, the immigrants on Ellis Island, who waved and threw their dreams like streamers at its dome, which were incubated into vast clouds by the bright light of the Southern Cross. The dining room, where dark waiters in white gloves tiptoed by with steamy samovars, was as palmed and humid as the Raffles'. The oak billiard tables, exact copies of those at Smedley's Matlock Bath in Derbyshire, had been crated out from England with the pages of illustrated weeklies stuffed inside their pockets. In copper tanks in the pumproom were stored the mineral waters of Baden-Baden which had curdled on their exposure to the mountain climate.

It is no wonder, crammed as it was with the grand dreams of elsewhere, that the air also fermented around this pleasure palace until it tickled our nostrils like champagne.

As I walked over those thick lawns with their brittle crust of snow for the first time, I could tell that even Mark Foy felt a little drunk on it that morning, having at last sacked the Swiss doctors and overseen the dismantling of the long, tiled spa rooms with their mysterious spigots and stopcocks and guttered tables. It had surprised him that so few of us had shared his enthusiasm for mud baths, milk cures and total friction. By the third birthday of his hotel, he had already abandoned his sanatorial ambitions. He had given up on his plans to trace the edges of our bodies with vaseline and wind them in wet sheets. He had ordered the night-watchmen to stack away the Bath Books, with their instructions on resting after hot baths and passing glycerine enemas without straining. He had to admit to Les Curtain, as he sipped a glass of his own tar water by the fireplace, that it really was more pleasant, now that the sounds of spinal slapping and centrifugal douching no longer echoed through the halls.

Mark Foy realised now that we were too confident for all of that. We had laughed at the thought that he could improve upon this climate. We had refused to take our pleasures in homoeopathic doses. We smirked at his machines. Instead, with our love, we had inflated the Hydro Majestic like a gaudy zeppelin. All that remained was for Les Curtain to remove the ribbon gardens, those tender guy ropes which bound it to the earth, and let it float up in the air.

'I recall,' Lady Harding had said, earlier that same morning, 'that we could only eat farinaceous foods.'

'I endured a week of indignities,' said Sir Wilfrid, 'in the torture chambers of that hotel.'

'Yet I cannot remember,' Lady Harding continued, 'a single food which that term signified. We were not even permitted to eat hot buttered toast. And Sir Wilfrid was denied his breakfast kidneys.'

'I was spouted and kneaded, sprayed and sponged, douched and nozzled.'

'So many foods were banished from the table: hare and pork; salad and watercress; duck and goose; mackerel, sardines, anchovies and eel. Anything which remained had to be swallowed down dry because we were forbidden flavoured sauces. In my sleep I dreamed of climbing suet mountains and swimming in forbidden lakes of gravy.'

'I think, but I am not certain,' Sir Wilfrid mused, 'that I was also sitzed.'

He wandered, distracted, to the gate, where his groundsmen were taking delivery of a new species of fern, its roots bound with canvas, which had been freshly dug up from the valley. At the end of the long pebbled drive two men hauled it off their cart. Viewed at a distance, from the house, their hands gave the appearance of being grotesquely swollen because of the many pairs of gloves they wore against the cold.

I waited eagerly for Lady Harding to continue, for I had only glimpsed the Hydro Majestic in the refuse of its renovation which Mr Medlicott kept in the storeroom behind the pharmacy: in those metal pans and canvas belts and tubes attached to rubber balls resembling car horns. He had also reserved for his own use a large box, containing seventy lightbulbs which, once electric power was connected in Katoomba, would direct the heat of that healthful fluid onto his naked trunk. That was one variety of treatment in which Lady Harding was prepared to concede some pleasure. 'I felt silver all day,' she said, 'as if a lightning bolt had lit up the inside of my heart.'

The groundsmen walked, invisible, beneath the windows, holding the fern above their heads. It glided past us like a frozen shuttlecock through the air.

Les Curtain stood as far as he could from the fire, and stared out of the window, resting his thick fingers on the sill. He held his weight on his back foot. I saw in the stillness of the muscles in his neck and shoulders the habits of the public bar. Although he was not much older than I was, he was already known for his accurate advice on the laying out of gardens. He had begun recently to advertise in the *Echo*, offering for sale his hybrid seeds and bulbs. Years of exposure to the sun had baked the lines of judgment around his mouth. When he entered the room I had watched him with scarcely any movement of his head turn his dark eyes on Lady Harding's spirit drawings and the samplers stitched by children in the Fresh Air Homes which hung framed above the velvet dado, as if he wished to prune them. I had the impression that our conversation was another ornament which he did not like.

Now Les Curtain also regarded me as if I were some kind of deeply rooted weed. For when he had mentioned that he was due to consult with Mark Foy that afternoon at Medlow

Bath, Lady Harding had determined to turn this trip into an excursion to view the newly converted hotel. It was all decided, she informed him. I would share his carriage while Lady Harding, her fox terrier Hutton, and my aunts travelled ahead by car.

'I need you,' Mark Foy told Les Curtain as he led him to the tight geranium beds, 'to restore a sense of humour to my gardens.'

I followed behind the two men, in order to avoid my aunts and Lady Harding who stood on the long verandah above the cliff. From their gestures in the distance I knew that they were discussing my sullen intractability and its effect upon my marriage prospects. I had already heard Lady Harding whisper, loudly, as they passed through the doorway, 'Has Eureka *become a woman* yet?' It was of particular concern to my aunts that I rarely smiled for they feared that this expression would set upon my face. An hour later this would be remedied by Harry Kitchings. Yet their words were prescient, for ten years later a worse expression would settle there; the edges of my lips would curl as if I had tasted poison.

In addition, I wanted to discover what was contained in the boxes draped with sacking which had rattled and shivered in Les Curtain's cart behind us all the way to Medlow Bath, disturbing the icy stillness of the afternoon.

The flower beds had remained untouched around the gabled house which formed the core of the hotel since Mark Foy had bought it. The man who once lived here had made his fortune by finding specks of gold dust peppering a river's banks. As Harry's grandfather in his studio had observed, it turns a man's head to find gold growing like potatoes beneath the muddy ground. From that time on he is offended by the sight of ordinary things: he seeks out soft sheets and polished sunsets; he requires mantelpieces free of dust; he can only be happy on mountains. This man had moved to Medlow Bath and ordered flower beds to be cut into the lawns and planted as thick as Persian carpets. The yellow and purple petals pressed each other tighter than a Mason's handshake, for he could not bear the smallest glimpse of earth. Long lines of flowers also ran along the paths and cliffs. In spite of their name, these ribbon borders did not have the fugitive character I recognised in my father's strips of cloth. Instead they were stretched straight between the gardens and the valley, as taut as the tape at the finishing line of a foot race, waiting to be breasted. I saw what Mark Foy meant when he had spoken of the grimness of this garden. The beds and borders were as clumsy as stage cogs and pulleys, as if they had been put there to heave up the scalloped edges of the clouds.

Les Curtain nodded and drew on his pipe. Squatting, he pulled some of the dead stalks from the ground and put his fingers in the soil beneath the frozen surface. Neither of the men spoke. They did not seem to notice I was there.

According to Lady Harding, Les Curtain's family were poor Irish gardeners, who had lived for some time around Wentworth Falls, finding work breaking the ground and following the directions of architects from the city as the large estates were built. Then, one day, Les Curtain's father had looked up, sweating, at the heavy houses and the blank grounds around them which stretched towards the bush, and imagined lines of trees, as thick as stone columns, as sharp as steeples, marking the edges of each estate. As if he beheld a vision he foresaw that the men of his century would fill their footsteps, and line the streets of their towns, and the edges of their lives, with great dark avenues of pines. Slowly, grubbing the money together with his brothers, he had set out in business for himself, travelling to the city, speaking to captains at the docks, and arranging for them to obtain for him, on their travels, the seeds of Norfolk and radiata pines. He met with great success. He had left Les Curtain, motherless, with his uncles. He had travelled with his seedlings to grand home-steads and country towns, and opened up his palm to men as if it held a Christmas wish. He had seen springing from the ground all around the state the tough foliage of his dreams. At last the larger seed companies, seizing on his idea, had bullied him and bought him out. For years after that Les Cur-tain's father had lived in the city and caught the ferry to Manly, stopping holidaymakers in the streets, and demanding that they take his photograph beneath the slim young trees which grew along the Corso. He wrote letters to councils, claiming that he was responsible for the beauty of their towns, telling them that he ought to be honoured with some remu-neration or a plaque.

Les Curtain, who did not get on with his father, or share his desire for travel, had taken his small inheritance and invested it in a selection of Barr's daffodil bulbs, some greenhouse glass from England, and the newest Radium sprays. He had bought a house and several acres of land at Wentworth Falls. The blooms he bred were becoming famous in the Blue Mountains. It was his daffodils which appeared in vases in hotels and made the English homesick. It was his roses which lovers carried. This last thought made Sir Wilfrid laugh, since he could not imagine Les Curtain giving any girl a posy; which was not to say, he added, that he did not spend time with the lower types of female. 'However, on the whole,' Sir Wilfrid said, 'I suspect Curtain prefers the company of seed catalogues and spirit levels.' Given the young man's brilliance, Lady Harding said, she could overlook this arrogance, and the faint odour of the shed that always clung to his clothes, but she could not forgive him those heavy peasant's hands.

Now at last Les Curtain stood with his hands on his hips, and thought, then lit his pipe and spoke.

'I should be able to do that for you,' he told Mark Foy. 'Fortunately horticulture is full of satirists, like the man who recently grew a beard upon the iris.'

He walked back to his cart and returned with a handful of orchid bulbs which sat like cloves of garlic in his large palm. For the first time I saw him smile as he introduced Mark Foy to his 'girls', those plants of his own design so delicate that he had named them after actresses and women's slippers. He explained how, in the wild, some orchids were so inaccessible that the pollen could only be transferred between them by mice or moths. In his greenhouse he had to open them with his fingers to place the pollen inside them with a brush. He cut a bulb in half now with his knife and lifted out the spike which had grown inside it in preparation for the spring.

Behind the hotel, we ducked beneath the flying fox which delivered food from the hotel's farm in the Megalong Valley to the kitchens. The wire was anchored to a high white pole, disappearing into the clouds as mysteriously as a fakir's rope. Here at the back of the building steam passed, sluggish, through the hinges of the doorways. I heard shouting in a foreign language and thought at first that the voices were raised in anger, for they were as loud and rough as the barking of possums during the spring, until I heard raucous laughter. I peered through a window which was blind with condensation. Through a clear line where the steam had run, as small as the passage of a tear, I saw those two small Turkish boys who had been photographed and written of so many times by the newspapers as they waited on the tables; they had snuck downstairs and removed their tight red uniforms and thick white gloves. They sat naked now in an old hydropathic bathtub which they had filled to its rim with mink. Several large trunks, so recently delivered that they still bore a bloom of ice, lay open beside the boys, who reached their arms into the drawers and laughed at the size of the women's shoes. They rubbed noses. They threw snowballs at each other. They pulled the thick collars of the coats around their heads. One held a walking stick as if it was a fishing rod against his chest. At last I realised that they too had forced this place to take the shape of their desires; as they played at being Eskimos, the domed roof of the hotel seemed to turn into the hard curve of an igloo's ceiling filled with cold blue air.

I have often wondered since, if we had ever for a moment looked into the brute face of the clouds and not seen the spires of another country, whether we would have fled from the mountains in our carriages and trains. Yet I must acknowledge now that I have looked for even stranger things in the faces of men.

My youngest aunt called from the verandah above, 'Eureka, you will catch a chill!' I pretended that I had not heard her and ducked into another old spa room where Mark Foy was pressing a boiler and sheets of glass upon Les Curtain for his greenhouse. Les Curtain ran his fingers along the latter as if he could already feel the sun caught in its surface. 'This will save more buggering around with suppliers in the city,' he said, before both men turned, and fell silent, their faces blank, when they saw me standing there. Then, swiftly, they had to turn again. For the wire of the flying fox outside had begun to vibrate like a bow string. It bent and shuddered. Sharp icicles snapped off and shot into the air. Inside the basket, which hung over the vast drop, a dark object moved, dimly visible through the cloud, and grew nearer as we stared.

How many things is it possible for the eye to observe and record in the space of seconds? I saw Mark Foy run out into the snow like an angry polar bear. I saw Les Curtain briefly count the sheets of glass before he followed, walking slowly, with his head down, bending once or twice to pull dead heads off the saxifrages. The Chinese waiters and the little Turkish boys ran shouting and pointing from the kitchen doors while

Hutton barked and trembled and threaded himself between their legs. Even my aunts and Lady Harding walked as quickly as they could without actually running across the grounds. I saw that they averted their eyes from the bedpans and hoses which were piled up by the doors.

There was a man standing in the basket as it jerked over the rough edge of the cliff. His hair had set into fine golden points upon his head; the ends of his moustache were frozen; his cheeks were furred with ice. His fob watch had fallen from his pocket. With his good hand he pulled himself along by the rope which ran beneath the wire, while the other, its fingers splayed at an odd angle, clutched a large tropical camera to his chest.

'What in God's name are you doing?' Mark Foy demanded.

I had already recognised the frail set of this man's shoulders from Katoomba Falls. Now I saw his lean face with its high cheekbones and fine chin. He looked back at us with blue night-hooded eyes.

'I am serving the clouds,' Harry Kitchings said.

Not long afterwards, as we sat in the dining room, and the Turkish boys moved around us in their national costume pouring tea, Harry Kitchings told us how he had come to the Blue Mountains to take photographs of God. He told us what he had learned from John Ruskin—that the greatest work of the modern artist is to draw our attention to the beauty of the air. Yet, he said, with all due respect to that great writer, the effects of paper and light were more democratic than paint. When he looked at his negatives, and saw the clouds caught like God's breath by the silver on the glass, he said, he was reminded of those frail prehistoric insects, almost too delicate to live, which by some miracle had left their perfect shapes pressed into the cores of rocks. He hoped that, by printing them out and selling them cheaply, they could be carried about in lockets and pocket books and be taken out, creased and warm, to be searched at leisure like lovers' faces; that we would all learn together to stare into the clouds until we saw God's face. He spoke until we seemed to taste cloud in between the dainty layers of bread and cucumber we ate, like those wool sandwiches which were fed by Mr Medlicott to children when their parents feared that they had swallowed pins.

The snow began to fall again, so that we could not see where the long cliff ended and the great drop began until, as the sky dimmed, only our own reflections hovered before us in the darkened glass. Les Curtain smoked his pipe to ease the tightness in his chest and watched Hutton, who lay upon his stomach with his back legs splayed, sigh and twitch with dreams of buried shin-bones by the fire. Lady Harding ran her index finger along the edge of a Willow Pattern plate, as if to confirm for herself that the scones balanced high upon its little bridges were not another piece of oriental conjury which might disappear upon her tongue in a quick blue puff of powder. My aunts' shoulders relaxed and they touched their hair and faces with their thin wrists often as they spoke. For a brief moment, by some trick of the light, I thought I saw from the corner of my eye the lighter faces they had worn as girls, which I had seen once or twice at home when they unwound their hair and it tumbled white down to their waists. For the rest of their lives their eyes misted when they spoke about that day: of how they had sat in the dining hall where two years later Dame Clara Butt and the Rajah of Puduka, celebrating the King's birthday, would eat Potage du Roi.

As I watched Harry Kitchings, I noted the faint electric tremor at the corners of his lips, which moved as if the words he spoke were luminous. I thought, *If he treads on one of those glass globes buried in the snow it will not break. Instead, light will spring up from his step.* In spite of this I had not noticed yet that he was handsome. That required a talent for the kind ordering of details in which my clinical gaze was as yet unschooled. It demanded in addition a confidence in the steadiness of appearances which my mother could not teach me. It is possible, however, that I had read that knowledge already in the quickened gestures of my aunts and Lady Harding, and in the studied indifference of Les Curtain. Yet soon after this, with Harry Kitchings' help, I would learn to change the pace at which I lowered and raised my eyelids, and acquire a faith which would last the length of eight blue years.

As Harry Kitchings spoke I also saw the strange purple lines of text upon the back of his hand.

I felt that if I took his slim fingers and opened that hand up like a bat's wing I would be able to read the pattern of his life.

Years later, as we drove for the last time to Medlow Bath through the charred morning light, too thick with smoke to cast our shadows across our laps, Harry Kitchings spoke with fondness of that evening when Mark Foy had asked him his opinion of the new plans for the gardens, as we walked in the casino after tea. He could recite their conversation without omitting a punctuation point, even as he flinched from the sharp pains in his gut. I noticed with sadness as we drove that there was a different sort of tremor in the deep creases on each side of his mouth.

He recalled how Mark Foy stood under one of the new electric lights: how his shadow with its broad yachtsman's shoulders was split into three upon the polished floor: how the dark shapes did not waver like those shadows cast by gaslight. He remembered that it was the first time that he had seen quizzical eyebrows of white wood cocked over every door and window, a decorating craze which later swept across the mountains. It made one's feet allergic to straight lines, he smiled, so that they slid by their own volition in strange dancers' arcs across a carpet.

He remembered that Mark Foy had said, as if he were a royal guest, *Does that meet with your approval?* and his own reply, breathless with the pleasure of being asked, that he was not keen, personally, on the idea of pulling out magnificent beds of flowers to make room for croquet.

Yet, fifteen years later he could not recall the wink of surprised amusement Mark Foy made at Lady Harding or the angry look Les Curtain gave him—for he had never seen them.

But back then our eyes followed Harry's good hand as it made supple arcs and circles in the air. He said that he had heard of men who had constructed alpine gardens in which the rockeries were shaped like little mountains and decorated with the rarest mountain plants. He said he could also imagine a garden filled with fuchsias, the colour and shape of the dome of the casino. He said that he had once passed a garden near Echo Point and seen these flowers break off from their stems during a storm. They had formed a scarlet cloud of petals high above the valley, he said, moving light and swift upon the gale, filling the sky like stubborn parachutes. It pleased him to imagine, each time the winds blew, these little Hydro Majestics rising into the air. And it was as if we could see that garden growing up before us, its shoots crowding up and unwinding through the dark blue shadows on the white snow outside, like a cold Willow Pattern plate writhing into life.

I heard the snowflakes brush against the windows as they fell. Mark Foy turned with the beaming aspect of a proud nabob to Les Curtain and asked him what he thought.

'It would require a lot of compost,' Les Curtain said, reaching for his pipe.

That winter night we could only see romance, beneath the jewel lights which cast a hard white mineral glow around the vestibule, and love was everywhere around us after that. To please Harry Kitchings we would lash the mist like ivy to our houses. From then on we would listen to the winds as they thrashed like ocean waves through the branches of the trees. The next day Lady Harding would write off to England for a special diary with a marbled cover in which she could record her observations of the weather and count off the stars each evening with the dedication of a nun.

Before that evening ended Harry Kitchings had offered to print the annual reports of the Fresh Air League on his own Wharfdale Art Press, which at this moment waited on the docks at Pyrmont, crated like a piano, until it could be brought by rail and craned into the back room of his studio. He told Lady Harding that its eighteen rollers were so subtly weighted that they could print a love sonnet on a piece of voile. He arranged with Mark Foy to photograph the Hydro Majestic as it rested on a nest of clouds. His panoramic camera would be required, he said, to capture its full length. He promised that he would search out the envelopes from his aunt so that Les Curtain could have the foreign seeds and bulbs which rattled in their corners. He recalled that she had written in one of her letters of visiting the orchid auctioneers in London with some beau, where the famous growers' bulbs were displayed like lumps of precious ore and gentlemen with kidskin gloves wagered on the precious hybrids which grew inside them. He thought she may have placed these strange hard sacs in the mail when she tired of the chafe of suede upon her arm. I remember this clearly yet I do not believe that Harry Kitchings could have said it.

We hugged our breath around us in our collars as we walked with quick cold steps along the icy drive. Because of the lateness of the hour I was squeezed into Lady Harding's horseless carriage. I sat warm between the cushioned flesh of her hip and the slim thigh of my eldest aunt, on which the skin moved like a crumpled cloth beneath the stiffer fabric of her skirt. I felt Hutton's cold nose touch the back of my hand and his hot breath before he turned three times in a circle and sank deep into Lady Harding's lap. The scent of gardenia perfume which hung thick beneath the roof of the car did not, as usual, make me toss my head to breathe as if some thick handkerchief had been pressed across my mouth. I did not smirk at the high-pitched noises of the chauffeur's stomach. Instead, I trained my eyes upon the dart of road which the headlights opened in the darkness and did not see the black shapes which played beyond its edges. I felt the architecture of my bones settle in my flesh in some new shape.

In the long gallery next to the casino, where ten years later the running carpet would be rolled up and the champion skater of America would cause a sensation by streaking up and down the floorboards on sparking wheels, his arms scissoring across his chest, Harry Kitchings had turned suddenly towards me. He asked me if I had ever seen a single cirrus cloud, floating near the ceiling of the sky, like a long curved pinion feather from an angel's wing. I shook my head and held his gaze. He was the first man to look into my eyes as if he expected to discover something there.

Now I saw my life stretch out before me as bright and silver as the searchlight outside Mark Foy's hotel.

I imagined that Harry Kitchings might one day like me in the same way that he liked clouds.

And my heart, like the Twayblade orchid, a flower so delicate that it sprayed pollen at a touch, unfurled and directed my love towards him.

CIRRUS

$$=== 7 ===$$

These, Harry Kitchings told me, were the three characters of clouds. *Stratus*, flat fog blankets, were of the least aesthetic interest, for they refused to take a shape. Yet sometimes, in the form of mists, when they probed the valleys with ermine fingers and soothed the fretting angles of the cliffs, they acted like draperies to beautify the landscape. *Cumulus* were the most expressive clouds, as great as continents, as massed and fibrous as the foam which lifts up from the surface of a boiling sea. When the rains were hammocked in their bellies they darkened and drew out the brooding colours of the earth. At other times they crossed the sky, stark white where the sun bleached them, like the ghosts of icebergs, hauling their own shadows. *Cirrus* clouds inhabited the ecstatic regions of the skies, where the high winds tossed and parted them like hair. It was these clouds, according to Ruskin, which exhibited the greatest order, being closest to God's presence. It was these clouds, Harry told me, which sometimes caused haloes around the moon.

In this way, as we stood on the lookout at Honeymoon Point, held by the wire that curved around our waists, Harry Kitchings began the education of my eyes.

That afternoon, as I passed the door of his studio, he had come out backwards, clutching his camera with his damaged hand, and peering at the sky. He had pressed the long, unbroken fingers of his right hand down his ribs until they found his watch. He had forgotten to read it when he turned to see me standing there behind him. I had noticed that he matched his strides to mine as we walked down towards the valley.

At Echo Point the blue scent of eucalyptus drifted over the box hedges of the large estates and leached into the stillness of their gardens. The air was jellied, and the promise of thunder lay beneath it like some volatile emulsion. Far below us, I heard the cold pulse of water in a hidden vein of river.

We took the path which ran parallel to that famous spine of rock where the Three Sisters stood in silhouette, until it turned again and wound back around the valley's rim to Leura. As we stepped over tree roots and slippery humps of stone, Harry Kitchings' fingertips had brushed my elbow. The thin grain of the cotton briefly held their shapes, as soft and damp as moths' wings pressed against my skin.

Now we stood high above an amphitheatre of rock, and watched the sunlight as it faded like applause.

He gazed at the clouds so intently that he seemed to look for something far beyond the sky.

Then, Harry said, there were the intermediary clouds: *Cirro-Stratus*, *Fracto-Cumulus*, and *False Cirrus*; the *Mammato-Cumulus* with the appearance of soft bosoms on its lower surface; the *Cirro-Cumulus* which caused a mackerel sky. There was the *Cumulo-Nimbus* which took the form of turrets or of mountains. He told me about the *Fracto-Nimbus* or 'scud' described by sailors. He spoke of iridescent, ovoid clouds lenticularis which appeared during a föhn, sirocco, or mistral.

'And what variety of cloud is that?' I asked him, pointing to a small still scrap of vapour which hovered beneath us in the centre of the valley.

When Harry turned and bent his head to mine I was surprised by the tender humour in his eyes.

'That one,' he said, 'I call Eureka—it is a wild orphan cloud which stands aloof and looks stubbornly towards the ground.'

Truly, we had not seen the shape of our passions until Harry Kitchings took their picture for us.

By this I do not mean that we had not loved the Mountains or one another. Indeed, if anything, we had been too well coached by the French artists who arrived with the explorers on horseback with tender pastels in their saddlebags and left them rubbed into the rocks, and by those poets and fern fanciers who followed later with the railway and made their homes within the mist. We had begun to take our sunsets for granted. We spent more time indoors. We had become vulnerable to fads. The town drowsed in a soft haze of insinuating feeling.

With his enthusiasm for clouds and his cameras and ropes for catching the face of God, Harry caused the precipitation of a pre-existent madness.

Later he would wonder if he had not captured our love so perfectly that he had exhausted it—if he had not caused it at last to disappear.

Even in the first months after we met at the Hydro Majestic there were certain phenomena I noticed. There was an increased demand that spring, for example, for cures for influenza, from those citizens of the township who had been unable to resist the urge to go out walking hatless in the rain. We sold more perfumes with exotic names for scenting letters, as well as sleeping draughts and remedies for palpitations. We saw bicyclists who had fallen, suddenly distracted by a cloud-rise in the valley as they sped around a bend. The backs of girls' hands bore the marks of love from practising their kisses, which at first I did not recognise but later saw upon my own. The young men from the Bohemia Apartments wept openly at the lookouts when the mountain distances turned a particular shade of purple. Outside the shop people would stop suddenly in the middle of the pavement to stare up at the sky. Even Mr Medlicott was heard to remark one morning that the Mountains were as blue as the tubercule bacillus under Koch's stain.

From this evidence I deduced that the whole town twitched and shivered as if it felt the closeness of God's breath.

And Harry Kitchings had not even begun to sell his view-books yet.

His telegraph theory. There were points around the world where the telegraph wires crossed, as tender as the nodes where nerves ended in the human body. There, where the wires swelled and quickened, electricity leaked into the air. These were the sites of train derailments, shipwrecks, and explosions.

It is a long time since that winter of 1907 when Harry Kitchings first came calling for me and I thought, *My life has now begun.* I have since seen my face reflected as the mask of a spinster too many times in other people's eyes to think of it in any other fashion. For years I have heard my features remarked upon, with no attempt to soften the words or keep them from my ears, as Flinty and Hard Bitten, although that is the effect of years of swallowing and squaring my back in order to disguise my feelings. In this time I have also observed the strange phenomenon of husbands and wives who seem to share a single visage. That has caused me to wonder in turn if men and women do not make the best matches before they have learned to see each other clearly, when they are like rocks whose edges are still wet, moulded together by the history and dreams which move around them. I have suspected that men, in particular, cannot marry a woman once they know her; when her secret thoughts have been exposed, it seems, they cannot recognise her as a wife. In the darkest moments of my loneliness, as I recalled these years by Harry Kitchings' side, I have dismissed love as a literary conceit. I have doubted my own memories as febrile misinterpretation.

There is another thing. When I speak of these years now, I realise that they were made up of odd lunchtimes, Saturday evenings and perhaps four hundred Sunday afternoons. Yet those rare times are all I can remember. After he came to my aunts' house, and I began to see the clouds through Harry Kitchings' eyes, my weeks shrank until they consisted only of those moments—lustrous, slippery, discrete from one another—while the hours around them were shadowed and haunted by anticipation. It was only when I felt my feet fall into step with Harry's on the mountain paths, that these bright hours were pressed together, as tight and sequent as a thread of pearls.

That string of light which we seemed to walk along together has been broken for a long time.

So it is not surprising that my memories of these years have the character of snapshots. They are stark and luminescent. They are strangely dismembered. I see myself—from a great distance—with disbelief—as if I am a traveller in a foreign land.

For I abandoned my historical eyes for Harry Kitchings.

And now, when I recall these moments, I cannot get the seams and shadows back.

These were his tools for hunting God: a panoramic camera with a lens which swivelled in a leather mounting as black and oily as a bat's wing (a switch, attached to the spring, could be set at *Lent* or *Rapide*); a tripod; a leather satchel filled with glass plate negatives in dark slides; a stout coil of manila rope, the same type used by Edward Whymper in his alpine scrambles; a canteen of water and a small bag of brazil nuts; a mahogany Sanderson Tropical Reflex camera; and, much later, simply because he admired the beauty of it, an Ensign Carbine made of brass which opened like a compass in his hand.

My aunts could not afford wood so they bought coal instead from the thin man who passed along Cascade Street with his cart. He had no English words but sometimes juggled for the children with the brittle lumps or pretended to extract them from the freckled anus of his horse.

It was a Sunday evening in August, a month after that first meeting, and each house still had a fire burning in its grate. My aunts wrote letters to unsuccessful applicants on behalf of the Fresh Air League while I sat with my feet on the grate and re-read my mother's columns. We were so unused to visitors that at first we thought the rapping was the work of spirit hands and leaped up to check the cupboards and the fireplace; until at last we opened the door and saw Harry Kitchings standing like a thin ghost summoned by my longing from the fog.

When he removed his jacket in the hallway I noticed how it still held the points of his shoulders. I saw mist uncurling from beneath the frayed lapels. The high collar of his shirt was tight around the muscles of his neck.

Each night, for a month, I had imagined him standing there.

Now I smiled but could not speak. I was scornful of my own shy silence. Yet I did not know what women said.

He held a flower larger than a fist which he handed to my aunts. The petals were as furry as the skins of peaches and covered by a silver net of water. Two hours earlier at Sublime Point in Leura, Harry Kitchings said, he had sawn it from a branch which was wet and darkened by the fog. When he saw the bloom he had leaped over the guard rail and leaned towards it with one foot on soil and the other on the slippery throat of sandstone which stretched beneath the lookout. The cold damp air had come rushing up his trouser cuffs. The sawdust had darted around his hands like a swarm of eager insects. He had watched the gas lights of Katoomba jump like stars in the darkness far across the valley and seen the clouds pressed flat and white beneath him like an altar cloth. Yet it was that flower, and not his own feats, which he regarded with surprise. He said it always amazed him when he turned from a fading sunset and saw that these arid flowers had turned into lush cloud fruit—night-blunted, violet, filamentous—hanging in the air.

After supper my aunts spread their disease maps on the table and drew his attention to the dark stains of typhoid and tuberculosis in the city of Sydney far below. Then he leaned back at last into his chair and told us what had happened in those first weeks after his mother had kissed his cheek with dry lips and watched the Steamed Fish pull out of Redfern Station. At Katoomba, he had walked down Lurline Street towards his lodgings, and felt God's presence quivering in the mist like the warm shape of a rabbit beneath a magician's scarf. He had spent the next days in his rooms sleepless from the fever and the pain in his crushed hand. He read about clouds in Ruskin's *Modern Painters* and sometimes lifted his uncle's cameras to strengthen the muscles in his arms. He rigged up a small darkroom in the corner by the sink. He found that he moved by instinct. He had no need for any of the manuals. When he recovered he had walked into the bush towards Mount Solitary, sometimes closing his eyes, and found that the cliffs formed ladders beneath his feet. He returned after three days with his first images of clouds.

He had recognised the sky as a vast photographic plate.

He asked us if we had ever observed an X-ray: how the skin became transparent and the shapes of the organs that sustained it emerged, frayed and milky, on the glass. He said it was a technology we had stolen from the sky. For in the same way the clouds were air given shifting substance by the sun. Yet the X-ray machine, he said, distinguished itself by detecting the invisible vibrations which had always moved around us through the ether but which could not be made out with the naked eye. From this he had deduced that it might also be possible in this high place to take a photograph of God.

'Do you believe,' my eldest aunt asked, her voice suddenly sly, 'that such principles might apply to the spirits of the dead?'

Harry Kitchings replied that he should not be surprised. Indeed, some progress had been made in America photographing ghosts. And once his aunt, who had slept with a photographic plate beneath her pillow, had sent him the boiling image of a nightmare.

These he understood as omens of God's presence: ragged storm clouds which crossed the sky like islands; lightning; a rainbow or a fog-bow; clear water gushing out of rocks; wind suddenly lashing a young girl's unbound hair.

On his next visit Harry Kitchings told us how in that first month he had glided on a flat-bottomed boat along the cold black river which passed beneath the Mountains—how the keeper of the caves had felt his way with padded fingertips along a blind tracery of ropes—how by the sudden light of his camera flash the roof high above his head had exploded into a velvet waterfall of bats. It was only when they had disembarked and reached the Bone Cave through a narrow passage that the keeper lit the torches. The shadows played across a ribcage and a skull, half-sunk into a glittering shelf of rock. The skeleton had lain so long since it tumbled from the surface, lapped by the limy waters, that it had turned into a thing of stone, its limbs awry in patterns of hard falling, like those fossils of shattered prehistoric birds. Yet, Harry said, there was still a marrow of soft human panic gathered in the bones, which he had felt stirring in the base of his own spine. And beyond him there were endless avenues of darkness, bottomless and black. With his pale skin and white beard and pearly cataracted eyes the keeper hung with one hand upon the ceiling rope, as translucent as an axolotl, suspended in the torchlight.

Another afternoon, Harry Kitchings said, he had walked in a forest near Mount Wilson where the air went emerald green into his lungs and out in pallid shades of lichen. His ankles brushed the furry snouts of fungus. Mosses crept thick and damp across the ground. Up in the trees the roots of vines sagged from the branches, as scaled and sinewed as the bellies of goannas. Squeezing things grew fast there. Always he could hear around him as he moved the tight sounds of constriction.

That same visit he told us how he had been caught in a storm cloud on Mount Solitary. He had dug the tripod of his camera into the soil at the summit and clung to it as he leaned into the wind. Grey vapour lashed against his eyeballs. The thunder left him deaf for days. He saw the insides of his eyelids lit up red by sheets of brilliant light. Yet, strangely, the lightning would not strike him, although the air was alive with thin blue veins which wound crackling wreaths around his temples.

It was then he knew that he was in the presence of that greater power. He had felt the electricity in the vapour kiss him on his lips. He felt it run its tickling fingers through his hair.

That was his aim in his photographs of clouds, he said—to make others experience that emotion.

I looked down and saw neat teeth marks in the melon rind on his plate, as if it had been nibbled by some nocturnal creature.

When my aunts left the room to go to the outhouse together, as was their habit, to compare the colours of their water, Harry turned to me and said he supposed that I was too young to have had these feelings yet.

I blushed that I was so unknowing.

I was as ignorant as glass.

A photograph always told him when it wanted to be taken—
he said it was like pulling the silver ribbon which tied up the
gift of time.

Mr Medlicott wrapped an Electro-Galvanic Suspensory Belt
for one of those thin young men who came to us to buy sal
volatile. The boy had nodded at his urgent questions about
Debility and Nerves, and blushed when my employer took
him behind the curtain, placed the little noose around his
finger, and described the effect of Soothing Electric Treatment
on the Weak Parts. Mr Medlicott suggested that he give up
Indoor Pursuits for some more Healthful, Invigorating hobby.
He allowed the cartilaginous muscles of his lips to form a
smile.

Like the rest of the street he had been observing the movements at the studio which Harry Kitchings had rented out
that week. He had noted the cirrus strips of photographs hung
from thin fishing line inside the window. He had read the
advertisement in the *Echo* in which Harry Kitchings offered
to meet picnickers on their walks and take artistic portraits.
The sparse bachelor's furniture which he saw being conveyed
from a cart to the upstairs rooms had made him sigh a little
with nostalgia.

Now, when he saw the heavy machines being dragged
along the street, he could control his curiosity no longer.

He had found Harry on the cart, his sleeves rolled up, his
shoulder against a Summit Fine Art Wharfedale press, struggling with the men to steady it as it was lowered on a crane.

'Mr Fowler's competitor!' Mr Medlicott said, his hand extended, stepping forward from the crowd.

That was not the case, Harry Kitchings said, as he jumped nimbly from the backboard. He wiped the grease from his hand with a handkerchief before he gave it. Mr Medlicott noticed that his grip was firm.

'If we cannot share the view,' Harry added, 'then there is no hope for us at all.'

'Indeed, indeed, none whatsoever,' laughed Mr Medlicott, who winked and slapped him on the shoulder.

Harry Kitchings had invited him inside to inspect the Caxton Art Platen and spun the flywheel to show him how the platen crushed the paper against the letters on the press. There were sharp guillotines and a linotype-machine like a madman's piano which made words from molten lead. Harry Kitchings pointed out the thick leather pulleys which he would harness to the flywheels and run up to metal shafts. These would spin like dervishes on the ceiling, driven by the seven horsepower Otto. Mr Medlicott drew out his notebook and soon had the story from him of how his hand had burst.

His vocabulary: valleys were *sylvan*, the mountains *rock-ribbed*, oceans were *shark-haunted*. The sun's rays were the *searchlights of King Sol*.

On his third visit, when he gave my aunts another flower, Harry Kitchings said, 'I have something for Eureka, also.'

He still smelled of tent and dust and eucalyptus from his last expedition to the Grand Canyon. From the pocket of his waistcoat he took out a folded handkerchief and unwrapped a piece of glass. He handed the rectangle to me by its edges, gently, as if he offered me his heart. There was a silver skin of dried emulsion on its surface. When I held it to the light I saw the pale ghosts of trees and clouds which were like black marble shot through with veins of sky. Then I made out the shape of him, his coat slung over his shoulders, balanced on a heady pinnacle of stone.

It was a photographic negative, he said.

He supposed I could not guess where it was taken.

My eyes had already recognised that anvil-headed rock—the trunk of a dead gum which leaned at an angle from its summit—their shapes familiar even in this odd world of reversals. I replied that he was standing high above the valley on the bluff we called the Ruined Castle. I could even see the string he used to pull the shutter on his camera, which he had anchored on another outcrop. It was faint but taut as a trout line, as if he had hooked a leaping picture in the air.

'Eureka,' my eldest aunt said, bending her face over the negative so that the lamp cast the clouds' shadows in her lap, 'there is nothing there. You cannot possibly see that!'

Yet Harry Kitchings said I was correct: his voice expressed his admiration and surprise.

'The whole world,' Harry said, when he showed me the lens of his Ensign Carbine, 'squeezes through this little hole.'

Each Sunday morning now my aunts prepared for Harry Kitchings' visit. After church, they carefully peeled the skin from the ox tongue which they had boiled, pinned it flat to a board with two forks through its tip and root, and coated it with gelatine until it shone. To make Angels on Horseback they trimmed and rolled rashers of bacon around oysters and sweet herbs. Their account books from 1907 and 1908 record these new expenses. Looking at those columns now, written in my eldest aunt's tight hand, I am reminded of the orchid auction attended by Harry Kitchings' aunt. In our case shrimps and cinnamon biscuits, not bulbs, were the brittle currency which passed across the table.

This particular spring afternoon he brought the new Sanderson Tropical Reflex camera he had just acquired, to show me; it had a leather focusing hood and knobs made out of brass. It was as large as my chest, and so heavy that I could scarcely lift it from the table. He steadied the base with one hand as he stood beside me and showed me how to move the camera in the opposite direction—as if I was steering a boat he said—so that the image of my aunts' busy mantelpiece, displayed in reverse, was caught inside the viewing lens. Patiently, he explained the action of the reflex shutter, the strange paths of refraction taken inside the camera by the light. For the first time, as I asked my questions, and he said I showed a natural understanding, I thought, *This is how it feels to have a proper conversation with a man.*

My youngest aunt, stepping into the parlour from the kitchen, called out to my eldest aunt, 'Sissie, come and see Eureka holding Mr Kitchings' camera!' I blushed and hated them. My aunts laughed and refused to touch it when he offered. He took the camera back, and placed it beside the hallstand. His lean arms did not seem to register its weight.

As he drank our tea, he told us how he had begun to enlarge and print the negatives he had collected, to see if he had caught the face of God. It was strange, he said, to see his photographs reveal new details, becoming unfamiliar even to himself. Under the light of the enlarging lantern he could clearly see the grains of silver, like seeds of images, which made up the picture on each plate. He had spent sleepless nights returning to touch the images thrown up on the easel— watching his hand slide beneath the shadows, becoming scaled with silver like a dappled fish—at last feeling with surprise the slickness of the photographic paper. Beneath his gaze, as he enlarged and focused, each mountain seemed to turn back into the sand from which it once was formed. A print, left in the developer and forgotten, continued to ripen, until those clouds which had emerged white and fibrous on the paper were filled with shadows and receded into darkness.

In his studio, beneath the quiet moonlight, he had felt that he watched the very beginnings of the world.

For the first time in his life he experienced vertigo and had to grab at the table's edge.

He recognised it as a testing of his faith.

Sometimes, Harry Kitchings said, when I train my camera on the sky, I feel as though I am falling through it, diving for some pearl at the tufted centre of a cloud.

In the months that followed, Harry Kitchings' photographs began to appear on mantelpieces and walls around the town. He took portraits with his panoramic camera while his subjects stood on small damp ledges in the middle of great filmy waterfalls which passed like the phantoms of water over rocks. Or he posed them in the shadows at the base of tree ferns whose upper fronds flared into fluffy parasols of light. In other photographs his subjects stood staring at the clouds, dwarfed by pitted cliffs. This made them marvel at themselves. They felt heroic and defiant. A visiting lecturer from a mission society even claimed that the sight of himself in one of Harry Kitchings' portraits, balanced on a mossy boulder in the Valley of the Waters, had cured his nervous ailments.

As the evenings lengthened, people began to gather at the window of the studio to see if they could find themselves in Harry Kitchings' pictures. In one photograph taken in Katoomba Street, some Mountaineers had stopped their bikes and carts in the middle of the road and others had crowded beneath the awnings to stare back at the lens. We had not noticed before the gentle curve of Main Street, the width of it, the way it followed the railway like a riverbank. It was from this photograph that a boy first conceived of a building as rounded as a belly which he would later erect upon this corner. It would give the impression that our town had been carved smooth out of mountain stone by the passage of swift water.

The crowds also marvelled at a photograph Harry Kitchings had taken of himself, posing with his heavy camera, his hair neat, his blond moustache immaculately waxed, in the high fork of a tree.

Late into the night we could hear the mysterious sounds of Harry Kitchings' presses groaning and slapping in the darkness.

Each evening after work now I would head directly from the pharmacy to Echo Point. As I passed Harry Kitchings' studio, I walked swiftly and turned my head so that he would suspect no deliberation if he saw me. Yet my sharp eyes had already glanced into the shop and picked out the curve of his jaw as it glided through the shadows. His chin was as smooth as the bottom of a wineglass. I imagined it, warm and frangible, in my hand.

At the lookout I sat on a bench on a great rock heated by the sun and took the negative Harry Kitchings had given me from my pocket. I held it out until it seemed to be balanced on the soft palms of the clouds. Forced to focus through those silver trees my eyes were no longer distracted by a lost glove hanging from the railing or one of Mr Medlicott's prophylactics, grossly inflated and bobbing in the updraughts, anchored to the bushes at the valley's edge. Instead I concentrated only on the beauty of the landscape. And everywhere I looked I saw the figure of Harry Kitchings, dark-suited, wiry, balancing with his camera like a dancer.

I preferred the strange scent of the chemistry to all the bush flowers on the cliffs around me.

Leaning back, I closed my eyes and saw the blood hot and red inside my eyelids.

I held the cool negative against my lips.

At last, that afternoon came, in the middle of the summer of 1908, when I walked past Harry Kitchings' studio at the same moment he backed out, and he smiled, and tossed his key in the air before he put it in his pocket. In spite of the heat, there was a tight pride in the way he held his back as we walked swiftly past the little lanes and guesthouses, and received tired greetings from the few people who stood looking over their fences into the street. As the footpath ended, and we began to hear the bright streamers of sound the parakeets and cockatoos trailed behind them as they flew, Harry told me how clouds played out the secret life of mountains, how they hinted at the former tenderness of rocks. They were reminders, he said, of how thousands of years ago stone had melted and risen again as swiftly as the mist, how it was squeezed into these great folds and elevated ridges. The Pluvial waters, he told me, still ran fast and ancient in the caves beneath this road.

When I mentioned my mother and how she brought her dreams of going as the clouds went to the lookout on the morning we had first arrived, I noticed that he glanced at me, kindly, the frown-line deepening between his eyes, as if he intended to speak, and then did not.

Instead he smiled at me and began to hum as the bush opened up around us. I saw that his cheeks were freshly shaved and smelled of Rexona shaving lotion. His moustache was neatly clipped. I heard the reed in his throat vibrating.

We stood leaning over the safety rail at Honeymoon Point as the purple silence rose beneath our feet.

Then Harry Kitchings told me—'In the six months since we met I have not seen a cloud which I have not wished to show you.'

$$=== 8 ===$$

'How do you find it, living with your aunts?' Harry
Kitchings asked me. We were walking back towards
the town after watching the sunset at Witch's Leap. The great
sandstone flanks of the valley had flared orange, turned deep
purple, and faded into violet. Now darkness crept over the
rocks, hung from the trees, and turned our faces into masks,
while the sky pressed down like a blotter to absorb the noises
of the bush. I could smell the pollen falling from the hairy
nostrils of the flowers where his tripod brushed the scrub.

'Life is a notion,' I replied, 'like Radium, which my aunts
have heard of but regard with some suspicion. They have
closed their doors upon it. Death, on the other hand, is an
abiding hobby, as you may have noticed. And charity, which
they exercise upon me with an iron will.'

'That is rather harsh,' Harry Kitchings said, but I could hear
the quiet laughter in his breath. I thought I felt his injured
hand hesitate for a second, before withdrawing, when it
touched my hip.

'On the other hand, I have a scientific temperament,' I told him. 'I prefer to investigate things for myself.'

He offered no reply and we walked on in silence. He was so certain of the way, that when the path narrowed, and we had to walk in single file, I did not look down at my feet, but instead watched the top of his bright head, gold where the moonlight caught it, as it bobbed and fell ahead of me, and took from it the rhythm of his feet. On either side of me I heard the passage of startled lizards up the dry embankments. A spider swung across the pathway on a thread of silk and bounced against my cheek. Once or twice we came across the trace, as sharp as ink, of a possum or a bat. It was only when we reached the stairs that I stumbled in the darkness. Then he took my hand and placed it in the crook of his elbow, holding it there firmly with his own cool fingers. As we walked along the road, we did not separate. I felt the muscle of his arm, as hard and rounded as a quince.

At last, at my aunts' house at the bottom of Cascade Street, we stood apart, and he looked down at the ground as if he read something there. Then he said I should be patient with my aunts. For he imagined I would be married very soon. He walked across the road and into the bush.

I watched his quick shadow pass between the beehives.

They were as white in the darkness as pieces of the moon.

It was 1909 and we walked without resistance. Things yielded and gave way. Roads, unpinned from gravity, turned into shimmering mirages. Sandstone paths slipped away to cliffs beneath our feet. Houses opened like steamed mussels and bodies parted to make room for Harry Kitchings and myself. Couches, left empty by design, turned into lovers' seats around us. A looseness seemed to afflict the township as we passed.

We owed this in part to Lady Harding, whose experienced eyes had observed certain physical symptoms which she diagnosed as love. She had noticed that my cheeks were flushed, that I was hollow-eyed, that my hands trembled slightly when they counted change. She had asked my aunts if I was constipated and whether I called out often in my sleep. Sir Wilfrid had been dispatched to the King's Hairdressing Saloon and reported that Harry Kitchings had been making frequent visits. From the Misses Moon she learned that he had asked them to darn the fraying collars of his shirts. She had noticed that he always looked up sharply when he heard my name. She had also detected, although she was too discreet to remark upon it, a keen new scent like basil in his sweat. The women of the Fresh Air League had carried her directives rapidly around the Blue Mountains so that we received many invitations.

Since Harry Kitchings had given me the first viewbook from his press I seemed to see him always, moving quick and straight-backed through the streets—as if the hot bright air at corners had been peppered with some silver madness. Each time I hoped that I might see him it leaped to take his shape.

Often I would glimpse him carrying a new delivery of glass plates or paper to his studio from the railway office, or returning with his viewbooks to be sent for sale in the gift emporiums of Sydney, although he would often open the

boxes and distribute half of these as presents to the people
who greeted him along the way. I would pass the schoolyard
where he stooped over his tripod and watch secretly as he
composed a stubborn group of children dressed as wood
sprites into order. Sometimes, when I looked up through the
window of the pharmacy, I saw him briefly, looking in, held
no longer than a heartbeat at its centre, behind the large cream
Specie jars with their ornate crests. Then the breeze seemed
to take him at another angle, and he darted, swift as a hum-
mingbird, away from the abstracted flowers in the glass.

And always, when we came across each other in the street,
Harry Kitchings smiled as if he also had expected it. He turned
his mild eyes upon me with such close and pleased attention
that I felt I had been skeletonised like one of Mr Darwin's
birds. For the rest of the day I felt the soft weight of unboned
flesh inside my clothes.

If he had taken photographs that morning in the valley he
would have a lyrebird's feather or some tart bush fruit for me
in his pocket. If I carried an order of strychnine, or Dr Collis
Browne's Chlorodyne wrapped up in brown paper, he would
rush to take it from my hands and walk with me to Alderman
Bronger's factory where the mice left sticky footprints, or to
the shuttered house at the bottom of Lurline Street where a
woman and her pale son with Russian eyes slept during the
day so that she could walk him to the lookout in his leather
harness late at night. 'Eureka,' Harry said, when I began to
tell him their story, 'you would find the dusty corners in
Paradise!' Yet his voice was gentle and when I spoke again
he bent his head to catch my words.

There were other secret symptoms.

For a month each time it rained Harry Kitchings had been haunted by the salty stink of kelp. For three weeks after that the sky had filled with mammilated clouds: in his darkroom, beneath the developing fluid, he saw nothing but downy breasts. Much later Les Curtain would tell me that Harry's dreams back then, when he eavesdropped on them, were thick with the cucumber smell of angels' beating wings.

Every evening Mr Medlicott complained at the marks he found on the dockets in the shop—I had traced the photographs in Harry's viewbook so often that my fingertips were silver.

His means of summoning sleep. He counted Hannibal's elephants as they swayed across the Pyrenees—in his imagination they always carried snowballs in their trunks, mistaking them for fruit.

It was around this time, I seem to remember, that Harry Kitchings explained to me how the cores of stones still held spores and grains of pollen from the lush plants which once grew in these dry valleys. He said from these scientists would one day be able to trace great changes in the climate. It would be possible, he imagined, in this way, to recover the temperature of an age.

Sadly, that is my own project now.

After my love became an embarrassment which stuck out

from the mountains as clumsy as the rib-bones of a dino-saur—after people turned cold faces away from me and closed their doors and retreated down long corridors of ice—I would feel my heart grow hard and dry inside my chest, until I no longer believed that it had ever been so tender and eager that it could be nudged open by the clouds. Recalling these years now, it is difficult to convince myself that Harry Kitchings had any feelings for me in return; that it is not a fiction I am writing.

Yet perhaps by his own logic I may claim he loved me.

For, if I was mistaken, then I was not alone. Our partner-ship was reflected as a fact in the eyes of many others.

An examination of the bedrock from this time would reveal the intense sapphire colour of the air.

Surely this proves that I planted at least the seeds of an affection in Harry Kitchings' heart.

When I ignite my flash, Harry Kitchings said, I feel, for a moment, as if I inhabit a second atmosphere, as round and silver as a dandelion, inside the darkness of our own.

One morning the previous year my employer's chin had appeared from behind the pages of the *Echo*, swiftly, as if it had been jerked up by a hook.

'Have you seen this?' he asked me, laughing. 'Poor Mr Fowler. He has been inoculated against the muse. But he does not let that stop him.'

He placed the newspaper before me on the counter. There was a photograph of the Weeping Rock, reproduced in the top left corner of the page, which I recognised instantly as Fowler's work. The falls were positioned stoutly in the centre of the picture; grey waters as sullen as lead fanned out over a rocky ledge. Mr Fowler had cropped the image so closely that no vegetation could be glimpsed at the edges of the stream which ran out of the frame. It resembled the Styx interrupted on its passage to the lower regions of Hell.

I saw that Mr Fowler had left the lens of his camera open for too long until the vision curdled.

'I believe that Harry Kitchings' work is far superior,' I said. 'I would also guess that Mr Fowler has been frightened into advertising by his presence.'

'No no. Not there. Here. *Here*,' said Mr Medlicott, who, as if to confuse me, did not look where his rapid index finger tapped on the opening line of a verse beneath the photograph, but up into my face with surprised intensity, as if he made some kind of mental calculation with my words.

The first line said, 'I will meet you at the falls.'

The next line said, 'Bring the babe but quell its squalls.'

'Ghastly!' Mr Medlicott placed his hands on either side of his small belly and rocked back and forward, laughing, like a seahorse with live young in its pouch.

'Take your portrait anywhere!' he wheezed, as the tears ran down his face.

'From Wentworth Falls to Blackheath fair,' I replied, and laughed and gasped, until my hair fell loose about my shoulders. Mr Medlicott threatened to strap a nebuliser to my face, then coloured at the thought. 'You had better tidy yourself,' he said, his voice suddenly tight, as he walked out into the street.

His method of descending cliffs. He closed his eyes and tried to think like water.

Today when I open that viewbook Harry Kitchings gave me, there is a dirty crease down the centre where it has been folded over for many years inside my trunk. There are long stains like tears in the margins of some pages. The blue of the cover has faded so that it resembles the sea after some disturbance of the sand.

Yet if I close my eyes I can imagine that it is 1908 and he has just brought it to me with its pages still damp from the press.

It was a Friday evening and my aunts were inspecting catalogues when Harry Kitchings turned up at our door. The Fresh Air League was about to purchase typewriters for poor women in the city. Not only did they hope that these machines would assist the women to find work but that they would also engage the fingers of 'silkworms' and 'placers' in some more useful way. My aunts had learned about these petty thieves from Reverend Stonestreet's lecture, 'Why Women Steal'. Sometimes in their minds they confused it with his other recent lecture, 'The Creatures of the Deep'. My eldest aunt could not understand how a typewriter functioned, until her sister told her to imagine it as a kind of loom for spinning words. Then she shook her head and said that it might mean the end of spirit writing. I looked up from my diary and observed that she ought to regard it as a kind of evolution of this occupation—that the typists would still sit at attention writing down men's words. My eldest aunt replied that I had become more insolent in the last year since my mother's death. She said I should submit myself to Mr Tuke the optometrist's new antropometer so that he could investigate the peculiar workings of my eyes.

When I opened the door, Harry Kitchings walked in, breathing hard, and stood in the middle of the room. His thin hair was, for once, not neatly combed back so that it made a pale arc above his forehead; instead it fell in a damp fringe across his eyes. Sharp whiskers broke like golden needles through the skin around his jaw. His wrists and fingers were still stained by ink, although I could also see the clear streaks of soap where he had attempted quickly to make them clean. He said he was sorry to disturb us, and that he would not stay, but that he had wished to give me the first book off his press.

The title, *Seventy-Five Views of the Blue Mountains Wonderland,* was printed on the cover in cobalt script, the bases of the capitals curled like vines around each other. The book was two feet long. My aunts remarked, as I held it, that it sagged over my knees like a sampler waiting to be stitched. Harry Kitchings said this had a purpose—in order to view the photographs inside, people would have to open their arms out to the clouds.

I have looked at those pictures so many times that I can still recite them.

The first photograph was taken from the Orphan Rock at dawn when the Jamieson Valley has filled with mist. To the left a dark cliff curved around the vapour like a forearm; the Three Sisters, black shadows, drifting from its summit, resembling the turrets Harry Kitchings had showed me lifting from the surfaces of storm clouds. In the distance, the stepped summit of Mount Solitary pushed through the clouds. In the centre of the photograph a long platform stretched—empty—as if it had just bent and shuddered beneath a diver's feet.

In the thirty-first photograph, of the National Pass at Wentworth Falls, he had turned his panoramic camera on its side so that the great length of cliff filled the right half of the frame. Beneath slab upon slab of bedded sandstone a group of tiny picnickers looked out across the chasm, the stone above them sharp and corrugated—as if it had been freshly split—the hatted men and women mute witnesses to some mighty crashing in the valley.

The fortieth photograph, of Grose Valley, taken from Govett's Leap, showed the bushy slopes, like the subtle swelling of an Adam's apple, climbing gently to a chin of rock. Tender shadows filled the hollow where the neck and shoulders met.

My aunts leaned over my shoulders to see if they could recognise anyone we knew in the little figures at the lookouts. Harry smiled and moved about the room, pretending to examine the books about Ruskin on the mantelpiece which I had borrowed from the School of Arts, and glanced occasionally at my face. I felt my skin turn red. I could not find the words to tell him how beautiful I found his photographs. At last I simply thanked him for the viewbook and took it to my room.

The next day, over cream teas at the Coffee Palace, when my aunts told Lady Harding of Harry Kitchings' visit, she said she was surprised that he had not come to see her and offer her the first fruit off his press, but she supposed it was less distance from his studio to our house than to hers. She continued to listen in silence as my aunts recounted the details, of the way his sleeves were still rolled up above his forearms, of the way he had wrapped the gift up in a length of silk, of his enthusiasm and my ingratitude. On the way home, she had her driver stop at Harry Kitchings' studio and walked out with a present of a viewbook.

The body's lightning. He said when we shiver suddenly it is because the electricity in the air has found its way to earth along our spine.

The 1909 season had ended. The Carrington Hotel had closed its doors until the spring and the last tourists had sent their trunks on to the city. In order to relieve the winter boredom Mr Medlicott had constructed 'Facts for Mothers', a small museum of childhood disasters. He had removed the Specie jars from the window of the pharmacy and in their place displayed the objects removed by Dr Summergreene from the ears of children in the district. There were moths and marbles, gramophone needles, bullet cases and dried peas. He had taped X-ray films of small bones broken by motor carriage wheels and wringers to the glass. To these he had added clippings from newspapers and scientific journals which warned of the increased risk of post-nasal growths among children who refused to blow their noses, the insanitary nature of domestic cats, and the ease with which a splinter could pass from the skin into the bloodstream, and onward, to the heart.

He had also devoted a corner of the window to that invisible world which demanded a mother's special care. In a sly homage to Mr Fowler he had composed his own instructive poem on the hazards of bacilli lurking in the kitchen:

How doth the lively little germ
Improve each shining hour,
Within the tea-cup's dark brown crack,
The dark brown crack so sour.
How skilfully he wanders in
The tea, and there doth swim;
And when the drinker drinks him down
He breeds more germs in him.

It had been set and printed by Mr Thornelow on the presses at the *Echo*. Beneath the text Mr Medlicott had added in tight copperplate that mothers might also wish to inspect our stock of dark measles glasses, chickenpox gloves and sterile baby feeders.

It had been a busy week and many of our lines were now exhausted. Mr Medlicott had even sold the last of the metal pans from the Hydro Majestic as infants' baths. I was counting nipple shields for nursing mothers when Harry Kitchings entered carrying his viewbook. He greeted me and said he had an appointment with Mr Medlicott. When he noticed the little pieces of tin I sorted with my fingers, I saw him blush for the first time. Until I finished he said nothing and looked down at the floor.

On the other side of the curtain I heard Harry present his work to my employer. He told Mr Medlicott that he planned to publish a guide to the Blue Mountains for the coming season which would feature his photographs and articles describing the area's natural advantages and beauty. He said he hoped that local businesses might care to advertise inside it. I heard the pages of his viewbook swiftly thumbed and closed. Then, as I sold and wrapped some toothache drops and a packet of Bonnington's Irish Moss, there were enthusiastic words from Harry which I could not make out. I heard Mr Medlicott's reply that, personally, he preferred to rest his eyes on the cool green felt of billiard tables. As they walked to the doorway later both men shook hands and laughed.

'Why is it, do you think,' Mr Medlicott asked me, scratching his belly as he returned behind the curtain, 'that God always chooses to appear on mountain summits and never from a tin of Lactogen or Glaxo?'

A photograph, he said, holding my hands around his camera, is always taken in the space between two breaths.

Harry had received no answer when he knocked at the front door. He went to search for Les Curtain in his fields while I sat in the cart. Les Curtain's house was set back a little off the long dead-end street which ran off the Great Western Road to the picnic grounds above the Wentworth Falls. There, Harry had said, he had noticed a persistent cloud effect which he wished to show me. He told me how, at a certain point, it was possible to stand between the sun and the valley and see one's own shadow upon the fog-blanket. He wished to photograph my silhouette hovering like a quick dark fractonimbus among the lighter clouds.

It was the spring of 1909. We had driven past small sanatoria with smoking chimneys, and paddocks and the driveways of invisible estates which caused minor interruptions to the bush. We had stopped at last to deliver to Les Curtain those envelopes Harry Kitchings' aunt had sent him from London in which smooth bumps had formed in the soft paper around the withered shapes of bulbs, and others from Japan, filled with tiny tortured branches and rare papery flowers which smelled like tea. Now, as I waited in the cart, a faint drift of dirt rose up in the breeze behind the house while, in an unseen garden bed, a young boy swore and coughed. A ginger cat slid out from behind a row of hydrangeas and when it saw me ran out across the road. There were some old hoses from the Hydro Majestic, I noticed, rigged up to a tap beside the driveway.

When Harry returned, holding a paper bag, I asked him what was in it. 'Nothing,' he said, and tossed it on the floor between our feet. He flicked the reins hard across the horse's neck. His back was stiff with anger.

The bulb room where he had found Les Curtain was like a crypt, he said. Its long racks were filled with thousands of bulbs, as pale as skulls in the darkness. He had seen piles of catalogues from daffodil conferences, and forceps for emasculating plants; rubber bands and little hangman's caps for binding roses before an exhibition and a syringe for spraying them with dew. The room also had a charnel stink about it from the great piles of lime and bone dust and blood manure and German potash salt which Les Curtain stored behind the building. He had told Harry he used it to improve the soil here which, until he had arrived, was not even fit for weeds.

'I have never met anyone,' Harry said, 'with such a disrespect for the Lord.'

Then Les Curtain had shown him his Lunatic Asylum. In this plot, at the far end of the garden near the valley, he kept the failed results of his experiments—irises with obscene flesh hanging from the flowers, dwarf narcissus too weak to raise their heads. It amused him, he said, to walk by and find some interesting monster.

'I profit on God's mistakes,' he had told Harry, 'just as you do with your camera.'

We walked along the Undercliff Track, which wound like a ribbon around the cliffs, and kept going for some distance. When we stopped, at an oblique angle to the falls, Harry Kitchings ripped open the bag, took out one of the bulbs which he had been given, and hurled it out across the valley.

He watched it fall. He pressed his lips together and released a long breath through his nose. He said, 'I am afraid that was not the action of a Christian man.'

I laughed at his expression of shame and the mottled redness of his neck until he also had to smile.

I said, 'I will wager that I can throw the next one further.'

I flicked my wrist as one of the young machinists had once shown me by the Yarra River during a staff picnic from my father's work. I thought I saw the bulb skip like a pebble on the cloud below us before it disappeared.

'Eureka!' Harry Kitchings called me.

He had jumped onto a misshapen rock which jutted out from the cliff below the path.

I threw another bulb—he leaned out across nothing and caught it in his hat.

Perhaps he did not believe me when I said that I would join him, or it surprised him, the ease with which I leaped. He called to me and stepped forward with his arms held out, standing exactly where I aimed to land, so that I fell hard against him. I felt the smooth flesh of his cheek against my own. I felt the hard muscles in his thigh between my legs as he steadied us above the drop. The trees jumped up towards us, and subsided. We stood together for some time, surprised by our own wild laughter.

Then Harry frowned when he saw that I had scratched my wrist against his belt. He held it for a moment near his lips as if he thought to kiss it and I felt his breath and then he said that we should go. I told him not to worry. I said, 'Women are not such fragile creatures.' Yet he would not look into my eyes. He said he thought it best to take me home.

His gifts to me: a piece of sandstone bearing traces of the feet of starfish; a snakeskin; a stalactite; a bracelet carved from the pale inner growth rings of a fallen tree.

'When tempted by a pair of thighs,' Mr Medlicott said,
   'A gentleman should botanise.'
   I heard Alderman Bronger laugh behind the curtain.

This high-pitched sound surprised me, since lately the alderman, who was possessed of a gloomy temperament in the best of circumstances, had been troubled by many things. As he walked up Main Street from his factory he counted the cracks in the pavement and the overflowing gutters. Improvements to the sewage works were proceeding at a snail's pace and he had begun to fear an epidemic. He dreamed of discharging waste from the septic tanks over the cliffs to turn great turbines in the valley and generate electric power for the town, but so far only Mr Medlicott had expressed enthusiasm for this project. Now he was faced with a conspiracy to promote surf-bathing and snow at the expense of the Blue Mountains.

In the last two years, he told Mr Medlicott, the whole eastern seaboard had gripped the public imagination. Commercial men had realised the lucrative potential in undistinguished coastal hamlets; advertisements had been taken out; doctors had been paid to write pamphlets attesting to the healthful properties of sea water; and people had actually begun to bathe in it, ignoring the stench of dead jellyfish and brine. Then suddenly—in spite of their lack of scenic grandeur—the Snowy Mountains were also being boomed. Public monies were being spent on a new road to Kosciusko and a government hotel. Indeed the Tourists' Bureau seemed intent on supporting these new sights at the expense of the Blue Mountains. It had refused the councillors' applications for assistance to advertise Katoomba at any forthcoming Exhibitions. The Railway Department had ignored their requests to increase the service of the Fish. He could not help thinking some deliberate sabotage was afoot.

'What pleasure could possibly be found,' Alderman Bronger asked, 'slipping down a frozen slope on planks?'

Mr Medlicott replied that he would like to see the statistics on frostbite and compound fractures.

He also thought that Harry Kitchings might offer some assistance. 'To my taste he makes rather too much chin-music about the Lord,' he said, 'but the man is a born Booster, there is no doubt about it.'

A week after that, Harry Kitchings was invited to lunch in the private rooms above the council chambers which were as planked and planed, he told us, as the insides of a ship. It flattered him enormously, he said, that the councillors did not even wish to view the samples he had brought. Alderman Bronger said that this was not an interview: that the councillors already had the highest regard for his work and therefore did not need to see it. Alderman Spry said he doubted whether there was anyone in this township who did not have the clearest image of them in his head. Mayor Gordon promised to advertise his real estate office in the next *Kitchings Guidebook*. The councillors also agreed that they would subsidise the lantern display Harry was planning to tour around the state. They would always be eager, the mayor said, to hear first of any of his new plans. Encouraged by his friends on the council, Mr Thornelow subsequently published a small piece in the *Echo*. 'In his new viewbook,' he wrote, 'Harry Kitchings takes us on a tour of the fairies' eyries. Mountaineers are strongly advised to secure this ethereal freehold, cloudy fixtures included, passed in at a bargain for a shilling.'

Once—and sometimes I think I must have dreamed this—he gave me my name written backwards in a block of lead by his linotype-machine, which I pressed in ink and printed on his forearm.

My mother's proposal had tasted of nectarines. In order to encourage her to kiss him my father had visited her home and fed her fruit in the mulberry shadows of the garden. She felt the skin burst and the sweet flesh and my father's lips between her own. By the time she reached the stone, his fingers had torn the ribbon from her hair and they were engaged. She felt her body tremble as if it had been caught by the vibrations of a low sad foghorn.

I had begun to imagine my own proposal, which would taste of glass, and tent, and bellbird, and Rexona shaving cream.

For Harry and I had launched leaves like gondolas across rock pools below the Marguerite Cascades; he had read me Wordsworth's poems in Sassafras Gully where the air was thick and warm with moss; and, as we had walked up the path which wound through the ferns in Nellie's Glen, Harry was delighted when I imagined that the workman, who held a cigarette between his lips as he laboured, had carved into the mountain the soft zigzag pattern of curling smoke. He had taken my photograph standing in the middle of the Leap Road at Blackheath; a picture in which I was so small, and the sky so large behind me, that the marks of cartwheels in the dirt seemed to slide around me like the pale grooves made by skaters' feet. He had shown me Water Nymphs Dell and the Bridegroom's Cave.

As 1909 ended, the summer of 1910 came and went, and Harry Kitchings' presses rattled through the night, I found I was not the only person in Katoomba to suffer from a kind of photographic madness. There were accidents at the lookouts as groups of men from the guesthouses clambered over guard rails and clustered onto rocks to compose themselves at the centre of Mr Fowler's lens. There were candlelight processions to recite Dante by the Leura Falls. I lost count of the people who came to the pharmacy complaining of bright mirages which shimmered at the edges of their vision. Others were troubled by clouds of silver insects which buzzed around their heads and spelled out the names that they kept secret in their hearts. Harry Kitchings was seen in a hundred different places—a lithe figure catching at some porous ledge—a shadow swinging out, impossibly, across the air, on the corded strands of our desires.

And all that time I waited for some declaration.

Each day I expected to be kissed.

— 9 —

The invitations to Lady Harding's lightning party were edged with silver. She was confident of lightning in this winter of 1910 for she had rarely wished for a thing in her life which had not been granted. Even Sir Wilfrid, once she set her mind to the task, had been easily acquired in the woods near Bath. Growing tired of waiting beneath the trees while he fossicked in nests and climbed down with eggs cradled like hot ginger in his mouth, she had contrived to faint, and torn her bodice as she sank back against the bark. At the sight of her pale nipples Sir Wilfrid had swallowed two wren's eggs and fallen like a shot bird in her lap. He had spent their honeymoon two weeks later crouched over the commode in the best room at the Savoy. I could see in his face now that he had never quite recovered from the association of Lady Harding's eager hands and the agonies of passing shell.

Because she had begun to make a study of the weather more than a year ago between the marbled pages of her journal, Lady Harding also felt that her close attention to the skies ought to be rewarded. Nevertheless she had taken the precaution of asking Mr Thornelow to consult the weather records at the *Echo*. He reported back to her that for the last twenty years lightning had always struck upon this day.

For a fortnight a steady traffic of delivery vans and motor carriages from the city had passed along Lurline Street toward the Hardings' estate. From the road the staff could be seen struggling between the frosty pebbles of the driveway and the house with the large carcasses of fish. There were also wooden trays of oysters which always reminded Sir Wilfrid of the eyes of rhinoceroses, a damp malevolence at each squinting centre. Sometimes the carts were queued so close to one another that the staff had to risk squeezing with their burdens beneath the damp necks of the horses. When a motor coughed and started into life the whole line buckled. Scallops were trodden into the gravel and horseshoes left bruises like new moons across sore insteps. For the next two weeks fish scales blew like sequins through the streets. Mrs Grudge had been stopped for directions by one of the drivers, who had told her that he must deliver his fragile load quickly before it perished from the cold. She saw something mysterious and tropical move in a glass tank draped with tarpaulins. She had continued along Park Street to hear her pupils recite with a piece of tentacle caught inside her morning. At last, to put Mrs Grudge's mind at rest, Lady Harding had to tell her that the tank was filled with eels from which her cook would make electric soup.

Two days before the party an ice sculptor with a mournful expression arrived in the town by train carrying a bag of chisels heavier than death. That first afternoon he tried without success to cut his throat with a spear of frozen water which he had snapped off from the Katoomba Falls. By night-fall he had recovered sufficiently to slump by the fire with a bandage around his neck, turn a tumbler of whisky in his long blue fingers, and make sad and indecent propositions to the barmaids at the Family Hotel. There was only one place now, he told them, where his hands felt warm.

Lady Harding had also summoned the Cassell Brothers, those famed telepathists visiting from Europe, who took rooms at the Clarendon, where they amused the other guests by producing strange condiments from their jacket pockets and, with innocent expressions, relaying the thoughts of lovers in bawdy and broken English across the breakfast table. Mr Hoffman, who had recently retired as the projectionist for a biograph company in the city to strike out in business in the Blue Mountains for himself, arrived at the Carrington Hotel in a motor carriage, his patent cinematograph, secured with ropes and tipped with a silken scarf, hanging out behind the backboard. In the dicky seat the pale boy who cranked his films was stretched out fast asleep.

Along Main Street we worked late into the night attending to those visitors who had obeyed Lady Harding's unusual command to come up during the winter. She had prevailed upon the hotels to open a month before the Season. The cabmen who waited outside the station paid boys to run across the sleepers to the Gearin to fetch them bottles and left a litter of unfinished cigarettes with wet tips along the icy kerb, which my employer commanded me to gather before they froze so that he could place them beneath his microscope to observe their wriggling life. Mullaney's Universal Providers took deliveries of firecrackers from the city, which arrived at unusual hours and had to be protected from children and young men smoking pipes who gathered around each cart. These measures were not successful, for every evening that week the Fish was forced to grind its brakes like a knife against the mountains as a series of explosions and bright fiery spirals issued from the tracks. Wicks were lit, bungers thrust through night-soil hatches, and outhouses erupted in fluorescence. The Misses Moons' cat ran beneath the wheels of a florist's cart with a chain of firecrackers tied to its tail, the last vertebrae bursting like popped corn as his mistresses stitched moonlight into dresses of white silk. In Alderman Bronger's factory, as the great tanks of frothy fluid were decanted into bottles with special commemorative labels bearing the Harding crest, part of a young woman's scalp was torn away by the conveyor. Mr Medlicott dashed down the hill with his Kodak to record the hanks of golden hair, still rooted in skin, entwined in the metal of the rollers.

At times like these I was forced to wonder how far our famous love extended.

Yet for the first time I was not troubled as often by such observations.

Strange things were happening to my eyes.

Close objects and faces now gave the appearance of being quite distant; they were languid, and beautiful, suspended at the end of misty pyramids of light. On mountain paths I often lost my way, and I suffered from persistent headaches triggered by the sun. I could no longer make out those features by which I once had navigated; the rotting wallaby skins outside a shooter's tent, the scar on a rockface of a convict's pick, the rusted cables left by a mining company which had dug kerosene shale from the valley before the town was founded. I only recognised it if I stood at the exact point where one of Harry Kitchings' photographs was taken.

If I was not in love with Harry Kitchings I might have understood these changes as the evidence of some grave physical disorder.

But I knew they were due to an event which had finally dispelled my sadness.

Harry Kitchings had invited me at last to that pungent room behind the studio where his photographs were made.

Harry Kitchings held my rain parasol in his lap and played with the sodden trim as we sat in his portrait armchairs. For over a week heavy autumn rains had fallen on the mountains, washing away the pavements and leaping over gutters. The stream which had its source in the old quarry shafts beneath the Carrington Hotel could be heard in the reading room as it rushed through the foundations. Alderman Bronger was sighted often, gloomy in his mackintosh, consulting with groups of workmen in the streets. Harry Kitchings planned an expedition as soon as the storms cleared to find and photograph the cold new waterfalls and streams for his seventh viewbook. Yet, he said, as we sat and ate the sandwiches which he had made, he felt no great anxiety to be on his way.

For even here in the town the torrents produced moments of unanticipated beauty. It always pleased him, he said, the sight of women walking beneath the coloured air bells of umbrellas. It seemed to him that they carried their own fragrant weather with them through the streets.

I had come to return the cloud atlas he had lent me.

Several weeks earlier he had told me that I need never wait for an invitation to come to the studio to find him: that there was a mug there which he always thought of as 'Eureka's cup'.

He asked me how I had enjoyed that bulky book in which the clouds were photographed and labelled. I said that I had memorised a new type each night and recited some of them for him—the billowy cirrus undulatus; cats' whiskers, scarf clouds, and cauliflower thunderheads; the bull's-eye which formed at the centre of a cyclone. I liked the mother-of-pearl clouds best, I told him, although the book only offered a written description, since they had not been captured yet by any camera. These iridescent clouds had appeared after the explosion of Krakatoa, and remained, cleaving to the curving ceiling of the sky for weeks, high above the highest cirrus, as if they were fragile coruscated shells which held in the pale blue flesh of the air.

'But not one of these photographs,' I said, 'comes as close as yours to revealing the presence of God.'

He ducked his head and smiled.

We drank our tea for a while in silence.

Then I confessed that the book had also produced in me a strange longing to see plump masses of white cumulus after so many weeks of thick grey skies.

He stood up and invited me to the darkroom.

He said he would make some for me there.

At the Harding estate oyster forks had been hung from the branches of the pines along the driveway in order to lure the lightning. The fernhouse was lit up from within so that the steam on the glass threw a marbled light onto the paths. I thought I also saw the shadow of two lovers moving among the heavy fronds. Already a number of motor carriages were parked askew beneath the rhododendrons on the shoulders of the driveway. Taxis passed us on their way back to the Main Street leaving behind them the hot scent of sweating horse. Around the bend, on the lip of the valley, I heard the sounds of champagne corks and laughter in the house. Harry Kitchings and I turned to each other to point it out at the same instant—at the far end of the garden beneath the hazelnut trees we had glimpsed the Three Sisters carved from ice.

My aunts, who sat in the back of Harry Kitchings' carriage, did not say a word as he directed the horse to stop beneath the trees. They behaved these days as if we played at cards, and Harry and I held the stronger hand. I also knew they were quite tired. They had consulted his cloud atlas, before I took it back, to make my dress of beaded lightning, for they suspected that it was here that my proposal might take place. Harry Kitchings, however, did not wear a costume. As he looked around, he said that perhaps he should have brought his cameras.

Inside the house Lady Harding had wrapped blue

cellophane around the gas lamps, and run a long white rug along the passage, so that we seemed to walk on luminescent stratus. A waltz passed from the new Victrola through the open door at the back of the house and echoed off the cliffs. For the first time in my life I saw people unaccompanied by illness. There were women as brittle as stalactites in luminescent dresses. I smelled mink oil and cigars and the warm wax of the piano. We walked between polished shirt-fronts, in a room of sturdy chests.

When Lady Harding saw us she said 'Harry and Eureka' and stood between us holding both our elbows. Dressed as 'Influence', she wore a silver gown of Japanese silk. Before we joined the party, she told us, I was to show Harry her postcard book which she had left on the table in Sir Wilfrid's study. She had acquired another Switzerland and three more Germanys, she said. When Sir Wilfrid moved towards us she told him to leave us be. She said, 'I am certain they have heard your old sea stories many times before.'

Sir Wilfrid took Mr Medlicott to the warm end of the room instead and showed him the new tank he had bought for the occasion and filled with neon fish.

Harry Kitchings' darkroom was narrow and no longer than the workbench. He had cut a hole in the window shutter and covered it with three lengths of orange and two of ruby cloth. Still the room was close, and dim as if the filtered daylight only served to tenderise the darkness. I heard the squeak of the rubber draught excluder as he closed the door behind us.

We breathed the pearly smells of glass and photographic paper and emulsion. He asked me if I felt warmer. Although it was foolish, he said, he always did, inside this weak red light.

I had to smooth my heavy skirt down with my hands so that he could pass me; but the hems still caught around his trousers.

He apologised: 'I am afraid it is rather cramped.'

'I do not mind,' I said.

He spoke quickly as he ran a damp cloth along the counter and unstacked his trays. He took a dark slide from his Sanderson camera filled with undeveloped plates. He said that Mr Medlicott had told him that the great photographic factories in America where these plates were manufactured were now the most dustless places on this earth. From beneath the counter he brought out another negative which had been exposed already to the chemistry and dried, to show me how the developed emulsion formed a brittle film on the surface of the plate. He moved the negative by its edges as if he was a magician holding up a card which would disappear at any moment up his sleeve.

He said that the fresh emulsion, by contrast, which was hidden inside the negative holder, had a creamy appearance on the surface of the glass. He thought of it as a supple skin which held in the juices of the light until he used his chemicals to release them in the darkroom. Like skin it was a substance which was sensitive to damp and heat. Once, he said, he had returned from an expedition to Mount Solitary where the sky was clear and found in the darkroom that heavy storm clouds loomed like bruises on each plate. At first he had been inclined to take this for an omen. Then he heard from the plate manufacturer in America that the calves they had used to make their gelatine had recently changed their pastures and that this had changed the chemical composition of their hooves. He said this incident had made him realise the effect upon us of different landscapes. He liked to think that we all had that capacity, if we wished for it enough, to hold the light within our bones.

I said that I had also felt that sensation sometimes in the time since we had met.

Our hips touched.

I noticed when he mixed his chemicals that he breathed hard as if in sleep.

He said I was the only woman he had ever met who expressed an interest in the fluids and shadows of his darkroom.

Some of the women in the parlour had costumed themselves as romantic victims of forked lightning. Their dresses were loose around their shoulders and they had unbound and teased their hair. I passed a merchant's wife who told Sir Wilfrid how she and her husband had left Singapore for Sydney because she could no longer bear the smell of monkey which drifted from the jungles through the house. In the next room the Cassell Brothers imitated magnets, drawing thoughts from people's heads. I heard laughter each time they willed Lady Harding's fox terrier to sleep or jumped back when they encountered the emanations of married couples or divined a young man's secret name.

There was so much silver heaped up on the banquet tables that staff were posted in the garden to stop any thieves from the town who thought to leap the Hardings' mighty hedge. In the platters there were vol-au-vents of oysters, caviare, and huge shining fish which had been baked inside their skins. Hands frequently refilled my glass with Alderman Bronger's Dynamic Soda. The label claimed that it was charged with that same mysterious liquid which flowed through turbines and copper cables and carried messages and light—that was why it prickled on our tongues. Standing near the table, in a velvet jacket, I saw the beautiful boy who cranked Mr Hoffman's films. He had bright red hair and the sleek expression of a statue. He ate canapés and watched our conversations from beneath disdainful eyelids.

Harry Kitchings was by now quite famous for his view-books, having printed nine so far, including two separate volumes on the Hydro Majestic and the Jenolan Caves. His recent essay on the mountain spirit, 'Adventures Among the Eucalyptus', had received a great deal of attention from the city press. If we approached a knot of people it would unravel and form itself again around us. As we passed from group to group, and Harry nodded stiffly and shook hands, I noticed that he kept his scarred fingers in his waistcoat pocket. Although he smiled, there was a tiredness about the soft creases at the corners of his eyes, as if they were bothered by the smoke. Once, as we stood together near the piano, an old mountain-climber came up and told Harry how he had lived in Paris as a young man; he had scaled the facade of Notre Dame one midnight on a wager, he said, feeling his way by the snouts of gargoyles and the blank faces of the damned. A rich man's niece stopped to tell us how she regretted the sale of the family's private railway station further down the mountains, for her earliest memory was of being held up in her uncle's arms and waving to stop the train. Another younger woman fell against Harry and laughed when she saw that her champagne had soaked his sleeve. She rested her cheek on his arm and told him that her feet became more ticklish when there was lightning in the air. 'Any minute now,' she laughed, 'I shall not be able to stop myself from dancing.'

Just once I glimpsed my aunts sitting on a long bench by the window smiling, as two lovers at the other end fed salmon to each other with their fingers. To my discredit I turned my head and made certain that I did not pass that way again.

Harry said that he needed to go out for some fresh air and went to join the group of men who were smoking on the verandah. Before they saw me following behind him I heard Mr Medlicott tell them that it was his suggestion that his wife come bannered as 'Suffragette', because, he said, bending over at the waist with laughter, he had never witnessed lightning without wishing one of those creatures might be struck. He was holding a magnetic helmet which, he said, directed currents to the brain and improved on the randomness of electricity in the air. He offered it to Harry Kitchings and said perhaps he'd care to try it. Harry replied that he would not and walked on towards the ice sculpture of the Three Sisters at the far end of the garden. Mr Medlicott called after him that he would have preferred to see Benjamin Franklin, attached to his kite at the moment of electrocution, rendered lifelike by the chisel's art. I heard Mr Fowler laugh.

I moved to the far end of the verandah and looked out across the valley, which was filled with still white stratus. On its cold lip I observed Mr Hoffman and the boy engaged in argument. There were strange canisters and contraptions scattered around their feet. No one but I saw Mr Hoffman pull the tie from the boy's white throat and hurl it into the valley, then call after him, trying to offer him his own watch as compensation, as he strode off into the night.

Harry Kitchings' hands seemed to move as slow and cool as jellyfish in those underwater shadows. When he took the exposed plate out of its holder he turned his back to the window so that his body made a darker pocket for it in the thin red darkness. He covered the developing tray with cardboard until he could wet the plate with the fluid from two bottles. When it was full he rocked the tray so that the liquid moved from side to side. With a plodget of cotton wool he swept the air bells which appeared on the surface of the glass. He told me that the brightest parts would appear first, then the half-tones, and finally the shadows.

For ten breaths I saw nothing.

Then I saw silver start like a blush to the surface of the plate. Beneath the developer I watched cumulus clouds emerging thick and fibrous on the glass as if they were reflections held in water. Then new, milky clouds of fluid spread out through the liquid, as if the image disgorged the stain of time.

Harry Kitchings lifted the plate out when his instinct told him it was ripe. He stilled the image with hypo and placed it under running water. At last he allowed me to reach my hands into the cold water and lift it out.

Then he asked me if I would like to try it for myself. 'It is a difficult process,' he said. 'Do not worry if you cannot master it at once.'

I could feel the heat of his cheek as he stood behind me. He told me not to move my hands too eagerly. He guided my wrist and showed me how to brush away the air bells without damaging the picture's skin.

I saw the silver rise beneath my fingers.

When it was thick I took it out and placed it in the fixer.

'It is a perfect density,' Harry said with some surprise, as he lifted the negative out and wiped the milky residue from its surface. He asked me how I had known, before he could even get the words out, the precise moment the development should stop. I said that I had watched and copied him. I could see the silver through the back of the plate when he took the first slide out.

For the rest of that afternoon we printed clouds out on his photographic paper and left them to dry on sheets of glass until their surfaces were polished. Late in the day he cut my name out of a piece of card and held it over the enlarging lantern. When he developed the paper, 'Eureka' was branded with light across the middle of a thick cumulus with bright, domed edges, its belly flattened by the wind.

As we worked he told me a little about the years before his conversion. For the first time I heard him speak of standing at the railing of the steam ferry with his father and how they had both seen the shadow of a shark glide as swift as death beneath their feet; of his mother's spoons of salt and her hands which hurt and wept when he was ill; of waking with his head on the bar in hotels in the western deserts and hearing the men around him spit women's names from their throats like dust.

I asked him if he had ever been in love.

Above our heads we felt the weight of his private rooms.

He blushed. He said some things were so sensitive, like photographic plates, that even in darkness they could only be uncovered in the body's shadow.

At last Lady Harding announced that Mr Hoffman had assembled the cinematograph. There was a rush for coats. The men emerged dark and quilted. In their furs many of the women appeared to have been wrapped up in soft vapour. As the group moved to the far end of the garden Harry Kitchings drew his shoulder behind mine as if to protect me from the cold. Our breath steamed. We smiled at each other. I leaned into the hollow of his collarbone as if it were a curving cliff and I was Harry Kitchings, closing my eyes, imitating water.

Mr Hoffman had turned his back on the large canvas sheet which he had earlier asked the boy to stretch between two pines. Instead he had pointed the nose of his small machine out across the valley. When he had stared us still and silent, he bent and opened up the lens. White light jumped and flickered and threw the jerking shadows of the branches at the valley's rim. 'There's the lightning!' someone yelled. Mr Hoffman ignored them and began to turn the handle at the side of the machine. We heard a sound like the spinning of a bike wheel.

Then, far below us, on the white cloud blanket, as if they had lumbered out of Harry's dreams, I saw three huge swaying elephants, climbing the gentle undulations with oddly shortened steps.

For twenty minutes, Mr Hoffman threaded and unwound his films while the sweat ran down his neck. Blooming and shivering on the clouds, we saw pyramids and Bavarian castles and bathing platforms on the Ganges. We witnessed, in their full magnificence, the Victoria and Niagara Falls. Then boats streamed across a busy harbour; the Statue of Liberty rose like a diver from the clouds and turned her blank face in our direction. We laughed and applauded at these ghosts of landscape which filled the clouds up with our dreams. Only Harry stood grave and straight-backed and did not clap. He turned his head a little to the side as if he listened for the voice of God. At last Mr Hoffman loaded his final reel and turned the handle of the cinematograph so that the Three Sisters on the edge of the valley before us were twinned by their sudden reflection in the clouds. We saw those three eerie rocks below us, black and solid and real in the new moon's light; and, beside them, their craggy forms repeated, pale and porous, as if they had turned back into dust, which briefly held their shapes. They twitched and shivered before they disappeared.

I reached into Harry Kitchings' pocket for his hand and squeezed it.

His fingers were cold and did not move between my own.

Harry urged the horse past the broken fern fronds and steaming horse manure and chicken bones which littered the Hardings' driveway. A stray dog ran about between the carriage wheels nosing in the gravel and barked when it heard Hutton howl inside the house. Lady Harding's groundsmen tried to clear a passage for the taxi drivers while the cars and horses backed and turned around them. I looked up and saw that someone had balanced the melting skeletons of the Three Sisters in the branches of a tree. My aunts did not notice. They sat in the back seat of the trap and spoke with wet eyes of those men and women who had been kind enough to greet them. I did not know what to say or where to look so I stared at the horse's neck.

Harry was also silent. His shoulders stooped a little as he drove.

I did not know it then, but I believe, now, that this was the first time, as we cheered the lightning which Mr Hoffman summoned from the air, that Harry Kitchings had smelled something rank which stirred and shifted its weight within the clouds.

═10═

Of all the cloudscapes, Harry Kitchings said, he loved this one most which he thought of as an oil-and-water sky.

The clouds above us were creased and swollen. Where their edges met they formed strange whorls of silver vapour: buckled, viscous, and seamed with light. He liked to imagine them as the fingerprints of God on the blue plate of the air.

We had parked the cart at Blackheath near some tethered goats which grazed on the yellow railway flowers by the train tracks on the other side from Govett's Leap. The path to the creek was thin and sandy. We walked up to our waists through purple heath, Harry moving ahead, as was our habit now, sometimes bending branches which overgrew the track. He secured them with his hip so that they would not sting me, and waited until our bodies touched. We ducked beneath a low stained shelf of sandstone and kept on until we reached the plateau, where he set up his tripod at the base of a great dark knob of weathered rock. It was as squat and solid as a paperweight on this windy outcrop—as if, without it, the shivering landscapes which stretched around our feet might lift up like sheets of purple tissue paper and derange themselves in the wind. I watched as he moved the focusing knobs of the camera with his fingers. It seemed to sniff for pictures in the air.

'You will need to shade the lens,' I said, for he photographed against the light.

He removed his hat and held it at the side of his camera as he bent to press the shutter. I smiled. It always touched me, this odd gesture of decorum.

As he worked, he told me how he had met a 'sensitive' on his recent lecture tour to Melbourne where he had shown his fifteenth viewbook. Harry had been leaning on the long pier at St Kilda when the gaunt American approached him. 'I could see in your face,' he said, 'that you would wish to hear my story.' As a child in Louisiana, the man told Harry, he had developed a facility for sensing creatures in the dark. Each night from the porch he had followed the nutria moving through the swamp by the luminous effluvia of their bodies. By the age of twelve he could stand in a pitch black room and distinguish a raccoon from a hound by its electrical emanations. With his father he had travelled around America, staying in small hotels, until they reached New York, where he had become a popular attraction, able to determine, blindfolded, the species of any flower. There, he told Harry, in a church on Fifth Avenue, he had begun to sense things for which he knew no names, felt the light itself stretching like a membrane, the shrug of sinew in the smoke. He said he had come at last to seek God in this less populous country where he would not be distracted by the human glare.

That encounter had renewed his faith in his own photographic project, Harry Kitchings said. Yet he had to admit that he also envied that man's capacity to approach so near to what he wanted.

I said, 'Perhaps his desire is stronger.'

Harry Kitchings doubted that.

It was more a matter, he thought, of overcoming fear.

Everyone had seen the cloud shaped like a dreadnought; everyone except Harry Kitchings who had disappeared from Katoomba again. The dark cumulo-nimbus was as long and turreted as one of those vast warships which now prowled the seas of Europe. A year earlier, on the first day of 1912, it had appeared in the empty sky over the valley and moved with swift deliberation until it hung above the town. Its base was flat while its upper surface had massed into great triangles of vapour, trails of false cirrus clinging like smoke around their peaks. The cloud was motionless, blocking out the sun. It was so thick that it gave the appearance of being armoured.

For an hour we had to light the gas lamps in the street so that we could find our way in the cold grey air beneath.

At last the cloud had released a barrage of hail which fell like lead shot on the town, denting roofs and punching holes through rusted gutters. The taxi drivers swore and their horses screamed as they tried to make them climb the kerb to shelter beneath the awnings of the shops. Yet, although the streets were empty of people, they had a strange appearance of animation; for every surface seemed to exceed itself in a lively blur of bouncing ice. The air was so thick and white that for a moment it seemed to my eyes that the entire town was a dream, an insubstantial thing made out of shifting particles of light. Mr Medlicott, who stood beside me in the doorway, said the activity of the hail made him think of those busy microbes which always swarmed around us in the air. When the hail turned finally to rain it fell so hard that soon we could see nothing from the pharmacy except a smooth curtain of silver water which ran from the verandah to the ground and blocked out all the street.

Then the cloud was gone and the mountains were a little duller as if the hail had battered some of the blueness from the air.

We were all rather uneasy after that. Many people were reminded of the German threat, while others were simply too timid to return to the kiosk which had shaken on its foundations and filled with leaves during the storm. In the valley beneath the Three Sisters, the branches had been broken off the ferns and the run-off had formed new byways which led alarmingly to the edges of the cliffs. For a week those walkers who risked the muddy paths were troubled by orphaned fledglings which ran at them with open mouths and cried to them for food.

However, by the time Harry Kitchings returned from Queensland where he had been exhibiting his photographs, and his fourteenth viewbook, Mr Hoffman had repaired the roof of the Empire Theatre, the red velvet on the seats had dried, and visitors were queuing in Katoomba Street once more to see *Trust* and *Polidore as a Policeman*. They were gathering again on the roof-garden at the Katoomba Amusement Company where they sipped iced drinks among the pots of damaged ornamental citrus while, below them, the Ladies' Orchestra played, and children and lovers skated in circles on the new asphaltum surface. In the heat of the day, when the streets were still and smelled of eucalyptus, it was possible to hear the sound of cool ivory balls dropping off the billiard tables into pockets in the air.

Harry Kitchings laughed when we told him about the dreadnought.

He did not seem to notice that we talked more loudly, struck the balls with greater force, and skated a little faster.

Once, near the oval at Mount Wilson, he had found a cricket ball covered in thick green moss and carried it all that afternoon, as soft as a planet in his palm.

It had been almost five years then since we met and still Harry Kitchings had not invited me to the Cosmopolitan Cafe and made a declaration. My aunts were so concerned that they had gone to Lady Harding's house to ask her advice on securing a proposal. The maid led them to the drawing room where the Persian carpets had been taken up, having been ruined by that unprecedented hail which had broken the roof tiles, melted in the rafters, and leaked from the ceiling throughout the afternoon. Waking from her nap, Lady Harding had failed in this instance to appreciate the ironic spectacle of rain pouring from the ragged edges of the ceiling mouldings while the sky outside was blue.

'I will not offer you any biscuits,' she told my aunts. 'I cannot risk crumbs on my new rugs.'

She had ordered the polar bear skins to commemorate Captain Scott's arrival at the South Pole. Now she did not know, given the uncertain fate of his party, whether she ought to return them. She led my aunts to the verandah, closing the door on Hutton, who stood in the hall, trembling and barking at those white heads with their rows of savage teeth. On the lawns below them, the young men of the Boys' Fresh Air Brigade marched with pea rifles on their shoulders.

Lady Harding said that she liked to think she had some expertise in the matter of proposals. In her experience men were unlikely to consider marriage unless they were encouraged. Indeed, it was best to establish the habits of a marriage, then stage a swift withdrawal—many a man had found himelf surprised into a proposal by a craving for soothing hands. Each time Harry Kitchings visited, she said, my aunts should cook him good plain meals. They should serve him the boiled fruit-cakes he most enjoyed until he could not do without them. While he worked I should take him mugs of hot beef tea.

It was possible, Lady Harding added, that Harry Kitchings was altar-shy because he had not made his fortune yet. To show that I was not a spendthrift, I should express a desire for simple, tasteful items each time we passed Mullaney's. Above all, Lady Harding said, I should not appear so bold.

She recommended that I place a pebble in my shoe each time we walked together. Nothing inflamed a man's desire more, she said, than feeling his own strength. She had to admit, though, as she bade my aunts goodbye, that Harry Kitchings' behaviour was in some ways a little strange: those vanishings, his tendency to lurk behind his camera, to leave any social occasion early. Before she closed the door on them, she called Sir Wilfrid from his shattered fernhouse to come inside and lift a little table.

I frowned when my aunts returned with sober faces.

I said, 'Harry Kitchings is an artist.'

I told them, 'Not all passions seek their natural end in wedding vows.'

Ancient peoples, Harry told me, did not speak of 'weather'. Instead, they found their deaths and fortunes in the trailing viscera of clouds.

By this time I had come to accept that Harry Kitchings might never ask me to be his wife. I thought: *He is too romantic for that.* For behind his high forehead, and the pale blue concentration in his eyes, I was certain that feelings as ecstatic and fine as cirrus cloud took fantastic shapes. He would not wish to give them any ordinary form. He would disdain to anchor them with proof. I also knew that he had no desire for me to perform for him all those tasks a wife did, boiling scraps on the stove and scrubbing with sandsoap along the sideboards. For he had told me how much it pained him to see me taking orders all day from Mr Medlicott.

This failure to propose did not preoccupy me. For I had realised a year ago that it was not something that I truly wished for either.

Instead, I was overwhelmed by one thought—that I had never felt Harry's firm dry lips against my own.

I had no concept, then, of how a man and a woman's bodies might come together. But I wished, more than anything, that Harry would, to use my aunts' mysterious term, insult me. I had no thought for my reputation. I longed only to see the raw face of his desire, as rough as freshly broken sandstone, turned towards me, to feel his breathing quicken like a climber's on close nights.

Contrary to Lady Harding, I suspected that Harry Kitchings withheld himself from me because he thought me weak. Since I had gashed my wrist on his belt at Wentworth Falls, he had regarded me with affectionate concern. On the mountain paths his hand hovered near my elbow. He often turned and asked me if he walked too fast. When I had reached for his hand at Lady Harding's lightning party, I decided, he must have considered it the gesture of a child. Perhaps he thought I was not yet strong enough to bear his passion, that my character was not fully formed.

That was why, without telling Harry, or my aunts, I had bought myself a harem skirt and begun to teach myself, secretly, to find steps and footholds in the cliffs.

His pinhole cameras. He told the children, when he gave them out, that he had placed a pinch of magic powder in each box and they must make a wish to conjure up the little landscapes.

For a week after Lady Harding's lightning party Harry Kitchings had disappeared. His studio was locked and the rattling presses no longer made the lemons quiver on the trees in the backyards of Katoomba Street throughout the night. That Sunday afternoon my aunts and I had waited for him in the parlour until the cream filling inside the nougat roll turned stiff and yellow at each end. I was tense and nauseated. When customers came into the pharmacy and asked me if I knew why Harry's studio was closed I looked down and shook my head.

I was surprised, then, three days later, to see him on our doorstep in the cold blue twilight, smiling. He had walked straight from the station, he said, to find his bearings in our faces. He told us, as he moved the fork through his scrambled eggs like an instrument for mapping, that he had left on a sudden impulse for Sydney to view the council's display, which had travelled around the country and arrived recently at Redfern. The council had purchased several boxes of his latest viewbooks, along with three large lantern slides of his panoramic views, which were placed like stained glass in the windows of a life-sized model of the kiosk. Mr Medlicott had furnished the generous amounts of cotton wool for the construction of the clouds. It was a popular attraction at the exhibition, Harry said, filled with pleasant music and refreshments, and surrounded by potted ferns.

Harry had stayed on for days, discussing his viewbooks, and passing through rooms filled with candlesticks and exotic carpets and films of the Taj Mahal. The display which had most pleased him was called 'Australia: Aviary of the World', featuring a choir of little girls, and a sign which claimed that songstresses were now among our greatest exports. When he had tired of the crowds he went walking in the Botanic Gardens and saw lovers carrying his viewbooks near the ornamental lakes. He had looked out over the harbour as it filled like a glass with the liquor of the sun. He heard the bats in the Moreton Bay figs above his head and it sounded to him as if someone played a high sweet note through a pipe made out of water. He felt his heart grow sweet and soft inside his chest like a piece of Turkish Delight.

He said he had a present for me and drew a hand made out of plaster from his bag. It was cold and porous; large veins like silkworms ran across its back. It had been cast from an ancient statue—he showed me how it was possible, even in plaster, to see the grain of the lunar marble.

I wondered if this was at once an oblique apology and a promise.

'Painters use these fragments,' he had said, I remembered now, 'to prepare themselves to draw from life.'

The kindness of rocks. In each new town he would find the mining museum and spend his mornings among glass cases filled with quiet lumps of stone: pyrites, chips from meteors, and quartzes, like thick rays of light, arrested and congealed.

It was not long afterwards that Harry Kitchings had seen the boy's face reversed from right to left through the magnifer as he stood on Narrow Neck and tried to coax the valley, which slipped and ghosted at the slightest touch, into the dimensions of his frame.

At first he thought he had seen an angel. Then he noticed the flies and left his cameras on the ground to climb down Dixon's Ladder.

This was not a ladder but a wire rope, attached to a hook in the sandstone, which dropped seventy feet into the air. As he descended he felt the grain of the metal between his shins measuring the inches, noticed the blood smell of it on his hands. Once a gust of wind took hold of the rope, and flicked it like a whip. He closed his eyes until it passed, imagining that he held the lashing tail of the sky. When his feet hit the ledge he saw strange comets beneath his eyelids like the undissolved grains of pryo on a glass plate negative.

The boy had rolled off the cliff's edge, but two supple branches had caught him and held him from the valley. Harry Kitchings leaned over and lifted the child as gently as a flower. He was unconscious and flies moved on the large scab on his forehead, but when Harry Kitchings held the boy's chest to his ear he heard a regular heartbeat as clear and tiny as a bellbird's cry.

He strapped the boy to his back with his manila rope and

began the slow climb back up to the plateau. He carried him through the bush, along the narrow spit of sandstone, past the market gardens and tallow works, towards the town. When Alan Davidge looked up from folding tablecloths in the Steam Laundry and saw them he ran to the Automobile Touring Company; there Mr Tabrett rang for the doctor and sent one of his motor carriages to convey the boy to his home. Although Harry Kitchings trembled and his hands were cut he would not accept a glass of rum. He drank the tea which Mrs Davidge made and walked back up to the crest of the Narrow Neck to collect his tripod and cameras. The next morning when he opened the shutters and looked down into the street outside his shop he saw Mr Thornelow with the press photographer from the *Echo* and a hundred tourists who had heard the story. Some of them slipped about on the ball-bearings of their rollerskates, he observed, as if there were mercury beneath their feet. Harry climbed over the back fence to the lane and walked quickly to my aunts' house where he spent the day hauling wood from the back lot and chopping it for them in the woodshed while they read to him from their spiritualist magazines.

It was Mayor Gordon who arranged the presentation. He had a medal struck and invited the minister from the Tourist Bureau to come up from Sydney to present it. The politician arrived by motor car with members of the city press. The councillors had only prevailed on Harry Kitchings to accept these honours by telling him that the ceremony would enhance the fame and reputation of the Blue Mountains. At the new Town Hall I sat in the front row next to Lady

Harding. Towards the end of the ceremony the lady vocalist sang 'Blow Thou Winter Wind' accompanying herself with the zither. Then a great cheer rose when Mr Medlicott announced that the boy's fractured skull was healing and he was wheeled onto the stage, bandaged, in a wicker chair.

Afterwards, as the pressmen gathered around Harry Kitchings, Mr Tabrett fetched the rescue vehicle which he had washed and polished and decorated with British and Australian flags. The councillors suggested that Harry Kitchings might wish to pose standing on the buckboard. He refused. Even from the steps of the Town Hall I could see their faces darken. The Sydney newspapers reported the next day that 'the mountain lens-man and hero expressed a preference for Shank's equine friend, stating that he had no desire to hurtle through the air with the force of a projectile. Having never travelled in an automobile, he thought it unlikely that he would succumb to the speed demon in this or any lifetime.'

His postcards. A single sentence, like a wire, across the back, to hang each picture on.

We sold so many patent medicines now that Mr Medlicott had discarded or forgotten a lot of the ingredients in tubs and boxes which he used to keep behind the curtain. These days he spent very little time there. The pill compressor was dusty. He had long since rid himself of the large lumps of beeswax from which he had once made his toilet creams, writing them off to the council at a discount, where they were used to polish the desks and honour rolls. Since the telephone had been installed, he was often absent, watching Dr Milton use his scissors to free broken bones from Pierrot and milkmaid costumes at the rollerskating rink.

This afternoon he had put down the receiver and dashed out to inspect a fire at the railway camp on the Bathurst Road. A methylated spirit lamp had fallen over and ignited one of the workers' tents. When he returned, he was pleased to announce that it was fatal.

A burned body, Mr Medlicott said, was always found *en boxe*, its legs bent, the hands raised, as if it performed a strange tango with the flames.

Sometimes, he said, he was afflicted by a certain sadness and had to go into the clouds until he felt himself filled taut as a dirigible with the bright blue breath of God.

'I have travelled all over this country, showing my photographs of clouds,' Harry Kitchings said. 'I have stepped onto railway platforms in northern towns smelling of caramel as the sugar cane burned in a hundred fields around me; I have travelled above the treeline near Cooma where limestone plugs break through the soil like teeth; I have visited red deserts where men lose themselves on the horizon and the salt lakes are as stark and cratered as the moon. But none of these land-scapes approaches the beauty of our mountains. Here, in the space of a hundred miles, I have seen sargassos of white daisies floating suddenly in the middle of green fields near Spring-wood, and parrots hanging upside down from fern fronds in the strange tropics of Mount Wilson. At Jenolan Caves, before the attendant lit the torches, I have stood in that original dark-ness which existed before time. Here, in the Blue Mountains,' he said, 'are united all the wonders of the world.'

He nodded to Mr Hoffman in the projection booth, and the first bright slide was projected onto the screen behind the stage.

The photograph, taken from his latest viewbook, showed Echo Point as a summer storm was clearing. A dark sky still curved above the lookout. From the middle of the valley, fat white clouds rose up to meet it. He had caught them as they circled just above the heads of the tiny suited figures at the railing—moving, nose to tail, as placid as a pod of dugongs, feeding on the updraughts.

The audience stamped its feet; they whistled and applauded.

I had watched the crowd move into the Empire Theatre from the wings. I saw girls from the Young People's Tem perance Society, who tied pieces of string tight around their fingers to remind themselves that they were happy; a cricket team in blazers and white piping; a group of young men from the Bohemia Apartments in brand new Panama hats. I sighted Lady Harding, and my aunts, and Mr Medlicott. Only Mr Fowler was absent. He said he would not attend a theatre which he suspected was German owned. Now, within the dark which still smelled of damp velvet in 1913 a year after the inundation, we moved and sighed as a single living thing. Many people fanned themselves with the large, ruby-covered copies of his eighteenth viewbook which Harry Kitchings, who had meant to sell them in the foyer, had given out instead as gifts.

Harry Kitchings stood with his fine hands raised like a conductor. Elsie Thorncroft's elocution students appeared on the stage and began to recite Shelley's 'Cloud'. Then he motioned to Mr Hoffman and more images sprang out of the darkness, luminous and strange, as if the flat screen itself had become a source of changing light. There were frozen waterfalls which resembled fallen chandeliers, and others, like soft skeins of silk, unwinding from the cliffs. There was a cloud, then a mountain, then a rock, each fulfilling the same shape. There were calcified willows and Egyptian needles inside the caves, and, outdoors, the great limestone sphincter of the Devil's Coach House which swallowed up two cars. Sometimes I also saw myself, posed at a lookout or the far end of a street at sunset while the three orders of clouds filled the sky beyond my shoulders, glassy and brittle, lit up like lamps from within.

'Mount Eureka—his favourite prospect,' a man's voice whispered behind me. I heard another laugh.

When the lights came up, I saw that the veins were tight in Harry Kitchings' neck.

His face shone with sweat like lunar marble.

When he said he would take questions a woman who was honeymooning at Hampton Villa raised her hand. She asked him if he would tell the story again of how he had rescued those three dear little boys.

He said he wished he had an X-ray camera. Then, just once, he could make me feel what it was to have one's body fill with light.

By the time Harry Kitchings had thanked Mr Hoffman and packed up all his slides the crowds had already left and been absorbed into the darkness. As we turned onto Cascade Street only the younger of the Misses Moon moved ahead of us, breaking eggs on the pavement for the stray cats which made their homes beneath the advertising hoardings and on the empty lots. Where the gas lights ended, and the steep hill fell away, there was the heavy smell of earth. Crickets formed air bells of silence as we passed, then began to call again behind us.

I had taken his arm and he had not withdrawn it. I could feel a nervous vein beneath the skin.

His eyes were bright with triumph. He frowned with pleasure when I told him.

'Sometimes,' I said, 'all I could see was your ecstatic face.'

It had surprised him, he said, how even his skin had opened up to the applause.

On either side of us, their windows unlit and lifeless, the houses seemed to recede into the shadows of the bush, and acquire a kind of mineral existence. A cow with a face as bleached as a skull looked up and stared from its paddock as we passed.

We did not stop at my aunts' house. We kept walking through the bush, towards the sound of the falls.

Our steps grew soft and slow, as if our shoes had filled with clouds.

He said, 'It is late.'

'Tomorrow is Sunday,' I replied.

I could hear in his voice that his chest was tight.

Where the track dipped, and he moved ahead, I stopped and leaned against a ghost gum, felt the resin catch against my back.

He stopped, then stepped towards me, then stood still again. He said it had moved him, with an odd suddenness, to turn and see me standing there. I looked as fragile and eva-nescent as a ray of light in water, he said, the shadows another darker liquid which threatened to engulf me.

I thought he was troubled by my weakness.

I said, 'I have never been frightened of the dark.'

We stood and regarded one another. The night stretched between us like a taut dark thread.

Then, as the wind freshened and began to blow the clouds up from the valley, he turned and walked me back towards the house.

$$=11=$$

We had reached the end of the long stairs which stretched all the way from the dry bush near the lookout to the foot of Govett's Leap. It was 1915; since that night at the falls two years had passed, and another hundred walks. Now we moved along dirt tracks and steps which descended further towards the smell of mossy stone. Below us, in its cold dark seam, the river moved between the ferns. Above us, visible at intervals through the branches of the gums, a long thin plume of water frayed and split as it fell away from the cliff. We slipped diagonally through columns of warm light, dropped into cooler shadows. It was like walking through a photograph, beneath the dappled skin.

We had passed no one as we drove down the long and dusty road which stretched from Blackheath to the falls. The trees on either side of us had been burned by bushfires early in the year. Their branches met above us like the spokes of an umbrella, the clear sky arching over them; a tight blue cloth, Harry said.

While I still longed for him to kiss me, sometimes to the point of bitterness, I had gloated on the small luxury of his elbow pressed against my own.

Down by the river, time squatted on its haunches. Long strips of bark hung from the gums, flayed by their own expansion. A large geebung tree had toppled sideways from the cliff; caught by the scrub, it was held in the act of falling, inches from the ground. Green creepers spread across it, like the veins on a man's forearm, tightening with sap.

Harry Kitchings asked what I was thinking.

'It is a slow catastrophe,' I said.

Although they were not the words he would have chosen, he said, he was pleased that I had grasped this sensation of contraction, the gradual gathering of force.

I was unable then to understand that this was true of all disasters, or to recognise the pattern of my own.

People agreed that the electrification was almost as exciting as the war. Mr Medlicott was particularly moved by the prospect of artificial sunshine. In anticipation he had already installed a series of wires and bells which ran between the pharmacy and his home. He had read about experiments in America using high-frequency alternating current to stimulate the growth of children, and was discussing with the councillors his plans to run an additional wire into one of the classrooms at the Katoomba Public School. He also believed that by spending half an hour each morning in the power plant, performing knee-bends by the generator, he might absorb that strange juice at its source, and eventually eliminate his body's need for food.

For more than a year the town had watched as the large brick chimney grew at Mr Joynton Smith's bidding on the vacant allotment in Park Street behind the Carrington Hotel. We had seen the Parson Bros' steam turbine, which once hummed in the basement of a hotel in the city, hauled into Katoomba on a special carriage of the train. Transformers had gone up on corners almost to the falls, and the wires which fed them crossed back and forward like silver streamers above Katoomba Street, as if it was a steep slipway, Harry Kitchings said, and an ocean liner had just slid from the town to launch itself into the pale blue mist below. One hundred and sixty-five new street lamps lined the roads, suspended from wires like the translucent abdomens of fireflies, waiting for that glowing fluid from the generator to fill them and make invisible their insect parts. Now, as the councillors and Minister for Public Instruction banqueted in the hotel dining room, only the touch of Mayor Gordon's finger on a switch was needed to enact this transformation.

In spite of the cold, Katoomba Street was crowded. I recognised some of the young boys who used to lean with their hands in their pockets at Expectoration Corner before it was sold and built on. Dressed in khaki puttees and slouch hats, they sat on an awning and used a broomstick to knock the straw boaters from civilians' heads as they passed. I saw two honeymooners wrapped up in a single coat, who kissed each other and regarded the bulbs with smug eyelids as if they were Christmas decorations in the hall of their own new house.

The ceremonial dinner had already run an hour over time. Some children threw pebbles along the driveway of the Carrington until they were chased by the doorman into the street. In the distance, in the shadow of the boiler room, I saw one of the stokers, stripped naked to his waist, shaking out the muscles of his arms.

Inside, Harry Kitchings leaned on his camera and waited to fix the long table—the pink sweet peas and asparagus, the shortbread and sugar in the shape of the chimney stack—in a blue puff of magnesium. Given the grandeur of the occasion, and the extent of the guest list, the councillors had explained, they could not spare him a seat at any table.

At last Mr Joynton Smith stood up to make his speech. He said it was a pleasure to be united in such a rare and happy occasion while, on the other side of the world, even as he spoke, many young men were paying full toll in the greatest conflict the world had ever known. While he was past proving useful in such activities himself, he noted that many of the councillors had given up their sons for service overseas and he hoped that, by installing this power plant, he might be considered to have made his own small contribution to the Empire. While he acknowledged that there had been some criticisms of his taking on the costs and responsibilities himself for lighting the municipality, he felt that private enterprise spelled the way forward for this country, and particularly for the Blue Mountains; the bright future of Katoomba and her businesses would soon silence the 'nay-sayers' among us.

Mayor Gordon thanked him and said that he was the kind

of enterprising man Katoomba wanted, who was prepared to stake his money and reputation on this town.

Then he pressed an oak and silver switch and the crowd gasped as a chain of light moved like gleaming drops of water down the hill.

Only Harry Kitchings, looking out of the window, saw the smoke from the chimney bloom and spread until it took the shape of the German eagle.

These he took as omens of God's displeasure: a heatwave which caused the edges of his negatives to frill and pucker even in the darkroom; the sound of a ticking motor which pursued him to the furthest reaches of the valley; a scum from the sewage works which formed on the froth of the Cascades.

It was August 1915, and in one month my heart would break.

You may wonder how, throughout all these years of withdrawal and approach, I could keep waiting for Harry to disclose his tender feelings, just as he hoped to see the face of God. I can only tell you that there is a certain point at which one comes to inhabit longing.

Each time he returned from some long absence, and raised my hand to his lips as if he kissed the earth, it seemed that we were closer. Each time, I thought, *Our hearts are moving towards each other, slowly, on caterpillar feet.*

I kept thinking, too, that only a thin second, a tiny movement of consolidation, as small as a finger squeezing on a shutter, as quick as a platen flattening a hand, was required to spill the feelings he had dammed for so long beneath his skin.

Whenever I doubted it, these were the moments I remembered.

In 1912, as we stepped out of the Allora Tea and Grill Room, the clouds opened up above us. Knowing that it would please him, I said that the fat raindrops were like minims falling on a stave. He smiled. He took off his coat. In front of the whole town he made an umbrella for me of his arms.

In 1913, he looked out of his studio towards the valley and saw a purple estuary of clouds veined by thin blue sky. He left the shop unlocked and unattended, walking swiftly to my aunts' house so that he might take me to the lookout to show me how they resembled the tufted islands of Venice curled around that quiet ribbon of lagoon.

1914, a year of elbows touching in the darkness. Each time he returned, there were tickets to a show in his waistcoat pocket. We saw Bud Atkinson's Wild West Circus, and Sam McVea, the Negro pugilist, who sped around Katoomba all week in his shining car. We saw a portrait of Christ in the School of Arts which wept fluorescent tears. At the Katoomba Amusements Company, Harry Kitchings applauded when Miss Faye, the midget aerialist of Tiny Town, stood on a silver wire above the stage, undid a ribbon, and let her chestnut hair fall below her ankles to the floor.

When I think back on these moments now, I am painfully aware that all I have to offer as proofs of Harry Kitchings' love are isolated gestures, as dumb as images on glass and a hundred times more fragile, now that the mood which summoned them has passed.

Soon the suggestion that I could ever have been the object of a man's affection would seem improbable, even in my own imagination.

There were other portents: a gush of muddy water from the taps; the diminution of the Bridal Veil Falls for two days during the filling of the swimming baths; the dark shapes of Russian bears and British lions appearing in the clouds.

It had been Alderman Dash's idea to construct the clubrooms behind the council chambers in order to spite the Masons. He had been troubled for years by the fact that he had never been invited to join their lodge. With great pleasure he had overseen the installation of ornate floral windows, requisitioned from a demolished Rosicrucian church, which filled the room with strange pink light. His only disappointment was that his motion for a secret mayoral handshake had been vetoed by one vote.

It was here, in 1913, among the obese armchairs and low hexagonal tables, that Harry Kitchings had drunk soda water and waited with Mr Medlicott and Mr Joynton Smith, who had recently purchased the Carrington, for the councillors to arrive. Mr Tabrett stood over by the bar and appeared to be distracted by an article in the *Echo*.

Mayor Gordon entered first, sweating like a teapot in a cosy beneath his new mayoral robes, which he escaped with the struggling motions of Houdini and cast on one of the chairs. He apologised to Harry Kitchings for the councillors' tardiness in arranging this get-together which he recognised was overdue; given the thriving business during the last season, he said, they had been preoccupied with approving land plans for subdivisions, entertaining members of the Public Works Department, settling a small dispute over the Sanitary Scavengers' wages, and arranging fees for the loaning out of the council's flags. Aldermen Dash and Bronger poured themselves port and put up a wager over the next meeting of the Rifle Club. Mr Medlicott brought up the recent visit of a group of medical students from the university, the human heart that had been found on the track to the Three Sisters, and the Complex and Delicate Negotiations which had followed. Mayor Gordon laughed when he remembered how the Chancellor had arranged to have it smuggled back to the faculty museum by his wife in a hatbox filled with ice.

Harry Kitchings, who did not laugh, said that it was unfortunate that this sort of behaviour was becoming all too common in the valley. Tree vandals had been so active of late souveniring foliage from around the falls that the shrubs there had assumed agonised shapes, while on Sunday afternoons the Sydney-bound platform of the railway station often gave the appearance of thick moving scrub. Signs were stolen by the young men who frequented the guesthouses and those which remained were peppered with buckshot. As a result a number of the tracks were now so perilous that they were rarely attempted by the average walker, while others were suffering from overuse. The ferns which lined the path to the Leura Cascades, for example, were frequently coated in dust or trampled in the mud. All these factors, Harry said, had the effect of keeping people from the beauty which they had been invited here to discover. Many were too timid to tackle the walks at all and hovered about the kiosk and the Katoomba shops. Some hired cars and motor carriages to take them to the lookouts.

If the council seriously wished to encourage visitors to enjoy the natural benefits of the mountains, Harry Kitchings said, they ought to engage a warden to protect them: the keeper who had been hired at Jenolan Caves had swiftly put a stop to the young men who snapped the stalactites from the roof and walked around Mount Victoria and Blackheath with them beneath their arms, frightening crowds of young children and tourists by passing them off as the horns of bunyips. The warden could police the popular attractions and clear and sweep the paths. He could erect new signs which not only pointed the way but calculated the distances and times between the sights and towns.

Mayor Gordon coughed and thanked Harry Kitchings for his thoughts. It was a shame, he said, that the secretary had not been present to turn his ideas into minutes, but he was confident that he could speak for all the others when he said that they would hold Harry's ideas in their hearts. Once the new roads had been built, and more funds had been freed in the next budget, they would invite him to make a written submission and refer it to the Finance Committee. After the toast Alderman Bronger began to entertain the group with scurrilous rumours he had heard regarding the Dutch Fleet's recent visit.

That day, when he returned to his darkroom he found the first sign: a group of mice, like tiny cattle, grazing on the sweet emulsion on the surface of his plates.

Mr Medlicott had once demonstrated the importance of antiseptics by placing a shallow dish of gelatine in the window of the shop. Beside it he propped up a sign which invited the passersby to become scientists and observe for themselves the transformation as it was exposed to the various animalcules which inhabited the air. Within days a delicate bloom appeared on the surface and extended itself into clotted filaments until at last the gelatine was hispid and opaque.

In the years since the lightning party that is how I experienced Harry Kitchings' silence.

I filled it with doubts and questions.

My desires grew into shameful shapes.

There were days when I no longer saw objects clear and islanded by light but walked instead through downy shadows. There were weeks when I did nothing but dwell on the possibility of touch. I had dreams in which I ran my hands across his photographs and each a whiskered map of silver threads. Sometimes they knotted and caught around my fingers. Sometimes they chafed beneath my skin.

I had begun to suspect that arms and legs might move as seamlessly as water.

I wondered if there were some steps too halting or uncertain to leave any traces of themselves.

One day, in 1914, we walked past Chas Turner's cash butchery, where pale carcasses hung like polished shirt-fronts in the window from the racks of brass. I told Harry Kitchings that if he stood his camera at the railway station, and trained it on the corner for an hour, opening the lens for a second every minute, he might catch the blurred passage of hems and cuffs, imitating the arcs of waterfalls, as they brushed the kerbs and lintels.

His time was geological. He measured all things by the slow formation of rocks.

That same year Mark Foy had discovered the 'Medlow Mermaids' on a motoring excursion through North Africa, caught in a fish trap which had been hauled up on the beach. The Arab men pointed and chattered and for a moment in the heat he thought that their voices had become the white glare from their clothes. Through the net he had glimpsed sad eyes and tusks, and something magnificently fleshly, the voluptuous paleness of Dutch portraits, already turning red beneath the sun. He had purchased them and had them stuffed and crated. They reclined now in the Hydro Majestic on a bed of straw. The whole population of the Blue Mountains was travelling there to see these mysterious creatures, human above and fish below the waist.

I asked Harry Kitchings what troubled him as we drove towards the hotel.

He smiled and said it was nothing.

We passed the Explorer's Tree, which had been recently killed by vandals who smothered it with tar. Only then was Harry Kitchings prompted to say it was another omen, and tell me the strange portents which he had seen. I replied that I did not know what to make of the skulls and torpedoes in the sky, but perhaps his photographic disasters only signified that he was in need of some assistance. I offered to come to the darkroom, where I had not been since the day, four years earlier, when he had made a cloud for me, and help him sort his damaged plates. He thanked me but said he had already arranged to pay Charles Eldridge, a local amateur, to help him—a man he barely knew.

We drove on in silence while, ahead of us, the pink domes and turrets began to appear and disappear between the trees. He did not seem to see the disappointment in my face.

The casino was crowded and filled with the steam from cups of tea. On the stage I saw a male and a female dugong, wearing crowns, stiff and filled with sawdust. They stared back at us from unfocused eyes of glass. Beneath the hot lights I could smell the solution in which they had been pickled. It had turned their skins dark brown.

'They are a magnificent couple,' Harry Kitchings said.

'There is no proof for that,' I answered. 'They are not a pair simply because they swam in the same ocean.'

I pointed out the scars where the Arabs' spears had torn their skins.

'*There* are your omens,' I said.

Later I asked him whether he had ever wondered if his Sanderson camera, with its springs and shutters, was also a kind of trap; if it also inflicted scars and wounds.

That was also the year Mr Medlicott had joined the summer drink battle and determined he would win it. The first soda fountain had been purchased some years ago by the Niagara, which announced each of the new fruit syrups it imported from the United States in a regular advertisement in the *Echo* beneath an illustration of an eagle. The Popular, above the Katoomba Amusements Company, had followed later, installing a polished Dudley Carbonator encrusted with silver, ebony, and coloured marbles. They were the acknowledged leaders in the department of 'fizz'. Now Mr Medlicott had knocked out one of the leafy pillars towards the rear of the shop and installed his own long counter clad in hygienic stainless steel. Each year he had contrived to destroy a few more of the floral decorations: he had long since knocked over the vases with his elbows and a whole wall of gilt-edged pansies had perished in the construction of the fountain.

At the opening Mr Medlicott welcomed the crowd and told them that I would introduce them to our own special lime juice and kola flavours, which they were invited to enjoy free of charge this day with the compliments of Alderman Bronger. He noted that the milk products we used were fresh and had been obtained that morning from a dairy which, he could personally guarantee, met with government health requirements. It was a promise he could not, as a scientific man, make for other establishments in the mountains.

'No ring yet?' Mr Medlicott asked me, as I stood and washed my hands in the little sink behind the counter. 'Perhaps Harry Kitchings has more in common with that eminent virgin Ruskin than an eye for pretty clouds.'

Sometimes I thought it was only the heart of a landscape which he prized, that frail ornament, harpooned and reeled in on a string of silver light.

It was five o'clock when I had knocked, a year later in July 1915, at the door of Harry Kitchings' studio and already the short man who lit the gas lamps was moving along Katoomba Street in a heavy coat, hearing above his head the gentle advent calendar of glass doors opening and closing on a new blue night for one of the last times in his life. The air was clear and so cold that it hurt my lungs. At the far end of the street the last traces of the winter sun formed a thin yellow lymph which filled the space where the clouds had drawn back from the black land.

The shop was dim and filled with shadows.

I saw that Harry had emptied out the window. Lengths of fishing line and strips of photographs were arranged neatly on the counter where he was making a new display.

I followed his stiff back, and thought: *He has a skeleton of glass.* His steps were deliberate and swift, his hands scarcely moving as they hung beside his hips. He was even thinner than when we had first met. These days I felt the passivity of his body as a calculated insult and often wished that I could crack his rigid bones.

Harry Kitchings no longer posed clients in the portrait armchairs, which were covered now with correspondence and cuttings from newspapers on the subject of prophesy and clouds. The room behind the counter had filled slowly over the years with half-empty canisters of ink and discarded type and the metal plates for the twenty-four viewbooks he had made by now on which acid had formed the shape of mountains. Piled up in the corner I saw copies of his last book which the councillors had voted not to purchase, because, they said, the major sights were too obscured by mist. There were other packages of viewbooks which he intended to send as gifts to the boys from Katoomba who were fighting in the war. After clearing the chairs he rushed to make me a mug of tea.

When he returned, I felt it again: the cool length of his fingers, as chaste as porcelain, briefly held against my palm. How can I describe its effect upon me? Harry Kitchings' broken hand never pressed quite hard enough.

I had not been to visit him for some weeks. I hoped that he would ask me what was wrong.

He said nothing. He did not sit. The shadows lengthened but he made no attempt to light the lamps, moving instead like a nocturnal creature at the edges of the room.

As I watched him I noticed, with pity, that his skin, since he had turned forty, showed the grain of age. I wanted to touch the cleft at the base of his Adam's apple, to feel those creases, like tiny watercourses, which had made new paths and deviations in the flesh.

At last I said, 'I am thinking of resigning from Mr Medlicott's pharmacy and seeking new employment. I have thought for some time that I might even leave the mountains.'

He stopped, and I thought his chest rose faster, but he did not say that he would miss me or try to make me stay.

Instead he looked at me kindly and asked, 'Where do you think that you might go?'

I told him that I had dreamed of a bed, sheeted and tucked with photographic paper, and asked him what he thought it meant.

Over the days that followed the electrification, as letters began to arrive from Europe which bore disturbing news about the Empire's progress on the Western Front, the whole town seemed to move more quickly, as if each one of us was attached to some powerful generative motor. Lady canvassers from the School of Arts moved about the station and the shops, rattling wooden boxes and badgering people to buy tickets for the Patriotic Fund. While the councillors met to consider charging a penny toll on all the major sights, the Kookaburra Girls performed in the hall beneath them, and the young women of the Polly Anna Club sold jam from trestle tables below the steps. There were special war services at the congregational church and pro-victory demonstrations. Younger sons and single men in khaki moved about the town arranging their affairs. Mr Medlicott attended lectures in the city on Whitehead torpedoes and skin flap amputations, and when he returned spoke with fondness of the Rexer automatic rifle which could fire three hundred bullets in a minute propped up on its two steel legs. Each day there were open houses, send-offs, and scandalous elopements.

Only Harry Kitchings stood for hours in the middle of Katoomba Street, staring at the sky, willing a still point to resolve itself within the scudding clouds.

The next day he was gone.

I waited for three weeks for his postcards and they did not arrive.

My aunts sent me in their place to Lady Harding's Officers' Farewell. They waved to me from the hallway, wearing their nightdresses, with their long white hair tied back in plaits. Since Harry Kitchings had told them about the omens in the sky, they had been too terrified to leave the house, even to scold the chickens in the shed. As I carried the cake they had given me past the beehives and through the scrub I thought that Harry must have travelled somewhere so far-flung this time that he could not find an agent of the post. I was so used to his absences by now that this did not concern me. I imagined as I walked through the dusk that I felt his gentle shadow hanging from some distant cliff edge, twitching and flinching, as if he did not grasp his manila rope, but held my heart instead by a satin cord of light.

At the Hardings' house, the Ladies' Orchestra from the Katoomba Amusements Company sat in the bay window of the parlour and took the officers' requests. In the spirit of the occasion they even consented to play the cancan. Charles Medlicott, my employer's son, stood by the piano, wearing his new captain's uniform, and opened the silver shaving kit which his friends had bought him, while out on the verandah his father questioned the artillery men about the Turkish snipers' telescopic bullets. I passed another knot of soldiers who spoke of their eagerness to join that 'hot-shop across the water'. One young man from the Signal Corps spoke with passion about the secret languages of cloth, of messages conveyed by coloured flags and the shifting angles of arms. Another showed Charles a wooden box which he would take to Paris and fill with bright red garters. I saw the bright red ash from cigarettes smouldering on Lady Harding's bearskin rugs.

I can recall few details after that.

For I glanced up and saw Harry Kitchings in the doorway, looking around him with that soft expression of surprise he always wore when he had come back from the clouds. In front of everyone, when he saw me, he smiled and kissed me warmly on the cheek, and took me to the far end of the garden by the hand. There he told me that he had just returned from Sydney.

He said that he had married, and that he would soon be returning there, and bringing back his wife.

STRATUS

— 12 —

'The worst lungers are over here,' Matron Coan said.

I followed her across the courtyard. Behind a high wall I heard a spade strike earth. In a distant hallway, a metallic echo and a curse, as a foot kicked over a spittoon. Several women appeared, crossed in front of us, and disappeared again into the mist. A small man came after them, pointing the way with his stick towards the hidden cliff. When the matron introduced him to me as the Captain of the Walk, he briefly touched his cap and turned back into the cloud, cupping his ear to catch the wet sounds of the women's chests.

We walked on through the dark smudges left by slippers on the silver lawns. This was the first time I heard that blood cough which would follow me for the next four years. I thought of birds shaking out damp feathers in the rain. Some nights, as I stood out on the verandah to smoke a cigarette, I would imagine that the ward behind me was filled with sodden wings.

In the corridor the mist pressed around us like a clammy

membrane. To my surprise the men's ward, when we entered it, was also filled with fog. There were rows of beds along each side and at one end I could make out the pale grey shape of open windows. Somewhere, at the edges of the gloom, the stink of phlegm and carbolic acid rose from the spittoons. The room had the glassy cast of an overexposed negative, as if it had been passed over and discarded during some bout of photographic madness. The bodies in the beds were ill-defined and faded, their edges dissolving in the milky light.

From the bed beside me, I heard a cough as thick as boiling rice and felt the hot splash of blood against my hand. A small voice, softer than a cobweb, caught my heart.

I looked down and saw Les Curtain, stooped over in the bed, his right hand pressed against his chest. His fingertips were lost in the deep clefts beneath his collarbones. He was oddly diminished, packed within the curling of his spine, like some dormant version of himself. Yet his cheeks were pink and his eyes retained a morbid brightness.

He whispered, 'There are nipples in the sky.'

'It is the *spes phthisica*,' Matron Coan said.

The sanatorium for consumptives at Wentworth Falls had been built in the middle of the last thick cloud which still clung to the Blue Mountains. As they balanced along the cliff's edge above the Valley of the Waters with long planks for the verandahs on their shoulders, the labourers had used torches and ropes to mark the line where the sandstone ended and the vast drop to the valley floor began. They had invented a language of shrill cries and whistles to find each other through the pressing corridors of whiteness. The waterfalls which rushed through that blankness far below had made them nervous, for it seemed that at any moment the soil might turn to liquid beneath their feet. The cement was reluctant to set in the foundations; the red bricks, when they fell on the soft earth, made no reverberation. And even when that building and its outlying cottages had been completed it would not take shape before their eyes; the vapour creased and shifted, as cool as bats' wings, the solid brick glimpsed only through the gaps which opened between its translucent folds.

Few people in Katoomba had noticed the slow emptying of the skies. In the last year of the war, they were too busy planning for the future; saving silk and lace for honeymoons, imagining long nights without the dead, or caring for the wounded. The men who returned from France no longer bought pills from the pharmacy to make the landscape look like Europe, but dug their backs instead into the hollows of familiar chairs, filtered the light through stained glass windows, and perused catalogues of furniture from city stores. They did not wish to stand at the lookouts where the faded colour of the mountains reminded them of the blue haze of mustard gas. They were relieved that winter when it did not snow. I doubt whether even Harry Kitchings marked the disappearance, preoccupied as he was with his failing business, his strange son, and his new wife.

As a result, perhaps, of this indifference the clouds had continued to withdraw. First the pink snowclouds had stopped resting like huge sea slugs along the full length of the mountain ridge, hushing the valleys and smothering the light. Then the alto-cumulus clouds no longer stacked themselves in fractured shelves and ridges above the horizon as if in soft imitation of the geology beneath. No great black thunder-heads forced themselves into the valleys, heavy with rain, to crowd out the frayed white ribbons of false cirrus and stain the mountains with inky shadows. The mists which rose up from Echo Point were thinner than an invalid's breath dulling a mirror's glass. At last, only neat clumps of cumulus or cumulo-nimbus floated overhead, their edges sharp and dis-crete, like illustrations cut out from a magazine, always passing on their way to somewhere else.

It was only around the site of the new sanatorium at Went-worth Falls that the fog still lingered, rising each morning, as stiff and luminous as egg white, from that deep valley, where bright fungi shone like jewelled pins around the bottoms of the tree trunks in the gloom, and the ferns were damp and bent by the heaviness of the air. It was only here that the clouds climbed up the pleated cliffs, filling the groove of the National Pass which had been carved halfway up the orange sandstone, and the scar of the Undercliff Track near its rim, and spilled over the Queen Victoria Lookout and the Edin-burgh Castle Rock, to flow across the Great Western Road, as if they formed a ghost wave, recalled by the valley in the dawn light, of the great sea which once had carved it.

Nurse Coan the corsetiere had taken charge of the sana-torium when her stocks of elastic ran out in the last years of the war. It had taken no great adjustment for her, after she had stopped fitting foundation garments, to learn to run the

King George Homes. As she told me, it was simply another means of disciplining breath. In spite of wartime shortages, at the opening of the new hospital there had been brass instruments and champagne cup and wordy dedications. The patients had waved banners from the windows while the band played 'God Save the King' upwind. When Lady Harding told me how Harry Kitchings had stood on a stepladder to take the photographs I shrugged to show I did not care. She said his wife had sat in a chair to watch him and each time the ladder trembled she begged the men to steady it. It was the nervous agitation, Lady Harding whispered, which preceded a confinement. At last he had to hold her hand and promise it was safe.

It was a year after that, in 1918, at a Red Cross lunch that Matron Coan had offered to employ me. Perhaps, as she had projected her lantern slides from the battlefields of Europe onto the wall—of women with bold browned faces and dark driving glasses pushed back from their foreheads, who leaned back against their ambulances—she had seen some corresponding emotion in my eyes; a grim decision to be practical; the promise that, in spite of this, I would be careless in the face of death.

That night three years earlier, when Harry announced that he had found a wife, he had sat by me and freely taken my hand as he expanded on her charms, as if some secret catch had been released within his chest. For the first time, the thumbs which touched my wrist felt warm and filled with blood. For the first time, they seemed to express a confidence in flesh.

She was a young widow with an infant son who ran a boarding house in Forest Lodge. She told him, when he came to see the room, that she had been forced to take strangers into her home because her husband, a seaman, had been struck with fever on a hospital ship and was lowered into some hot ocean in a dirty sheet—and here her voice had broken—because they had run out of flags to wrap the bodies in. There were gardenias and lace doilies on each table in the house, he said, and little baby things upon the mantelpiece. He had said he would stay and paid her for a fortnight. One night he saw her sitting in the front parlour, her head bent, making scented globes from ribbons and oranges and cloves, which he had later found, like strange sweet flesh, filling out the pockets of his shirts. When she cooked for her son, she made him warm landscapes in which sausage frogs snouted out of mashed potato nests. The next night, after Harry had commented on them with delight, she also prepared him special food: she turned the dish she placed before him into the Blue Mountains. There were blunt pumpkin ridges and butter waterfalls; golden sunsets breathing clouds of gentle steam. Broccoli—she called them 'little trees'—formed tender forests on his plate. Yet the whole time he stayed there he never saw her eat.

When she walked to her church in the Glebe, he had kept her company, in spite of her shy protests, for she feared the narrow streets which ran diagonally through the shade of painted sandstone and brick privy walls, past rough fences where dogs hurled themselves, growling and snapping, against the splintered wood. On the steps of the boxing gymnasium men in singlets stretched their olive legs out in the sun. Here she had drawn so close to him that he could feel the rapid beating of her heart. She had touched his hand with a glove so soft that it might have been stitched from a mouse's suedy skin.

I could not stop myself from interrupting.

'I am surprised,' I said, as lightly as I could. 'I have always thought that you are the kind of man who would be drawn to strength.'

'Oh, she is not weak,' Harry said. 'She is more powerful than you or I. She has the capacity to endure.'

I was less frightened by his impatience than by the sudden distance in his eyes. For a moment he had regarded me as if he felt no warmth at all.

One afternoon, he continued, he had caught the tram back early from the city. There was nothing more for him to do at Chalice House, for the tanned young men in uniform who crowded in to see his photographs had so moved him by making plans to honeymoon among the cliffs when they returned, that he had given them the entire supply of view-books he had brought down to the city for sale to take onto the ships. When he returned to the house he had found her struggling with the copper in the yard. She asked for his help to empty it and passed him the damp white cloths she held to wrap around the handles. He hefted it easily, surprised into a new emotion by the thought that she could barely lift so small a weight when she had laboured with the child. It affected him greatly, he said, to think of those small hips, as tiny as a wishbone, bending in the delivery of the baby, which she referred to as the granting of her greatest wish. In the mossy corner of the yard, hot vapour spread across his face and ran into his eyes. There was a gush of steaming water on the earth. They had both blushed when he looked down to see the undergarments, which still held the soft shape of her body, bunched up in his hands.

A few days later, when he had collected his new supply of viewbooks from Katoomba at the railway station, he spread one open on the dining table for her and she traced the shapes of the waterfalls softly with her finger. She had asked him then if she might hold one of his cameras in her lap. He leaped up to fetch the panoramic camera from his room. They had both laughed: it looked as improbable as an accordion in her tiny hands. After he had helped her prise the viewfinder out of its shallow cleft, she had peered through the crosshairs at him and growled, with a silly accent which made him laugh, that she was a '*vicked Germ-hun*'. She pretended to shoot at her son as she chased him about the room; until, at last, the child had thrown himself upon the floor, screaming with delight. Then, just as suddenly, her face had broken up like glass, as she remembered her poor dead husband and began to cry. Harry quietly lifted up the boy and put him in his bed. When he returned to the filmy half-light of the parlour, without quite knowing how it happened he had found her on his knee. Her hot tears hit her bodice so that he could smell the starch. When he had tried to comfort her by explaining the use of the camera's apertures, she said—and her phrase still made him chuckle—that all her life she had never understood the 'technicals'. At this point they had both begun to laugh and found they could not stop. Her hands were caught up in his hair. He had never imagined that a human tongue might taste of marzipan and mint.

I cannot recall at what point in this story Harry ceased to speak, and when I read this new knowledge in his face, along with the conviction that on his part some terrible advantage had been taken. They had been married swiftly after that for the sake, they told each other, of the boy.

'I am sure you will like her and make her welcome,' Harry said. 'I will guarantee that she is the daintiest creature you have ever seen.'

He was to fetch her from Sydney in two weeks, as soon as she had finalised the disposal of the house. From his top pocket he drew out a letter which was already as soft as a handkerchief from being folded and unfolded so often by his fingers. He withdrew it quickly so that I could not read it, but my sharp eyes had already seen more than the mauve script written in a large round hand. She called him 'My Darling' and wrote how much she missed him; especially, she told him, his crumpled morning face. In one corner of the paper she had made a small sketch of a robin, with a twig held in its beak, perching on its nest.

When Harry returned indoors, I ran into Sir Wilfrid's fern-house because I thought I would be sick. In the mulchy darkness I played those love scenes he had told me like a cinematograph over and over in my head until I felt a kind of vertigo of despair. With that strange sense dogs have for sadness, Hutton came out and found me and put his wet nose in my palm. I could hear his tail stump twitching as he sat and scratched his ears and moved about to urinate against the ferns. Beyond the noise of Lady Harding's guests, and the cliffs at the bottom of the garden, the suck and hiss of wind stirred the cold silver shadows of the mackerel sky. I could feel the ferns brushing like soft skeletons against my cheek. I imagined a hollowness which stretched up to the stars and ran beneath my skin.

When I walked back into the house I could see that Harry had made his announcement. The men who had gathered near the piano toasted him and laughed while he drank lemonade and firmly held his hand over his glass as Sir Wilfrid tried to pour him something stronger. The women stopped talking when I entered, and there was excitement and a malicious kind of confirmation in their faces. Lady Harding left the group and put her arm around my waist and took me out onto the verandah. She pressed a handkerchief into my hand and offered to have me driven to my aunts' house in her motor car. I started to refuse but Lady Harding glanced back inside and gave an exaggerated shiver as she hugged herself against the chilly air. The women sat waiting with glassy eyes, watching us, like the parched birds in Sir Wilfrid's cases, wishing I would leave so that they might animate themselves again. I saw that there was no place for me among them. I did not cry as I sat with an aching head in the back seat of the car and the celebrations started up again. In spite of this Lady Harding would later tell her interested friends that I had 'sobbed my heart out' all the way.

From this night on I marked the stiffening of age.

When I walked out of the fernhouse the light had gone out of my bones.

After Harry's announcement I began secretly to dose myself with every medicine in the pharmacy, attempting to relieve my loss. I swallowed Hean's Tonic Nerve Nuts and Pomona Tonic Wine, and Mr Medlicott's Acclimatising Tababules. I mixed purgatives in the long glasses from the soda fountain and used them to wash down aspirin and toothache drops. I took Ayer's Sarsaparilla for ladies' spring headaches and smoked all of the remaining marijuana cigarettes. I rubbed Ulano, the great healing salve, into the flesh above my heart.

I wished to veil my eyes, so that I could see once again, even for a second, the vivid blueness of the mountains.

I am ashamed to admit that I also clung to the hope that these remedies might so weaken me that Harry would be forced to recognise his feelings at my bedside, once he saw the softness produced by illness in my face.

Perhaps my grief and shame were too systemic to be relieved without the loss of life or—in spite of Harry's convictions—I had found my own capacity to bear. It is even possible that, by some quirk of the Pharmacopoeia, I had chanced upon a combination of opiates and galvanicals which all but cancelled one another out. For the remedies I prescribed myself seemed to have no effect, except to dull my sense of time. That was one small mercy. My memories of this period are still tender and easily exposed. Yet—and I am grateful for it—they are also tissued by that narcotic languor which for some time kept my historical eyes at bay, and prevented me from arranging the innumerable slights and omissions which followed this disaster into the pattern of my life.

As if I am a stranger standing at a distance, I can still see myself, wearing the new blue dress which I had purchased for the party, wrapping medicines for the women of the Fresh Air League who have given themselves indigestion by chewing on my misfortune like pork crackling, and for those who have simply faked their illnesses in order to see my face. I watch those men with kittens' eyes, who once asked me out to the Oyster Saloon and engaged in surly flirting, enter now to purchase some medicine or little trinket for their wives. They have plump bellies and hair as thin and yellow as unspun silk and dull red rashes burned by the sun across their cheeks. It is as if the first years of marriage have precipitated a sort of teething process, and offered some soft space in which they can indulge their second winds and squalls. Yet they smirk at me and slap pound notes and guineas on the counter as if they are bullets which their hands have grasped from deep within their pockets. In the corner of my vision Mr Fowler lingers about the shop, pressing digestive mints on me with clammy hands and hopeful sympathy. He has combed Marie Sheep Dip Jelly through his ginger hair. I see Mr Medlicott bend over his pestle to laugh again and address me with that casual roughness men use to suggest that women have reached the age of pantomime and can at last appreciate the comedy of our sex. He exclaims, for the tenth time, 'We always took old Kitchings for one of those ninety per cent chaps, didn't we?'

And adds, winking, 'This widow must have some charms!'

Yet my queerest memory of this time involves my youngest aunt. Indeed, it is so improbable that I have often wondered if it was not the single vision conjured out of the bottles on Mr Medlicott's shelves. When I returned from Lady Harding's party I did not tell my aunts of my disgrace. To my surprise, even after Lady Harding's visit, when she brought me a consolatory tapestry and needles, they did not mention Harry's announcement, although they could not have failed to hear of it by then. Several days later, I found a recent photograph taken by Harry of Charles Medlicott in his army kit propped up on the kitchen table. My eldest aunt consulted it as she fixed little strips of orange peel onto the shoulders of the porcelain figure which she would later place on an iced fruitcake model of the troop ship *Ulysses* for Charles' farewell banquet. I realised that, in order to spare me a visit from Harry Kitchings, in which I might betray my feelings, my youngest aunt had left the house for the first time in six months, in spite of her fear of the strange shapes in the clouds which pressed down on the street, and walked up to his studio to collect the photograph. She had carried a bucket in her hand, so that when the nerves brought bile to her mouth she could vomit into it and continue on her way.

That night she sat on the edge of my bed and made me drink a cup of tea. When she placed her warm hand on my forehead I felt the skew and knob of arthritis in each joint, as if each night her fingers had absorbed their own distorted shadows, a calcified darkness which continued to grow like those twisted parrots' beaks and rabbits' teeth which Mr

Medlicott collected. For the first time, with guilt, I recognised them as a rosary of work.

She had to unfold the letter with her thumbs.

I read it, too dizzy to believe the unfurling of the copper-plate, the ghosted letters where the quill had split and doubled with desire. The man who wrote the letter, my aunt said, had come to see my grandfather because of the bogong moths. These large black insects had arrived with the warm November winds and clustered, like seething fur, on every object in the house. They left great piles of wing dust on the wooden floors, drowned and clogged the gully traps, and made the maid scream when their cold abdomens fell like lead-shot on her shoulders. Only my mother, a child then, was fond of them, for upside down and dead, she thought they looked like little angels dressed in velvet. My grandfather worried that they might cause a fire, for already they had stopped the candles and effected flashing immolations in the lamps.

The man he consulted was an expert in animal behaviour. He had been, as a younger man in Melbourne, a member of the Acclimatisation Society at the zoological gardens, which had been set up to tame and find uses for the native wildlife. He had achieved some success training a Tasmanian Devil to retrieve fallen game, although it could not be coerced, like the spaniel, to give the dead bird up, and it released an offensive odour when he tried to prise its jaws. He knew how to stroke the downy base of a bird's chest so that it was compelled to hop up on his finger; and, faced with the larger emu, he could press the matted feathers near its tail until it squatted on the ground. He had schooled a budgerigar to gently place a cigarette between his lips. It was also rumoured that he could find the nodes in the neck of any living creature to make it purr and give its life into his hands.

As he paced around the grounds considering the problem of the moths, the man would stop and watch my aunts who worked at their tatting on the verandah. He asked if he might touch the lace, which he lifted and fingered like a pelt. He said it was a map of the infinite movements of tiny muscles in women's hands as they gave grain and pattern to the air.

Once, in the greenhouse, he had performed knee-bends with an aunt sitting on each shoulder.

He wound their curls around his fingers which bore the silver scars of beaks and teeth.

He appeared once beneath their window in the middle of the night, and coaxed the flying foxes from the trees with little bits of apple. He stood in the moonlight with the warm weight of fur and membrane hanging from his arms. When my aunts tiptoed down in their nightdresses and touched his chest, it was alive with warm wet snouts and flicking tongues.

A week later the man arrived at dusk with a bucket which, he told their father, contained a love potion irresistible to moths. After he removed the cover, and dipped all the mops in the house in it, he stood them on their ends like torches in the ground. A great cloud of insects flew out of the house until the air was heavy with them, and their bellies brushed like swollen eyelids against my aunts' brows and lips. The man's face was brown and dusty with the powder from their wings. From the wrists of his shirt, where the chemicals had splashed, the moths were suspended like soft, shifting ruffs.

My grandfather took out his pipe, which he had been unable to light for some weeks because he was invariably sickened by the taste of burning insect, and chewed the stem with admiration. The mops were thick with moths like fantastic feather dusters. When the man began to push them under the surface of the ornamental pond, my mother screamed at the sight of this massacre of angels, so that my grandfather had to hold her head inside his jacket and carry her back inside the house. It was then that the man had suggested an elopement and my aunts said yes with wings between their lips. They agreed. He would marry my eldest aunt, but live with both sisters as his wives.

In the letter my aunt showed me he cites the animal kingdom—the prides of lionesses who care for one another's young, the polygamy of sugar gliders—as evidence of the precedents in nature. He imagines sleeping on his back between my aunts as they press his ribs like two soft bolsters. Or sideways, as they all fitted inside each other's spines like seahorses, drifting in the warmth of one another's breath.

After some months, my aunt said, the sisters had sent their glory box on to the city, where he lived, with its cargo of lace collars and hose they had made, so fine that even a moth's sharp foot could not fit into the spaces between the stitches. Taking their shoes off so their feet would not echo on the floorboards of the empty rooms, they looked in on my mother and kissed the metal plate, the shape of a horseshoe, which the surgeons had placed there after a racing accident, in their father's sleeping head. When they reached Flinders Street Station there was no one at the other end of the platform. They waited for an hour. Then my eldest aunt took her sister by the arm and they went home, retrieved their letter from under the glass by the bed in which my grandfather kept his teeth, and never said another word about it.

'So. There it is,' she said, and smiled. She held the paper, with its brittle promises, on the flat of her palm so that its edges moved in the tiny currents of the room.

In spite of many searches, and even when I packed up my aunts' belongings some years later, I have not been able to find that letter since. Yet I am unable to explain the alterations which followed in my relationship with my youngest aunt unless I at least imagine that I once saw it.

In all these hours before his wife arrived Harry did not come to see me.

Of all his betrayals, that was the one which left me breathless.

Looking back, I see myself as one of the hatted figures in that photograph in his first viewbook, caught against the cliff at Wentworth Falls, standing beneath a huge rough scar of stone; it looks as if a ledge above their heads has only seconds earlier cracked and fallen in the valley, broken off by its own weight. They appear to have witnessed, in mute surprise, the final and decisive moments of a catastrophe which carried the force of many years; incredulous, and motionless, they maintain the pose of watching on the raw edge of a space they cannot yet imagine—observing, in the air beyond the frame, that solid, overhanging future which has crashed down beneath their feet.

I would grow used to this sensation.

Over the next three years I would give up all hope of ever being loved.

$$===13===$$

'The Hardings?' Les Curtain asked me.

'Gone,' I replied.

'Mr Medlicott?'

'He cannot accept the boy's death. In spirit, at least, he is no longer there.'

'And that odd fellow Kitchings?'

'The council doors closed to him, and there were visits from the bank. I have heard that his health has begun to suffer from it; he has moved to the city with his wife.'

Les Curtain sat, wearing his old gardening jacket and fingerless gloves, in a wicker cure chair on the verandah. Although his body was as insubstantial as light beneath the blankets, his head still made a deep impression in the pillow. The winter sun had worked its way through the mist all morning, so that at last it had thinned slightly, lifting to leave a clear band of thin grey air beneath. Since his relapse at the beginning of last winter Les Curtain's condition had shown a marked improvement. After a year of bedrest his fever was

reduced and his Gaffky Count was down. He had been transferred several days earlier from the men's infirmary ward, and
did not seem to remember the time during his fever when I
had stood beside Matron Coan in my new uniform beside his
bed. He seemed oddly pleased to find me here in the cure
galleries, which I attributed to clinical nostalgia. 'So. *Have you
"become a woman yet"*?' he had asked me as he shook my hand.
I was startled by his recollection of that cold afternoon at the
Hydro Majestic, when I had been almost invisible in my
shyness, and his accurate mimicry of Lady Harding's confi-
dential shout. I smiled and replied that I had tried and failed
and did not make the effort now.

'Two years I've been here,' Les Curtain said now. 'How
will I recognise the world if I am released back into it again?'

'You follow the threads back,' I told him. 'If you are bold
enough. Until you see how these things were taking shape
for years before they made themselves visible to your eyes.
That is if you wish to. Finding one's place in the scheme of
things is often too greatly esteemed.'

'So, you are telling me that even outside the san, it is a
matter of symptoms and diseases.' Les Curtain smiled.

'You should rest,' I replied, finding for the first time that I
liked him.

Matron Coan leaned back against the iron column of the
verandah so that heavy drops of condensation shuddered from
the gutters and splashed across our shoes. 'Men put great faith
in symbols,' she said. 'Show a man a statue and he will mistake

a paddock for a city. Wear a corset and ribbons and he will see you as a wife.' She struck a match and I saw the glow of two cigarette ends between her lips before she handed one to me. Its external skin was already damp and threatening to break. I watched the warmth of my breath curling and scrolling through the mist. We had moved the patients indoors from the cure chairs; some were sleeping now, while others had gathered around the table in the communal living room to play a game of whist. 'No matter what a man says, you can be certain,' she continued, 'that he will only fall in love with what he has already been taught to see.'

Matron Coan had moved me from the women's infirmary wing to the cure galleries after the first six months because she found me an interesting talker. She liked the fact that I was not the type to bore her with the details of my trousseau—she had seen enough foundation garments, she said, to last her for a lifetime. She was also pleased that I was not here searching for a husband. There were matches made of course, between the nurses and the patients, but she counselled the women against them in stern terms. She told each applicant that every marrying man on earth was looking for a girl to nurse him, so she might as well find a healthy specimen and save herself the extra work. Besides, in her experience, if a man recovered, he would be filled with bitterness, and seek out the company of other women who had not seen him when he was frail and vomiting his milk.

I was glad to be out of the infirmary. Even the patients with the hope upon them lost it when they were sent there, for they realised what their transfer meant. In that ward the electric lights were always burning. The air was sweet and heavy with the smell of rotten blood. There I had been shown how to tap a patient's chest above the clavicle to find the soft spots in the lung which made a dull sound like ripe peaches falling on asphaltum. I had been trained to listen for the râle, that gurgling rattle which preceded death. At one end of the ward, where there were two beds to which we moved the sickest patients, a door led to the morgue. On the other side of the wall, separated from the living only by the distance of a brick, the dead lay on their tables, their faces like statues covered by the sculptor's sheet. The regularity of these expirations was no secret. Matron Coan had recently sent a stiff letter of refusal to the director of a visiting cinematographic company, shooting a murder mystery in the Carrington Hotel, who had asked to hire a corpse.

In the cure galleries, by contrast, the mood was optimistic. The patients were, for the most part, ambulant, and forbidden to speak in the dormitories of the symptoms of their illness. Any man who forgot himself and broke this rule was forced to place a penny in the poor jar on Matron Coan's desk. Letters home were to be written only in rhyming couplets, since their nursery rhythms were incompatible with despair. Sometimes, as they sat in the cure chairs on the verandahs, reading and absorbing ozone, I thought that the men and women resembled haggard but hopeful migrants on the long deck of a ship.

Matron Coan had great faith in the philosophy of open-air treatment, which claimed that breathing soft clouds in a mountain landscape would gradually heal tubercular lesions on the lungs. The high air was purer, and more concentrated. It was visible. Its medicinal effects could be relied upon and gauged. Matron Coan was inclined to endow these facts with a moral aspect. In her opinion, the cure also put a patient's character to the test. There had been much talk, she knew, about the refined sadness, the fugitive mystery, of clouds. But here, in the sanatorium, the consumptives had to learn to master the mists which exercised a repellent fascination on them, creeping like the ghosts of caterpillars slowly through the wards. They must learn to ration the damp air or choke upon it. They had to expose themselves to the clouds until they conquered their own blank fear of death.

It was for this reason that Matron Coan had broken the days into segments so that the clouds were also cut like elastic into neat and serviceable lengths. In the cure galleries the day began at seven when we woke the patients and took their temperatures and made them drink their milk. After breakfast, they lay along the verandah in their beds or cure chairs until we called them in for lunch. Afterwards, they returned to their chairs, or were allowed some gentle exercise within the grounds. Matron Coan did not let them wander very far, and allowed the views of the Valley of the Waters only to the strongest. It was to keep this rule that she had employed as Captain of the Walk a small man with bent shins and hopeful eyes the colour of diluted sarsaparilla, who, as a child, had survived consumption in his bones. He was also to inform her if he saw any hawkers of patent medicines or cough lozenges lurking by the gates. In this he was less successful, for my keen nose frequently made out the smell of eucalyptus in the sputum mugs. Some afternoons the paths closest to the dining hall shone with the thin expectorated discs. At five we called the patients from the gardens for their dinner, after which they rested without talking for two hours. Then they were summoned for their supper; we exchanged their sputum mugs, took their temperatures, and settled them in bed.

It was, in addition, Matron Coan's opinion that romance was particularly dangerous to women in any dealings with the clouds. She had observed men in straw boaters and patent leather shoes tell their fiancées how they liked to feel their heads resting as light as mist against their collarbones and kiss the flowers of death which flared up in their cheeks. She had once discharged a patient when she found him in the infirmary making a young girl eat rice out of his hand while he stroked her hair and whistled in her ear as if she was a little bird. For this reason she had segregated all the wards. She had the patients sponged with icy water. She forbade them crimson foods like shrimp or lobster. She insisted that the reclining cure chairs were made of rattan instead of plush. Before Harry Kitchings left the mountains that summer for the city she had confiscated his viewbooks when they turned up at the san. In the first weeks after they were admitted Matron Coan would not even let the patients leave their beds. They ate their meals propped up on their pillows and had to call out for a bedpan, swallowing their food where they had passed their ordure; watched by the others as they used the pot, they soon learned to control the ecstatic impulse in their faces.

In spite of the wishes of the board and Dr Summergreene,

Matron Coan had prevailed in having the paths which led to the cliffs christened after famous thoracic surgeons rather than following the vogue for naming them for lovers: 'Juliet's Balcony', 'Honeymoon Point'. She tasted the names like salt upon her tongue as she recited them to me now. 'As if,' she said, 'the good Lord had designed the landscape with the sole intention of making men and women meet.'

I watched her freckled hand brush the ashes from her chest. For a moment my eyes mistook the fine grey flakes for dry skin which had been rubbed off by the starched grain of her blouse. I observed that there was no tenderness left in her chapped fingers. I had already noted the same change in my own. I doubted whether they would be able now to depress a small brass shutter on a camera, softly, as if it were the key of a trumpet, or brush the air bells from the surface of a photographic plate. For the first time for many years my hands did not wander from my body during the night to feel for openings and latches in the air. They had grown so used to the touch of washcloths and metal and rough sheets that it was a shock, each time I took pulses, to feel a heart jumping against the inside of a wrist.

I regarded these changes with a certain satisfaction. For at last I had abandoned that ambition which I recognised now as the cause of all my sadness. For that reason, six months after my first conversation with Matron Coan I had removed myself from Katoomba, where, in that clear air, each landmark was a sharp reminder of my loss, and I seemed to stumble always across the muddied tracks of my old self. I had chosen to live instead on this misty cliff with the other casualties of that exodus of clouds: coughing landscape painters from the continent and shell-shocked soldiers; those masturbators from the Bohemia Apartments, no longer youthful, whose skin had been ridged and desiccated by their illness; bookworms with the pinch-marks of spectacles around their noses whose longing for the past had transformed itself into a grim urge to taste and swallow the air like cotton candy. I had thrown out my harem skirt for climbing mountains, and left the negative and the viewbooks which Harry Kitchings had given me, still carrying about them the scent of chemistry like the rings of some dim planet, at my aunts' house, beyond the mist, three towns down the line. Passing darkened windows, I no longer looked for my own reflection, bright and suspended in the surface of the glass. Instead, as I walked backwards and forwards along the wards each day I kept my eyes fixed on the flat linoleum floors and breathed the fog through my nose in shallow, even breaths.

I thought now how much I liked to listen to Matron Coan talk, as she made her smoky maps of the secret places of men's hearts. I only wished that I had met her three years sooner when I had regarded the failure to win Harry Kitchings' love solely as my own.

Over the next six months, as Les Curtain began to move stiffly around the men's ward, stooping now and then to retrieve some fallen letter or piece of woodwork from the floor and place it on the end of its owner's bed, before he lowered himself into the armchair by my desk, I recalled for him the

events in Katoomba during the last two years. I told him how
Mr Medlicott had begun to walk in 1918 as if he saw mud
in the streets, holding the tops of his trousers like a woman
hitching up her skirt, so that the cuffs rode up past his ankles.
I described Lady Harding as she ordered the destruction of his
fernhouse after Sir Wilfrid's death; how, during the torching,
as the grass cracked, she had watched the fronds curl and
blacken, until they resembled the plumes on a funeral carriage.
And I went back further, to the middle years of the war, to
recount with an even voice the many times I had seen Harry
Kitchings, after his wife's miscarriage, squatting before the boy
with some gadget which spun in the currents of the wind, or
one of those bright horned flowers we mounted on pipe-
cleaner legs and called 'mountain devils', while the child
screwed his head around to watch his pug sniffing the verandah poles and listened for his mother's voice inside the shop.

Yet I did not tell Les Curtain about those weeks in 1915,
which I still counted among the worst hours of my life, when
I had waited for the arrival of Harry's wife. Each time I heard
the expression of steam as a train pulled in, or looked out
from the shop into the bright air of Main Street, I felt a muscle
in my cheek begin to twitch and quiver. As if, in a strange
way, I had become Harry Kitchings, disembodied, squeamish,
peering at the sky, afraid to see at last the brute shape of his
desire.

He had said her eyelids were so fragile that the violet veins
showed through them like the last hint of sun caught in the
membrane of the dusk.

He had said she wore so many layers of soft lace that, the

first time he kissed her, he had felt as if he reached for and touched the centre of a cloud.

Each evening I worked with the Red Cross women in the Masonic Hall making socks for other people's sons and husbands. If I stabbed myself with a darning needle or chafed my fingers with the khaki wool I felt these sensations as confirmations of my plainness. In the mirror I had seen my lips grow purpled from all the times I pressed them tight and swallowed bitter thoughts. A sharp frown-line had formed between my eyes. I drew the thread taut and broke it off between my teeth.

The day before his wife arrived, Harry had surprised me by showing up briefly at the pharmacy, where he bought a perfume atomiser with a pink bulb and tassel at one end, a nerve tonic, iron tablets, and five of Mr Medlicott's novelty sweets moulded in the shape of hearts. 'She is delicate; a delicate girl,' he said to us both, as if the term itself were a source of wonder. There was no diminution of kindness in his manner, yet he did not stay to talk. Nor did he seem to register the alterations in my face. Instead, as I said bitterly to my youngest aunt that night, 'It was as if his eyes shone with some kind of happiness emulsion.' They focused only on his wife. I noticed that his fingers shook with tenderness when he passed the pound note across the counter.

The next night, as I passed his studio, I saw the top rooms lit up, as if the moon had rolled on its orbit through the windows and now leaked golden light through the gaps between the curtains.

I felt a sharp pain in my chest, and knew that she was there.

You cannot guess what I imagined.

Harry's wife had taken days, confined to bed, to recover from the journey. The moment she came out I sensed it. From the doorway of the pharmacy I saw knots of people form at the other end of Main Street. They greeted her and pressed tiny pullets' eggs and boiled sweets and mandarins upon her son or teased him to lift his head out of her skirts. Yet I could not see her face. At last, when the reflection of her large hat appeared in the window of the Niagara, Mr Medlicott instructed me to stand behind the counter while he rushed out to greet her. He dropped the flap behind him so that it rattled on its hinges. There was a roughness in his manner which suggested that my presence was a kind of calculated insult.

Mr Medlicott helped Harry's wife lift the boy, who had sunk to his knees, across the step, but did not introduce us.

At last I saw her—a small plain woman with ambitious eyes.

She wore a pink dress of the new length which showed her narrow shins: her bodice and skirt and hat were trimmed with matching lace. She had caught her thin blonde hair into a chignon. While her gestures were girlish there was a certain stiffness about her waist and a brittleness to her skin beneath the rouge. That the boy was a late baby, the women of Katoomba had already guessed. As Mr Medlicott showed her about the shop her eyes narrowed slightly beneath dark brows in the squint of the near-sighted. She told him that she had already purchased flowers and japanned vases and curtain fabrics that morning in Katoomba Street, and a sailor hat for the boy. In his single life, she joked, Harry had mistaken the interior of his shop for another sort of wilderness, so that she risked losing her way among the junk, which she was currently engaged in sorting. She had already made up a parcel for the poor out of Harry's old shirts with the soft blooms of thread around the edges of the sleeves. She was taking his measurements to Bartle's Men's Emporium to choose the fabric for new undergarments and shirts and suits with padded shoulders.

When Mr Medlicott invited him to look out for beetles and spiders in the carved acanthus leaves around the poles the child began to cry. My employer apologised and ducked behind the curtain, promising to find some present to amuse him. I heard his quick footsteps upstairs in Dr Pritchard, the Molar Wizard's rooms. It was then that Mrs Kitchings came over to the counter and asked if I was 'Harry's dear friend Eureka' and said that he had told her all about me. She took my hand and whispered that she was glad that Mr Medlicott had left us to ourselves. We should soon have tea, she said, but perhaps now, while he was gone, I could recommend a potent women's tonic. 'These last few days,' she said, 'I have been so very tired.' She smiled and I noticed a line of bright pink gum between her teeth and her upper lip. To this day I do not know if there was cunning in her words. I was relieved when Mr Medlicott returned, holding a bloodied wisdom tooth wrapped in cotton wool with its own misshapen twin embedded in its side.

That evening, Harry had taken his wife to Echo Point where the honeymoon couples left trails of rice among the rocks, and garters and strings of beads and soiled handkerchiefs caught upon the shrubs. It was my aunt who stood at the kiosk, as invisible as air, and observed how sometimes his wife withdrew her hands from a large fur muff with artificial violets pinned onto the front, to cover Harry's eyes, or smooth his hair, or wind the ends of his moustache around her fingers. It was my aunt who found me in my room and reported that when they leaned out over the cliff's edge the wife had clung to his shirt-front and closed her eyes and made him promise that he would never bring her there again. We turned to see my eldest aunt standing in the doorway. She said this sort of talk was a waste of time and told me that I should ask God for the forbearance to accept what could not be altered, and the strength to change what could. 'And you,' she frowned at her sister, 'should encourage her to have more pride.' She retired to her room; these were her last words on that matter.

Yet I could not have lived through this time if I had not returned in the evenings to find my youngest aunt making slits in the surfaces of piecrusts: if she had not said, 'as thin as men's promises,' to make me laugh. When there were questions I could not ask, she moved without attracting notice about the town to ferret out the answers. When I said I had forgotten the taste of shellfish because I could not dine alone, she opened the housekeeping tin and took me at once to the Oyster Saloon. We sat in the front window and she nodded to the passersby as the dull shells piled into little hills between us. There she told me that when Harry visited us she had seen the love he bore me as clearly as she had seen the spirit babies in the air. When he entered, shimmering drifts of gold floated across the room. When he spoke, viny curls of silver probed the space between us and caught like moths' feet on the little tensions in the air. When he left, his love settled on the furniture and clung for hours like a purple mist so that sometimes she had been forced to gather up all the antimacassars in the house, she said, and bleach them in the sun.

'If that was the case,' I asked my aunt, 'why did he pass me over for this undistinguished woman?'

'Perhaps . . . I always suspected it,' she said ' . . . you made him quite afraid.'

I could not understand it. I had learned to climb mountains for Harry Kitchings. I had listened as he unwound and carded the orders of the clouds. I had squeezed my vision through the polished focus of his sight, until the leaves on the gum trees shone like lead crystal, and the mountains glowed as blue as stained glass, and our own hearts seemed transparent traps for light, with the veins and shadows of the same thoughts caught within their centres. I had tried to fit that panoramic measure which he held up to the sky.

And now, instead of something wide and luminous, he had chosen the cottage garden—the model railway—the Tiny Town—of love.

Could a man demand one thing of a landscape and another of a wife?

After that I began to wonder if men regard the time before their marriages as a barren place where they wait for their real lives one day to loom before them. I wondered if they ever truly notice those women who have been their friends before their wives.

When I made my rare trips to the lookouts, I found that

the mountains were no longer blue; they had faded to an ashen grey.

It was as if my own history had ended.

From then on I saw all the changes in the town take place but took no part in them myself. The truth is, I told Les Curtain now, I was no longer thought of. Once it was assumed that I had recovered from my 'disappointment', as the town referred to it, I was left to my own devices to perish like one of Mr Darwin's superseded insects. For two years I was not invited to a single dinner dance, since I could not play the piano or contribute decorations to a theme. Yet I was expected to turn up at every marriage and funeral as some kind of changeless and cautionary presence, like the fossil dragonflies which Sir Wilfrid used to weigh down the papers on his desk. For these four years people either spoke to me as if I was five or one hundred years of age: in each case they offered partial and censored information. Having not married it was assumed that I could have little sense of the common trials and enjoyments of adulthood. More than ever I relied on my powers of deduction. Whatever history found me out had to squeeze through the doorway of the shop in the remote form of its symptoms. For these reasons, I explained, my memories had the fleeting quality of images projected out of darkness which pass in swift succession across a fixed illuminated screen. They were clear but aloof, acute but oddly muffled.

I remembered how, in the window of the pharmacy, when

the news of the war still brought a flush of pleasure to his cheeks, Mr Medlicott displayed the bullet cases his son had sent to him from France. If a returned soldier came in with a Carne arm he asked to inspect it, tapped the hinges with his pencil, and asked him how and where he had been pipped. In Harry's window further down Katoomba Street, beside the novelties and wrapping papers purchased by his wife, there were letters from the soldiers who had received his viewbooks in the post from home. They wrote how even in the trenches as the mud of a dead Europe crunched between their teeth they had looked at his photographs and remembered those white clouds of Australia which stretched to its horizons like fleeces thrown out across the great table of the sky.

Some days there were so many white feathers passing through the post that the postman had to weight his sack with stones when the winds swept across the escarpment to stop it blowing down the street. At other times, he knew he carried dead men's letters, for he smelled the sweetness of gangrene, and when he finished for the day his back was wet with tears. When he tried to push these letters through the brass flaps of our doors, they stuck to his hands as if they longed for the world of living flesh.

In the grounds of the Hydro Majestic the Anti-German League burned the piano which had once belonged to the German heiress Bertha Krupp.

Later that year, I told Les Curtain, there was a panic as hundreds of Mountaineers mistook a large black cloud for a zeppelin when its smooth belly hung above the shops. As the thunder rumbled they joined hands across Main Street and sang 'On the Shores of the Aegean Sea'. I remember how, white with fear, they resembled actors of the cinematic screen: how the light stuck like powder to their faces. It was little wonder, then, that during this time people lost their taste for an immensity of sky. When they spoke of the air those days they referred to it as 'our servant'. The Fresh Air League had disbanded at the beginning of the war and many of the boys in the Brigade had already perished in the East. As a result, Mr Medlicott had begun to sell little tins which resembled containers for shoe polish; these swift-selling souvenirs, which sat flat in the tourists' hands, were filled in a factory near the Bathurst Road with Katoomba air. In Lurline Street Mr Fowler opened a successful studio where, for a shilling, wives could pose with limbless husbands in front of a large painted panorama of the mountains, safe from the disagreeable presences of shrubs and parakeets and rain.

This was the time, Les Curtain told me, that he had woken one morning with blood on his pillow to find that the plants in his lunatic asylum had jumped their bounds to seed themselves, so that his garden became a battlefield, filled with mutated scarlet and purple petals, like the livers of dead men.

Yet I did not tell Les Curtain, because that memory still disturbed me, about the dark evening in 1916 when Nicholas Hoffman appeared at the door of the pharmacy as I was closing up. When he touched my arm his fingers were moist with apology and skidded on my flesh. He asked me to sell him a razor since the Antiseptic Hairdressing Saloon would no longer accept his custom. For the last year, he told me, he had been receiving dark letters from the Anti-German League.

Anonymous patriots had accused him of working as a German spy in the letters pages of the *Echo*. One night, as he stood smoking at interval in the lane behind the Empire, two young men in khaki shirts had closed his fist around the ember and said that the next time they would break his hands to prevent him from using his cinematograph to flash the location of our town in coded signals out across the sky. The manager, he knew, was writing letters to the city to replace him, for when he shone his pyramid of light above their heads the audience would hiss, even if he offered Theda Bara. It was strange, very strange, he whispered to me at the counter; in the last few weeks, although he had never seen that country, German dreams had been unspooling through his sleep. He saw bare cliffs and dark swift-flowing rivers and squat turrets tiled with scales which shone like lizards' backs. That very morning, he said, he had woken with the chilly taste of ice wine in his mouth.

Three days later he was found dead in the projection booth. I knew that he had felt the tight vowels forming on his tongue and used the blade to slice it off.

In 1917, I continued, Harry's mother had died in Sydney, out of relief, perhaps, that he had found himself a wife. She left her daughter-in-law her jewellery, the salt cellar, and her homoeopathic kit. Several days later, in an anonymous package from the city addressed in a shaking hand, I received his great aunt's letters which I still carry everywhere I go.

By 1918, with so many faces absent from the town, the days were foreign landscapes. As the list of those men lost in action grew, we were scarcely able to believe in our own existence. There was so little proof. The last thing people wished for was to look up into the sky. Instead, they ate nursery foods. They danced harder until the Katoomba Amusements Company banned the tango, fearing the shuddering roof-garden would splinter and collapse. They married so that they would never have to take the trouble of learning the contours of another person's arms.

Yet I did not admit to Les Curtain that, in spite of myself, I had continued to scan the council reports in the *Echo* until he left later that year to make out the pattern of Harry Kitchings' life. I saw that he continued to deplore the expansion of the town while the sights deteriorated below us in the valley. The reporter noted how *Mr Kitchings had, somewhat eccentrically, remarked during the meeting that many of the smaller streamlets and waterfalls in the area had dried up or dwindled and seemed to infer, by his demeanour, that this was because they had been too often photographed by visiting Kodakers with little regard to the artistic precepts.* I wondered if Harry's optimistic blindness extended to blocking out the humiliation of it: the endless deferral to some slow committee of his requests for funding; the pittances offered for his slides; those descriptions of him in the *Echo* as 'Mr Kitchings, a Mountain photographer of the old school and friend to the eucalypt, who favours the pursuit of beauty over progress'. I knew that his wife lacked this necessary defect. For my aunt heard that she continually urged Harry to raise the price of his viewbooks, which he had not altered since the first day he opened up the shop. She regarded her husband, and did not care who heard it, as a benefactor of the town. Many of my aunts' friends remarked on how she consumed their sandwiches and sticky buns with quick little bites and not a word of thanks as if they were a necessary tribute.

And when I recounted that terrible winter of 1918, I could not find the words to tell him how Mrs Grudge, who had been widowed two years by the war, was found in her chicken shed, her cheek flattened against the faeces and pellets on the floor. I remembered how Mr Medlicott, just weeks before his own loss, had returned to the pharmacy to give an account of the post-mortem. He had stood behind the doctor as his government-issue scalpel made a red line from the tip of her chin down to the sparse triangle of hair below her belly. Before the muscle and the inner organs were revealed he saw pale beads of fat which spilled and gleamed. The voluptuousness, he said, had surprised him. Inside her womb the doctor had found a lump of tissue attached to a damp hank of chestnut hair, which he pulled taut with one hand while he detached the tumour with his knife. Springing from her belly, the growth bobbed from his gloved fingers like a shrunken head. When it was bisected there were two crude teeth caught like seed pearls at its centre. The doctor dropped the flesh and teeth and hair into a jar of spirits and took them to a sandstone building in the university on Parramatta Road, islanded by the traffic which made its way into the city from the west. All that day I was haunted by the thought of those damp secrets unwound on the wooden table. It was only when I recounted the story to Matron Coan that I could articulate how much it troubled me. Since the time Harry Kitchings had abandoned me for someone he could recognise as a wife because she did not have mountain-climbing legs and clouds caught in her hems, I said, I could understand what might drive a woman to turn her yearning for another body into hidden flesh.

I had already lost my future, I told Les Curtain. Then two events had occurred which severed my attachment to the past.

Three months before the war ended, Sir Wilfrid had agreed at last to the sale of Pinefield and planned to move with Lady Harding to some new apartments in the city. Mayor Gordon parked his new motor in the driveway and showed him the plans in which the gridlines of the subdivision were pencilled in with blue. Sir Wilfrid said it was a strange sensation: as if he had seen his own heart cut up before his very eyes. There was still a trace of scientific wonder in his voice, when he told Mr Medlicott, rubbing a pale finger along the parting of his hair, that for some time he had noted a similar principle of displacement in the world around him. It had something to do with the fact that he had suddenly noticed the rough young men around the town who slouched against the walls, still wearing their uniforms, and failed to raise their hats to him, although they looked into his eyes and flexed the muscles in their jaws with recognition and contempt. Then there was the young couple engaged in fevered coupling he had discovered in the fernhouse. Even the young woman, as she smoothed her dress, had stood tall and sullen, and returned his glances without shame. Later he had found their dope needles scattered in the sawdust. 'I knew that young man's father,' Sir Wilfrid said. 'I am an old man from another time. This new world seems very strange to me.'

Two weeks later he was dead. Lady Harding closed the shutters, for the blue of the mountains reminded her of the colour of her husband's lips the morning that she found him. Then, swiftly, she was gone, and the hazelnut trees were all cut down and the lawns were crossed with drainage ditches. Visitors, taking a short cut to Echo Point across the grounds, soon hacked a large hole in the hawthorn hedge.

Shortly after that, a telegram arrived at the pharmacy for Mr Medlicott. I can still see him, as he rushed back around the corner into Main Street from his house after I had pressed the electric buzzer. His face was half black with polish, his pin-striped vest unbuttoned, in preparation to perform at a Conscription banquet that evening with the Katoomba Nigger Minstrels. A week earlier he had received a letter which his son had written from a field in _____. The gaps made by the censors' scissors created terrible spaces for imagination. 'So many men had paid full toll before me,' he wrote, 'that the mud was littered with false teeth which shone when the moonlight caught them. Sometimes I find myself thinking for a mad second that I am in the Molar Wizard's rooms.' When he had ducked beneath the barbed wire the next day one of these broken dentures had gashed his knee and he had contracted gangrene. The telegram reported that even when the leg was taken off the doctors could not save him.

Mr Medlicott re-read the words. Each time he finished he nodded to himself and moved his lips as if he memorised a chemical formula, then began again. At last he said to me that he should complain to someone that his son's train had passed

Paris five times but he had never seen it. I closed the store and walked him home. His elbow felt suddenly unfleshed, as light as a dog's shank beneath my fingers. From that day on his mind quietly unhinged. If he came up to the pharmacy he soon misplaced his glasses. I would later find them in the Kodak cabinet or sticking out of a tub of toilet cream. Then he would sit and hold his notebooks open on the desk before him and say he could no longer understand them. If I spoke to him he would turn his head at the first sound and then forget to listen to the rest. Once he told me he had seen giant turtles grazing on his son, snapping his bones with their pincered beaks. After that his wife had kept him in their house. She made arrangements to transfer the business to his brother's son.

That day, in 1919, when I stood next to Matron Coan in the men's infirmary ward, and we looked down at their haunted faces, we agreed—it seemed foolish, in many ways, to declare that the war was over.

Matron Coan and I sat side by side before the fire in the nurses' quarters. We had taken the last round of temperatures for the day and supervised while the patients drank their milk and went to bed. I could smell the leather burning on our boots which we rested on the grate. I knew that the next day there would be itchy chilblains on my feet but still could not find the energy to shift them. In the distance, in one of the wards, a woman coughed until she retched.

'There is a couple marrying tomorrow in the gardens,'

Matron Coan said. She told me that she had counselled the woman against it but she would not be dissuaded. In this case, she said, it was best to follow the conventions. She had offered to find a minister to marry the couple at once within the grounds and then she would discharge them. She had suggested that they honeymoon at a particular hotel in Katoomba from which she received a small commission that kept her in cigarettes. The routine there, she told me, was almost as regulated as her own. There were cream teas and gentle walks along the Main Street. They would make the acquaintance of thirty other couples there who dressed and spoke alike. There were quiet runs in the hotel car to view the major sights and loving only after tea.

'There is nothing like matrimony,' I heard myself reply in Matron Coan's voice, 'to cool the febrile affair.'

—— *14* ——

The phenomenon had been observed so many times last century, Matron Coan told me, that physicians had coined the term *spes phthisica*: its symptoms included restlessness, the desire to travel to exotic countries, and the urge to find a mate. In its advanced stage, tuberculosis often worked against the doctors' efforts. The patients' bodies gave the false impression that they were quite recovered: their eyes brightened, their cheeks were pink. Afflicted with a false joyfulness, they displayed an unusual vitality; their passions and appetites increased; they discovered new vigour in their limbs and other neglected organs. Even after they had been shown their Gaffky Count, they refused to believe that the bacilli were multiplying in their sputum, and asked to be released. It was widely acknowledged in publications on the subject that artistic or literary habits made one most vulnerable to this unreasonable craving for life.

We were in the middle of an outbreak now.

Over the last weeks some of the men had tried to knock

the weights out of our hands when we made them stand upon the scales, while others had begun emptying their sputum mugs in the sinks, convinced that Matron Coan was falsifying tests. Thermometers went missing regularly and appeared tucked into the grooves of the skirting boards behind the aesthetes' beds. The artists had taken to collecting blue medicine bottles and boiled sweets and children's marbles beneath their blankets, as if they were bowerbirds, and comparing them, hoping to find that particular shade which would relieve their sense of loss. Long coils of French knitting spread across the floors like vines. Each day the Captain of the Walk escorted men and women back from the cliff walks whom he had found reciting poetry, balanced recklessly on rocky outcrops. They said that the mist stung their eyes: that it burned their faces when they walked; that they could see each drop of eucalyptus vapour, microscopic, faceted, suspended in the air. One thin man with eyelids like crepe paper had clutched the captain's arm and begged him to listen to the waterfalls—it was sex itself, he told him, breathless, gushing down the cliff.

Matron Coan knew that this hyperaesthesia of the soul preceded an increase in cough and fever. It was a process of refinement, she said, by which the body prepared itself for death. She alerted Dr Summergreene, who dispatched half of the patients to the infirmary ward, and confiscated letters and portraits of old lovers. He ordered that we confine the majority of those remaining to their beds.

Perhaps I was affected also by this peculiar state of mind.

For the first time in the two years since I had come to

work here I began to feel a diminution of the tightness around my heart.

The night he returned from the Hydro Majestic, Les Curtain told me, he had noticed the first symptoms. When he breathed the evening air he felt the weight of the darkness in his chest. He had thought his orchid bulbs rattled more loudly than usual in their boxes in the cart behind him until at last he realised that the sound was quite regular and issued from his own lungs which were clinging like thick damp clouds to the curving insides of his ribs. There was a sharp pain in his left side. He shivered and his bones ached as if his whole skeleton had been carved by one of the Chinese waiters out of ice. From that time on, he said, he had felt the weather in his blood.

We stood in the kitchen gardens where the homeless men who worked in the cemetery and the orchards pulled up the winter beds. Having been chosen—as I was too, I suppose— because they had little to lose from any exposure to infection, they moved about with no display of interest, as if they did not distinguish between digging vegetables or corpses. At Les Curtain's direction they began to uproot the rows of silver beet behind us. The plants had gone to seed, extending little tails of jade into the air, lined with dark green vertebrae of bud and leaf, each one smaller than the last as it grew towards the tip. Les Curtain said he was sometimes troubled by the thought that each plant exhausted its own idea of itself as it drew closer to the sun.

It was the September of 1920. For the last month Les Curtain had been allowed graduated exercise within the grounds. First he had taken gentle walks along the paths named after chest surgeons, then he was asked to help with the spring planting. He had attached a small bracket to the handle of his barrow to hold his sputum mug, which he referred to as his music box. I saw that his face had begun to brown again as he stood and chewed his pipe.

He told me, 'A strange dream had also troubled my sleep that winter night, although this first one, at least, I had not borrowed but could acknowledge as my own.'

He imagined that he had returned to the casino in the grounds of the Hydro Majestic, and lay on the crimson carpet while Nellie Melba sang upon the stage. He was so close that he could see her great jaw work around each note. The sinews moved and expanded in her throat beneath the powder. Above her head, the electric lights vibrated in their sockets. Slowly, he had felt his heart loosen in his chest and float up from his body, bobbing and weaving like a cobra's head. At last, as that organ hovered near the roof, her voice had forced it like a bulb so that it trembled and thickened with unexpected life. He felt bright creased fists of petal forming at its centre. The flowers shrugged and struggled to unfurl. Then, when he had all but given up expecting it, Melba threw back her head and finished her song with a note so pure and so extended that she seemed impaled upon it. It was then that he felt the tight muscle split and explode into a hundred yellow wings.

He woke coughing the next morning to find a thin blood

spray on his pillow. Telling no one, he had stripped the bed and destroyed the linen in the iron drum where he burned his weeds.

That had been the first, and the only haemorrhage for many years. Yet the experience had shaken him profoundly. It had forced him to acknowledge that his lungs might unravel at any moment—that, as if to defy him, they had grown into odd distorted shapes like one of the hybrid plants in his lunatic asylum. Indeed when the fevers came he sometimes thought it possible that he had inhaled one of those strange wind-borne seeds shed by the native trees which flew on sheaths of tissue as veined and brittle as cicadas' wings. He wondered if he had not spent too much time up to his elbows in this soil until at last he had turned into some monstrous type of hybrid. He fancied that small blue jacaranda flowers budded in his lungs and filled them up with sticky sap.

He remembered what Harry Kitchings had said that after-noon: that it was possible to be transformed by living so close to the face of God. Yet he was no believer and could find not a single grain of faith inside himself even as he contem-plated death. It also struck him that compared to the feelings that sometimes overwhelmed him, Harry's notion of the Lord was singularly tame. For even when he was not experiencing hailstorms in his stomach or feeling lightning building in his pelvis he was haunted by ungodly symptoms. He experienced an exaggerated tenderness which afflicted his mind as well as his organs so that he found himself one evening in his green-house weeping inconsolably over a bucket filled with salt and frothing cherry snails. He felt a desire always to have the smell of mulch about him, to the extent that he sometimes smoked it in his pipe to feel the dankness of it as hot and rich as chocolate in his throat. And, above all else, there was this greediness for air.

Yet his illness had caused no damage to his business. In fact he had been forced to take on two more boys to execute his plans as his reputation continued to increase. This, he told me, was because he had developed a facility for experiencing other people's dreams.

I could not help laughing, and then I could not suppress my laughter because of the anger in his face. 'Don't tell me that you are also succumbing to the romantic impulse,' I said. 'If you want to get well you will have to take responsibility for your own hallucinations.' He turned his back on me and refused to speak until, at last, to test him, I asked if he had ever heard from Mr Hoffman in his sleep. He replied—'Two nights before his death I dreamed of thick gold letters painted on the fronts of houses and steep vineyards ending in an icy river. I woke with the taste of sausage in my mouth.'

Then, when he began to recount a certain dream of mine in which Harry carefully raised my skirts with his cold hands and felt his way along the insides of my thighs until he found the hidden catch which made my body spring apart, I told Les Curtain he could stop.

On reflection I do not know that I could converse in an interesting manner when Matron Coan first arranged for my transfer from the infirmary ward. Each evening, in the nurses' quarters, while the others gathered around the wireless to discuss recipes or their plans for breeding dogs, I would describe Harry Kitchings' photographs to her in minute detail or try to interest her in the different orders of the clouds. As I showed her the cloud atlas I had purchased, she put aside her lists of Rules for Nurses and her orders for more shrouds, and peered through her reading glasses. After a full day's work, she said, they looked to her only like gobs of expectorated phlegm.

Once I had confided in her, I would return constantly in my conversation to that evening in the fernhouse and ask her if there was anything I might have done to secure Harry Kitchings' love. I scarcely paused to hear her interjections. As the moon rose, she would let me speak while her fingers tapped against the bottom of her glass.

Perhaps Matron Coan was relieved that I was one of the few nurses who did not regard her with condescension. I had watched them force their faces to stay sober when they asked her why she had never wanted children or whether she had ever been a suffragette. There was a titillated silence while she answered: as if she delivered the punchline of a joke. I heard her interrupt the nurses planning out their glory boxes, 'My girl, girdles make promises that your body cannot keep so you might as well dispense with them as soon as you are married. Lacy knickers give you thrush. You would do better to buy a sturdy pair of boots.' I could imagine how her voice had become more bold, then strident, until at last she had begun to parody herself.

Eventually, as the days lengthened, and the thick night air

rose a little later each evening from the valley, bringing the smell of ferns, Matron Coan would ask me to illuminate small details and connections, until—as if Katoomba were a tangled knot of ribbons—other stories began to loosen, and writhe, and find their own sleek pathways in the air.

Thus I told Matron Coan how, when I made my weekend visits to Katoomba now, I found my two aunts engaged in a battle over breath. Three years earlier my eldest aunt had taken to her bed. Each night since in her sleep she had seen her father in his nightshirt standing in her doorway, and heard her brothers and sisters hurling themselves like birds against the window glass, whispering all her secret names for death. She now refused to knock on the bedhead ten times each night, so that my youngest aunt had to do this for the both of them until she counted twenty taps. Yet because the sisters breathed for one another, it was impossible for my eldest aunt to die without my youngest aunt's cooperation, for her faith would not allow her to stop her little sister's lungs. And my youngest aunt had no intention of dying, having at last under-taken her own private studies in animal behaviour, caring for injured wildlife, so that some warm creature always curled, squirming and suckling on her thumb, in the pockets of her skirt. Yet sometimes, when my youngest aunt was walking in the valleys after windy nights, searching for fallen nestlings beneath the trees, my eldest aunt would make her chest grow tight until she had to return, gasping, at the end of that invis-ible leash of breath.

On other nights I told her of the pornography of pale faces and agitated feet blown up on the white screen at the Empire, and flickering elephants, and cities, projected onto clouds. I spoke of the ribbons which we used to tie my father's hands, dyed with Britannia Violet and Dust of Ruins. I remembered gritty envelopes from Luxor—a hail of knucklebones on polished floorboards—Mr Medlicott's description of the seven cuts in the bud of an opium poppy which made its resin leak.

As I spoke, Matron Coan nodded her head, and swore, and ground her cigarette butts into the wheeled ashtray which she pulled about behind her. In return, she told me that if she could ever save the money she would like to sail to San Francisco where women drove the trolley buses. Or she would travel to Vienna where she would learn how to talk sense into other people's dreams.

It was Matron Coan who told me there was a place in the world for reasonable anger.

It was Matron Coan who said I had historical eyes.

Les Curtain squatted over a long mound of loose, dark earth, poking holes with his finger, and dropping seeds into them from his palm. Beneath the gaping collar of his shirt, as he bent forward, I saw the vertebrae now as pale and delicate as a woman's. A damp heat rose up from the soil. It was a Sunday and I was not on duty. The day was warm, in spite of the fact that the sun, behind the high mist, was as pale and silver as the moon.

In the distance, on the lawn behind Dr Summergreene's house, I could see his children playing with one of the bantams from the farmyard. They had dressed it in dolls' clothes and wheeled it around inside a pram. Some of the old women in the cure gallery who were permanently confined to bed waved to them from the verandah. They applauded when the girl took the chicken out and covered it with kisses. It was well known in the Mountains that when the doctor began setting up the King George Homes and was petitioning for sponsors, the Governor of New South Wales had personally guaranteed his debts to honour his service to the Empire early in the war. Working as an army surgeon on one of the great hospital ships near Alexandria, Dr Summergreene had become suspicious of the great number of apparently fit young men who returned positive samples for tuberculosis, were invalided out of service, and were sent home to Australia with a pension. After making rigorous enquiries he had broken the black market in infected sputum singlehanded.

'Do you know what it meant to be able to read another person's dreams?' Les Curtain asked me. 'It meant that I could design a landscape for them before they even knew that they desired it.'

In his most famous gardens, he said, there were flowers which smelled like hotel rooms and seashores. There were weeping mulberries which shaded hidden lovers' nooks. At Mount Wilson he had left a stand of tree ferns like palms in the middle of a lush green lawn so that a retired sea captain could imagine that he still drifted through the heart of the equator. There were rose bushes in bachelors' gardens placed at the edges of the paths to catch at women's dresses with their thorns. There were cabbage patches in the kitchen gardens of the childless.

'And what would you put here?' I asked him.

'Too easy,' Les Curtain replied. 'I would divert that little stream near the graveyard beneath the wards so that it would run beneath our beds and lick all night at the base of the foundations. What do you think? Should I also run it through the nurses' quarters?'

I asked him how he had come to be admitted, after hiding his illness for so many years.

He said that he had begun spitting blood regularly several years ago, but since this had usually occurred while he was pruning his roses, or dragging his 'Iron Age' Orchard Cultivator through the beds, he had been able swiftly to cover his hot expectorations with the dirt. He was more concerned that people might notice the change in his tastes and habits which the acceleration of the disease had wrought. For he had become vague and, until he hired his cousin to look after the receipt books and ledgers, he often found bills and orders folded in his pockets when he fumbled for a handkerchief to raise up to his lips. He no longer enjoyed the texture of a cut tree stump, or the taste of cheese, or Guinness, or the flakes of stale milk floating on the surface of his mug of tea. When he used the old vaporiser pump from the Hydro Majestic, he did not move calmly along the plots but, unmasked, pointed the Radium spray indiscriminately at leaves and flying insects. The leathery feeling of his galah's tongue when it took sunflower seeds from his fingers no longer gave him pleasure. Instead, he thought constantly about the skin as soft as a petal behind a woman's ear, and developed a passion for playing chess.

Then, one day, when he was working in his greenhouse,

he had coughed up several cups. He said he would never forget the sight of it—bright scarlet—steaming—fringed with foam—splashed across the ground. During that spasm he had dropped a seed tray, and for some time he stood there, convinced that each seedling, which curled like a pale foetus in the frothy liquid, was the living matter, half-plant, half-human, which had germinated in his lungs. One of the boys, seeing him stagger from the greenhouse with a bloodied chrysanthemum held up to his lips, had run to telephone Les's cousin. Les had been found delirious in the bush which stretched behind his home, muttering that he only wished to step out from the cliff, and lay his face down on the cool white clouds as if they were soft pillows. The cousin had made Les lie in the back of his own truck while he whipped the horse towards the new sanatorium, a handkerchief bound around his face for fear of contracting the tuberculosis germs. Les Curtain had shivered and rolled from side to side in the truckbed and thought he was an orchid bulb. When Matron Coan saw him, he said, she had admitted him at once.

Les Curtain sighed between his teeth, stood up stiffly, and stamped the dirt from his feet. His thighs were lean inside his trousers. I observed how his rubber boots had barely left an impression in the soil. He was so light from his illness that it seemed as if only the large bones in his forearms and hands had any weight.

Strangely, since those first nights in the infirmary ward, he said, he had come almost to welcome the hot gush in the night, the sweet fullness of his life welling in his throat. Often, as his bones unhinged and elongated, he felt as if he were being drawn and quartered, gently, by the mist. Or he thought the clouds moved inside him, like little fish, nudging at his skin. Sometimes, when the coughing ceased, he lay, aware of nothing but the keen sensation of his sex, as soft and tender as an unshucked mollusc, resting on the sheets.

The Captain of the Walk began to move across the lawn, leaning like a shadow puppet on his sticks, calling the lungers to the dining room for tea. His harsh cry cut as sharp as a cockatoo's through the thickness of the air. Suddenly, Les caught my wrist with his hot fingers. I felt the veins on their undersides, swollen by the work, pressed against my skin. He begged me not to report to Matron Coan what he had said, for it was these strange melancholy thoughts, he knew, which marked him as an ill man.

Perhaps I first failed in my duty when I said, 'Not six years ago. These ideas would not have seemed so strange then. You must know that I loved a man like that.'

Except, I thought, this time when I touched Les Curtain's long hand, it was warm and relaxed beneath my own.

He blew smoke out of the corner of his mouth as he regarded me, his eyes narrowed in a squint.

He said, 'You are quite beautiful.'

I laughed.

I said, 'That does not count for much, except in photographs and landscapes.'

Each week, as the *spes phthisica* continued to rage, the kitchens reported that patients filled with a sudden hunger were stealing sardines and oysters in the night. Spades sounded late into the evening in the cemetery. Les Curtain showed me, glistening among his seedlings, the sticky throat pastilles of lovers, where they had spat them out in a stinging passion to suck each others' tongues. In the nurses' quarters, I heard of half-finished love letters of exquisite tenderness discovered in the infirmary under young men's pillows when the sisters had come to plug and wash their bodies, and of women who rejoiced secretly at pregnancies the night before they died.

Matron Coan stood on the verandah, and watched as the visitors with tanned faces and return train tickets in their hat-bands and posies of gardenias in their hands walked through the iron gates. She shook her head with pity. She would have to ask many of them to come with her to sit in the wicker armchairs in the room next to the infirmary and tell them not to hope. She would soon have to send them packages filled with the letters and lurid paintings from the patients' lockers, along with the three shirts, three sets of underwear, and single set of pyjamas they had brought, keeping aside the suit and the shoes for the funeral, and all three pairs of socks to keep them from slipping off the men's emaciated feet. Matron Coan cursed and told me that she hated the unhealthy melancholy of the past which ruined the patients' will to leave. I did not reply.

At first, when she had told me that I had historical eyes, I had found this an enormous comfort. But now I began to doubt the virtue of detachment. Each day my eyes were confronted only by symptoms, proliferating faster than imagination in this sealed-off place. The more I tried to sort them into the patterns of that one illness, the more the patients' hot cheeks and eager lips and flushed enthusiasms seemed to me to imitate the very force of animation. It was I, by contrast, who seemed oddly immobile. I was as numb as a Carne arm.

Secretly, on one point, I began to disagree with Matron Coan.

It was not so contemptible, I thought, this urge to seize at life.

$$=15=$$

I t was his lungs I first chose to love.

When Dr Summergreene held Les Curtain's X-ray to the light in his consulting rooms I saw seams and cavities within each lobe which curved and thickened like the strange dark pockets of Jenolan Caves. I imagined that they were filled with bright blood rivers and perished tissue which arched like limy wings.

Then it was his heart.

One day, early in summer, in a quiet corner of the orchard, Les Curtain unbuttoned his shirt and placed my hand flat upon his chest. Early in his treatment, when he had first arrived at the sanatorium, six of his ribs had been removed. I felt a short ledge of rib and the sharpness where the saw had cut it. Where it dropped away I touched the swelling of his lungs. I felt the muscle of his heart as it jumped into my hand—the heat of it—held only by the membrane of his skin.

There were brown hairs on his chest and a thin line of darker hair which began beneath his navel.

There were deep silver scars like dried up watercourses across his back.

I picked up an apple from the ground and held its coldness to my cheek. Then I dropped it and heard its weight cushioned by the thick damp grass between us.

I thought, *It is better to be dead than loveless.*

He said I was the first woman who took his face in both hands when she kissed it.

When Les Curtain told me that he had begun to eavesdrop on the other patients' sleep I kept his secret to myself.

It is strange how, half-empty, the wards in a hospital can give the appearance of being darker, as if faces and bodies are themselves a source of light. In the dormitories of the cure galleries, the shadows caught like dirt at the corners of the room. Stripped of their sheets, the exposed mattresses of the unused beds seemed to absorb the electric light. The artists and the soldiers and the men from the Bohemia Apartments were gone. At the other end of the long building, the infirmary wards were as noisy as the kennels filled with inbred dogs, which old Tom Pritchard used to keep in the bush near the Leura Falls.

There was a large man who had been in the men's ward for a month when the other patients nicknamed him the Rooster. He would wake them each dawn with deep clearings of his throat which began beneath his breastbone and reached a groaning climax in his mouth. He would fumble for his sputum mug, drag it to the edge of his bedside table, and heave himself forward for a spit. The men had taken to saving their porridge from breakfast and slipping it inside his slippers and the pockets of his nightgown. One of the younger men, who had worked at Alderman Bronger's soft drink factory before his illness, had even suggested that they swap his sputum mug with one from the infirmary ward so that he would be taken there and they might enjoy a week of deep, uninterrupted sleep.

Les Curtain told me that three days after that man's admission, he had felt the Rooster's dreams, as thick as butter, sliding through his sleep. Each night that man imagined that he had returned to his table at the Australia Club, where one of the waiters held his silver christening mug and raised it each time he gestured to his lips. Another opened oysters and placed them with an oyster fork upon his tongue. Yet the Rooster found, as he tried to swallow, that he gagged, for sharp fragments of shell were still attached to the flesh and caught against his throat. Another waiter came forward with a platter lined with parsley, in which he caught each shellfish when the Rooster coughed it up, and took it to the kitchen beneath a silver dome. At last, when the meal was finished, he had felt a sudden urge to defecate. He realised, with some surprise, that his bowels had begun already to purge themselves over the back edge of his chair. A fourth waiter appeared with a nut scoop and when it was filled he conveyed it gently to the kitchen. A fifth offered him a folded serviette.

At this point both men had woken up coughing and reached out for their mugs.

Les said, 'I guess that's what it takes to get better, his way of seeing the world.' For when he had looked about the Rooster's dream room, each waiter's face was as blank and gormless as a new-laid egg.

We both realised then that the bacilli were beginning to multiply again inside Les Curtain's lungs.

He said that he did not wish to treat them. He could not bear to leave the gardens where he had so recently begun to touch the earth again. He did not think he could survive another year in bed, peering into the terrarium on his bedside table that his cousin had bought him so that he could use a tiny fork and spade to redesign the placement of the paths.

After that, as his temperature rose, I entered it each day as unchanged on his chart. When he stood on the scales, he had stones in the pockets of his shirt and trousers to record a higher weight. That week, at the nurses' station, I took the label from his sputum mug and switched it with the Rooster's. I felt no guilt. Having seen death so many times, we had little fear of it. And Les Curtain had said that his only wish now was to make himself transparent to me so that I could touch the hot wick of his soul.

I will try to tell you how it felt, for the first time, at the age of thirty, to have a man touch me with desire. There is a surprise of the body which begins in the belly and leaps up to the surface of the skin. That was the first sensation. When I held Les Curtain's cheeks his skull was hot beneath them. There was the smell of soil on his fingers. Inside my mouth there was the blood taste of his tongue. His thin arms trembled against my back, although he said it was not from fever, when I asked.

He opened my blouse and my breasts fell out like apples into his hot palms. When his gardener's fingers moved beneath my skirt, and divided the secret flesh like earth, I thought that at any moment they would touch the pith inside my bones.

There was shock at the violence of another body's hunger. And pity, when he moved my hand between his open flies, for the softness of a man's hidden skin.

The hair was thick there, and damp as the thread around an ear of corn.

I squeezed his sex.

This was the first time I heard the moan of pleasure on another person's lips.

At last we heard Matron Coan on the other side of the orchard wall, shouting Les Curtain's name. The Captain of the Walk had not found him, and he had missed the call for tea. He kissed me as he unlatched the fruit-gate. He said that he would try to find somewhere undisturbed where we could lie together in the sun like lizards, and feel it make paths inside us as our bodies opened up.

In the following weeks my flesh grew to fill the maps made on it by Les Curtain's hands. My breasts lifted themselves high up on my chest. The muscles of my arms became as supple and taut as ribbons of fast water. Even the bitter lines were softening around my mouth. In turn, I saw that Les Curtain had begun to walk with the breeze in his feet, as if air had caught inside his bones. There was something close to photographic madness in his face. At times I wondered, Was he making himself over for my eyes?

If Matron Coan had any suspicions she did not turn them into questions. But sometimes, at the periphery of my vision, as we washed the stained cups left in the sink by the others in the nurses' quarters, I thought I caught her staring. Her fingers tapped on the edges of a saucepan, as if she made a mental calculation, and some strange emotion seemed to cross her face.

In spite of the recent spate of deaths there was no shortage of applicants eager to take the Fish up from the city to fill the empty beds. Late at night, when she was not going over the Gaffky Counts, which were finally descending, or writing memoranda to the board about the poor water supply on this high ridge, which had caused so many difficulties for the steam laundry on the premises that the cleaned sheets were often returned to us with pale brown stains of blood, Matron Coan had been sorting through their letters of application. Slowly, now, they began to arrive: rouged secretaries, the sons of the owners of soap factories, golfers, kindergarten teachers and quick young men who sold real estate around the new suburbs in the north across the harbour.

Among this group, a pretty coiffeuse from Double Bay was admitted and confined instantly to bedrest. She sent a note around the hospital, to which she had pinned her card, inviting any woman who wished to have her hair bobbed in the new styles which appeared in the American fashion magazines to visit her in her bed. The next afternoon, while she cut, with her straight back propped against the pillows, a party of ambulant men whistled and threw pebbles at the roof to protest the desecration of our sex. The Stott brothers, who had travelled to Australia in the chorus of the D'oyly Carte before their illness made them breathless, acquired two pairs of women's bloomers and performed a cancan on the lawn. They ran their hands through their short hair with an exaggerated primness while they twirled the ends of their moustaches. Some of the younger women leaned over the verandah railing and let their long hair fall on the men's wrists when they asked them to light their cigarettes.

By the time Matron Coan returned from the post agency at Wentworth Falls, the men had stolen the hairdresser's comb and scissors, and were weaving and feinting as they chased each other around the driveway. When Matron Coan ordered the men back to their dormitory her voice was quiet with rage. She ripped the ribbons from the younger brother's hair. He claimed that she had whispered to him, 'I hope your lung breaks up like a piece of china.'

Half her female patients looked like Clara Bow.

I did not care who giggled at my spinster's vanity behind my back. I had also queued and felt the weight of my hair fall onto the floor, the sudden rush of air upon my neck.

I had watched Les Curtain leaning quietly on the stair rail beneath the verandah, holding a sack, waiting to take the sweepings for his garden. When he planted his broad beans in April, he said, he would place the hair in the bottom of the trenches, so that the little creatures in the soil which liked to nibble at roots would lose their way and die entangled in its softness. Before he stored the clippings in his locker, he told me, he had picked out the thick strands which fell from my head. These he placed in the centre of his pillow. He said he had no trouble finding them because they were the same dark shade of russet brown as the pitch which runs from beneath the white bark of a gum.

He hoped that this precaution would protect him from the other patients' dreams of missed trains and vacuum washers and Tam-O'-Shanter Oats which crawled into his sleep each night.

He said he preferred his own dreams from now on in which I curled my body like a pale vine around him.

Matron Coan had recommended Les Curtain to Dr Summergreene as a candidate for his new treament program because, she said, his condition had been stable for six weeks now. The therapy was experimental. Each morning the doctor drove the hundred feet from his house to the cure galleries in his new motor, reversing onto the road, changing the gears into drive to turn into the main gates, and spinning his wheels on the white pebbles of the driveway. He suspended a burette on a frame above Les Curtain's bed. He attached a needle to the inside of his elbow, and ran a solution of gold salt from the bottle through a long tube into his veins. 'The gold is hostile to the bacillus,' he said, 'but harmless to the tissue. It should cleanse your blood of all infection.'

That first night Les Curtain dreamed that he stood in the

fecund quiet of his greenhouse and worked at hybridising daffodils. To prepare the seed parent to receive pollen from the plant which he had chosen, he clipped off its stamens with his forceps so that it could no longer pollinate itself. Then, when the flower was fully open, he wet the tip of a camel-hair brush between his lips, removed the pollen from another plant, and dabbed it on the sticky pad which had ripened on the stigma's tip. He continued for some time at this work, until his breath was sweet with honey, and he had to return to his house with a handkerchief across his mouth in order not to inhale the bees which hummed around his head. When he looked into the mirror of his hallstand, he saw that the grains of pollen which lingered on his lips were in fact little specks of gold dust. He turned to see Dr Summergreene behind him holding forceps and a paintbrush, who laughed and told him he was nothing but a prank made out of flesh.

The second night he imagined that he walked barefoot in the desert until his bones began to quiver and he knew that he had found Lasseter's great lost reef of gold.

On the third night he dreamed that I blew gently on his stomach so that his skin floated in thin sheets of gold upon my breath and hung like Spanish moss from the branches of the gums.

After a week of this treatment, when he arrived at tea from the garden, the backs of Les Curtain's hands had turned a vivid shade of purple. Mabel Pewsey, a minister's wife, shouted out that he had contracted scarlet fever. As she leapt up from the table she had scalded Alf Parr, a young motor mechanic, with beef tea. The ambulant patients rushed back to the dormitories. Even those confined to total bedrest leaped up in the panic and stood to watch Les Curtain from the doorway. He did not move. He sat still at the table peering at his hand. Matron Coan sent urgently for Dr Summergreene and soon we heard the squealing of his car.

The doctor still wore his sheepskin jacket and flapped cap and goggles, having returned minutes earlier from his weekly flying lessons. He took a small piece of Les Curtain's skin and examined it beneath a microscope in the morgue. He determined that the sunlight had caused an odd chemical reaction with the metal and decided to discontinue the injections. But, two weeks later, Les Curtain was left with those violet stains which marked out the thick lines and knots of veins across his hands.

I knew that Les Curtain had begun to hallucinate again.

For he had said to me, as he rested his hands on the table, 'There are jacaranda flowers blooming just beneath my skin.'

In the graveyard, the slabs of sandstone reflected the sun, which struck our chests and arms as we walked by so that Les Curtain said it felt as if we moved through doorways in the light and passed through overheated rooms. Clouds of crickets jumped up at each footfall, and landed with the slap of bellies on the dusty paths ahead. Near the fence the tall grass had turned to brittle stalks. Les pointed out the cats' nests there, the cool depressions where they lay and watched the birds with lazy eyes. One of them jumped up now from the hot earth piled on the hairdresser's grave.

Behind the fruit-gate, the apples were sweet and rotten in the heat, as the sun's rays burrowed to their cores.

I felt my blood become as thick as treacle when he lifted my skirt and placed his hot sex against my own.

He invited me to put my ear upon his chest so that I could hear the cooling waterfalls inside it.

It was here, in the cemetery, that Les Curtain told me, 'Some days I don't know where I am, but feel as if I am moving through a hundred different landscapes.' Once, he said, he had thought he was far beneath the ocean and the irises were jowly fish thrusting thick lips upwards to the surface. Another time, he thought he knelt in a cathedral where the pelargoniums loomed like stained-glass pennants in the sudden darkness. His hearing had grown so acute that he could trace the sounds of worms moving through deep tap-roots far beneath the earth.

Yet, he said, he felt no fear.

For the white of my uniform, he said, jumped like a dream out of the air, and seemed to float above the ground like a glass bell filled with concentrated light. When the hallucinations came upon him, he would always look up and see my skirt as white and cold as a moon on the horizon. Then he knew that I would find him.

One moment Les Curtain's lean back could be seen in the kitchen gardens pulling weeds from the trenches around his herbs. The next there was no trace of him, except for the bruised smell of basil hanging in the air. When he did not appear for tea,

Matron Coan called me to the nurses' station. She was expecting three new admissions that afternoon with their sad, slim bags, as well as their families, who would expect to be shown around the rose gardens and benches by the Captain of the Walk. In addition, she waited for the transfer of five other patients from the infirmary ward, whose neat beds and quiet fingers indicated that they had recovered from their *spes phthisica* at last. Before she raised a general alarm over Les Curtain, she said, she wished me to search for him discreetly.

The afternoon was closing over. All around that dark ridge, the mist had thickened and curdled in preparation for a storm. The cicadas were silenced by the shadow of the clouds while the bush flowers seemed like dead things pressed between the heavy pages of the sky and earth. I walked to the cliff's edge and followed the sounds of water, thinking they might lead me to his chest.

When I found Les Curtain at last, he was kneeling in a damp pocket of the cliff where the cold water leaching from the rocks had formed a tiny stream, its surface ruffled by the warm wind which issued from the bellies of the clouds. He had removed his clothes and folded them and anchored them with his mug. When he opened his mouth to speak there was no sound and his brown eyes seemed black with fever. He was so thin now that I could see the purple of his lungs as they gilled beneath his skin, and the rapid tremor of his heart. Only his sex was as pale and thick as a fennel bulb, alert and leaning on the air.

I removed my own clothes and lay down before him on my back. I braced my legs apart, as I had learned women did

from the stories men told each other in the ward. I squeezed
my eyes tight, anticipating harm. Instead I heard the click of
sticky sap and saw, when I opened my eyes, that he moved
his hands swiftly on his sex. Suddenly, his jism spattered on
my belly, thick, smelling of the dampness of the earth—like
the first hot drops of summer rain. When at last he knelt and
touched me, his hands were as slippery as light.

As he lay with his head on my belly on the mossy rocks
he whispered that he no longer thought of himself as a single
body, but as a riot of disconnected flesh. He sometimes saw
toes at the end of his bed and wondered whose they were
until he saw that they were connected to his leg. When he
asked me to map him with my hands I remember that I took
the puffy sac which hung beneath his sex, as soft as eyelids,
and found that I could divide it with my finger so that it
resembled my own sex. Then he showed me the tight seam
which ran between his legs. He said he sometimes touched it
and thought Dr Summergreene had stitched up another organ.

He was so slight now that he could sit across my hips: his
thighs were hot and shivered from the fever: he asked me to
put my finger in the icy water and open the tight flower of
his anus for only that would cool him.

Later, when he showed me how to place my mouth around
him—and flooded me—I felt little grains of gold upon my
tongue.

His own tongue was as pointed as a paintbrush when it
found the shoot between my legs.

I laughed from the pleasure of it. I felt my heart grow loose.
I knew now, from the way he had moved, that Harry

Kitchings had not known any of these things. I think, at last, that we may have performed that Great Act, as men define it. Sometimes it is difficult to remember. There have been other bodies since. I do remember that the brook stilled and the air grew lifeless and we slept. I can recall as if I am there how, when we opened our eyes, the mountain lay in its own cold shadow and the birds darted and cried, invisible, in the clouds, the sound moving back and forth as if they pulled in their beaks the last pale ribbons of the sun.

The close air around us was a startling shade of blue.

Indeed, that colour seemed to have its own life as it hung in a curtain above us, suspended, then stirred and shifted before our eyes, as thick as ground and sifted sapphires. The moss on the rocks was azure and like the powder of moths' wings to the touch. Even the sandstone of the cliff appeared to have absorbed the mountain's dark blue shadow, while the scribbly gums wore a strange bright fur of cobalt dust. It was a shade I had not seen for many years.

When I told Les Curtain we should go, he nodded and coughed a perfect jacaranda.

I caught it in my hand.

It was only as we climbed, and our palms were stained bright blue by the rocks, that I began to feel uneasy. The air was soft and granular and filled with bowerbirds which, in their greedy confusion, hurled themselves at our heads. The cockatoos were an inky blue and screamed out the love words they had picked up from the honeymooners further up the mountains. Our feet slipped on that steep path which water had once made, kicking up the thin brown soil beneath its bright blue crust. Les Curtain's head was scarcely heavier than the air as it rested on my shoulder. Sometimes he coughed up hot crimson blood which I felt foaming and trickling down my blouse. As we reached the top of the cliff I could hear men's voices shouting and the dull percussion of running feet.

We stood in the middle of a great disaster.

The patients had been evacuated from the buildings and stood out in the driveway looking at the sky. There were dunes of strange blue powder piled up on the lawns and at the edges of the paths where the orderlies were sweeping. The Captain of the Walk trained his hose along the verandahs and the wooden walls to turn them white again. Matron Coan and Dr Summergreene consulted with a policeman and two men in suits who wrote down observations in their note-books. Les Curtain and I stood unnoticed beside his tomatoes, which were dark blue and felt as tufted as peaches as they brushed against my legs.

At last, when Matron Coan saw us, she caught her breath and called two orderlies who took Les Curtain to the infirmary ward. In the nurses' quarters she helped me to undress and took my clothing, which was stained with Les Curtain's sperm and blood, out to the furnace with its great chimney where we burned infected waste. She drew a bath for me and made no comment when she saw the gold dust shining on my breasts. It was then that she told me how the government plane had whined and dipped so low over the hospital that it had clipped the roof of the nurses' quarters with its wings:

how the pilot could be seen struggling with his controls and reaching for a lever on the dash: how a hatch had opened and its load of copper sulphate had spewed into the air; how the plane had ascended quickly, banked, and then flown towards the west. She gave a thin smile as she recalled that the government men had dismissed her concerns and spoken with polished words about the crop-dusting trials on the fields beyond the mountains, even as they held their handkerchiefs up to their streaming eyes.

I slept for several hours. When I came down to the common room, I found Matron Coan seated at the table, eating peanuts and writing her report up for the board. She looked over her spectacles and told me that Les Curtain was gravely ill and had been scheduled the next morning for an experimental pneumothorax. In this new treatment, a needle was inserted into the lung to collapse it to allow the unused tissue to heal. She said that she and Dr Summergreene hoped that it would eventually supersede the need for exposure to fresh air.

When I returned to my room, I sat by the window and watched the lights burning in the men's infirmary ward for half an hour, before I drifted in and out of an inconstant sleep. Around midnight the storm burst overhead. By morning the rain, sheeting and sluicing to the bottom of the valley, had washed the blueness from the grounds.

In Katoomba, where Matron Coan had insisted that I rest for several weeks, my eldest aunt sat on a commode chair in her nightdress and nodded in the heat. Her eyes were reptile sharp but accorded me no recognition as they followed motes of dust around the room. The white cotton on her breast flinched every few minutes when she took a breath, as if an electric current had passed unbidden through her skin. My youngest aunt said that her sister's demeanour sometimes worried her so much that she found she had forgotten to breathe for long intervals herself. Although she was lonely, she told me with a tired smile, she no longer went out walking to the shops on Main Street. For there was nothing to see, she said, since she had reached the age where she mistook every face she saw for another she had lost. The week before, she had even thought she saw my mother as a girl, with brown limbs and soaking hair, in a group of children returning with their teacher from the baths.

When she heard that I loved Les Curtain and that we would be together when he recovered, my youngest aunt kissed me and said that before she died she might yet change her view of men. I hugged her back and laughed and told her many foolish things.

Back in Wentworth Falls, I dropped the bags which she had filled with quince jelly and tinned cocoa on the end of my bed in the nurses' quarters and headed towards the infirmary ward. The leaves had turned in the she-oaks outside Dr Summergreene's house so that from that distance, through the mist, they resembled paper lanterns filled with yellow light. The steam from the laundry moved like a thick white cumulus along the ground beneath the gauzy stratus of the fog. The air was cold. Walking across the threshold, I was struck by the stale warmth of bodies and tobacco.

As I approached Les Curtain's bed, I could see that he was sitting straight-backed against the pillows, holding a whispered conversation with the old man in the next bed, who pretended to swing with an invisible cricket bat at a phantom ball. When the man stopped and looked up at me and cleared his throat, Les Curtain turned around and saw me. I moved the cigarette cards and tobacco pouch and phosphorous matches from the chair beside his bed. The terrarium had spilled dark grains of soil onto his bedside table. The ward was quiet as I sat down. The other men watched us with amusement in their eyes.

At last I spoke first and asked him how he felt.

'Fair to middling,' he replied, and glanced up quickly at me. Although he was weak his eyes no longer shone with fever. Instead, they held the irritation of a boy who fears that his mother might stroke his hair or face.

I observed that his tan had faded, leaving a sallowness which sharpened the lines around his mouth. I noted how, beneath the blankets, his hands and knees were drawn tight together, no longer drifting as I spoke until they touched me, warm and eager and filled with a secret tenderness, as if they wished to find and stroke my voice. We sat in silence a little longer. When Les Curtain finally looked up I could see in his face that he found my looks bitter, prematurely aged. I rose. I said, 'I suppose you will be returning to your greenhouse.' He glanced sideways at the ward. His voice was a murmur. He rubbed his neck. He said that he was planning to embark on a new venture with his cousin when he recovered, breeding four-leaf clovers, which he hoped would make them rich.

A year later, as I stood with Matron Coan in the moonlight beneath a clear sky on the last night of my employment and laughed as each of us tried to spit date pips further into the weeds at the edges of the kitchen gardens, the furnishings caught fire in the west wing of the Hydro Majestic in Medlow Bath.

Perhaps it was due to the honeymooners' bellies rubbing together in the darkness like dry flints, or the fact that there was no hope of heavy snows which tasted of champagne, or because we no longer felt a European dampness in the air. Or perhaps something else had faded during the last season from the mountains.

For that night, 25th August 1922, sparks jumped onto the sweetheart sofas and made glowing holes which spread across the watered silk. The curtains bellied in the heat, touched the flames, and turned into blazing veils of light. The parquet flooring warped until the little rectangles of wood jumped from their settings as if they had been prised loose by the heels of tango dancers. The lightbulbs blackened and exploded. Inside their long display cases in the hallway, the hot pins in the butterflies' stomachs popped out of their backing cork. The brittle insects caught the backdraught underneath their wings and flew upwards through the broken glass. The first groundsman who came upon the scene said that he saw them darting like bright parrots beneath the ceiling mouldings until their wings ignited into golden streaks of light.

Soon the lawns were filled with running feet. Someone battered at the pine trees with an axe. The waiters tried to douse the flames with Baden-Baden waters from the tank room. At the other end of the hallway the grand house, which had once been owned by a man who discovered gold, was lit up from within. By the time the fire brigade arrived, the flames had already broken through the windows.

Inside, above the roaring of the fire, the strings of a piano snapped and echoed, as if the ghost of Bertha Krupp played Wagner with her fists.

—— *16* ——

It was one of those winter mornings, which had not occurred for many years, when the damp wound itself around Katoomba and the mist from the valleys threatened to hang sluggish in the streets all day. I stood on the station platform and smoked a cigarette. Shaking out the match, I had knocked my knuckles hard against a bench: the pain was intense and oddly personal, for the cold had made my fingers brittle. I swore softly in the way I had been taught by Matron Coan. I did not care who heard me talking to myself.

Although the season had not yet started the platform was crowded with sightseers from the city who had come to view the ruins of the Hydro Majestic and were heading home now with their pockets full of ash and marble. The stink of smoke like bacon bones was caught in the lace and flannel of their clothes. Some spoke of how the cliffs had blazed like limelight in the darkness, although they could not have witnessed this, for the fire had been controlled by morning and the crowds from out of town had only turned up later in the day. Besides,

I recognised this description from the *Echo*, which had offered word sketches of the fire from different angles, including the filigree effect of flames and trees the reporter had obtained by standing on the Great Western Road. I listened scornfully to these breathless men and women and ground the cigarette beneath my heel. Now, however, at a great distance from the Blue Mountains, I find I must remind myself that I too was not present on that night: that I did not see the clouds of smoke, rising and gathering slowly on the glowing ridge, bellying crimson and orange, as if in imitation of a summer sunset.

Further along the platform a group of young men played bowls with a row of beer bottles and a round sphere of marble, still bearing the polish of many hands, which they had cracked from the bend of a broken staircase. When the stationmaster came out to caution them the crowd refused to part. They jeered at him and changed the signs above the benches and moved the hands of the clocks around behind his back. At last he was forced to retreat into his office where he shook his head as he pulled the heavy levers.

The day after the news of the fire appeared in the Sydney papers I had received a note from Harry Kitchings. It was an odd letter. It made no mention of his wife and offered no account of the last hard years in the city, although I had heard that he had continued to produce his viewbooks in spite of his ill health and struggled to sell them in the shops. There was no suggestion of apologising for his silence. At the first sight of his handwriting on the paper I had fallen back, momentarily, on ingrained habits of interpretation. He said that he wished to return to view the damage. I wondered if he made some veiled allusion to my heart. Yet as I forced my eyes to slow I saw the words *Hydro Majestic* and *catastrophic fire*.

He had written as if the last seven years since we had last spoken had not occurred at all—as if he had just returned after a short absence from some expedition in the sky, the clouds caught like the ghosts of icebergs on his plates of glass, to request my company at some film or musicale. He had asked if I might come to the station to meet his train. I had agreed by telegraph. When I told my youngest aunt she looked up from the newspaper without surprise. She offered to keep me company although we both knew she would not, for recently my eldest aunt, who slept in her commode chair all the time now, did not allow her to breathe at all if she walked outside the house.

There was a hot press of steam before the train pulled in. When the doors were opened some of the crowd, thinking it was the train to Sydney, rushed forward while the conductors shouted and the passengers tried to force their way out with their luggage through the throng. Then, as the young men threw back their heads and began to hurl mournful howls into the air, imitating dingoes, I saw Harry Kitchings standing on the steps, his spine stiff with disbelief.

For some time I made no attempt to catch his eye and took a secret pleasure in watching as he searched for me. Then he turned and smiled and waved, threading his thin shoulders through the crowd, navigating by my face. His chin was pointed at my heart. Yet, when we stood together, we were held by our old shyness. We stared at one another. He did not take my hand. I did not kiss his cheek.

I had planned to greet him with some sharp comment—
'Thank you for your letters,' or, 'Won't you ask me how I
passed the war?' Now his silence was like glass. I could not
choose the first place to dig in. Instead I said, at last, 'Two
strange old rocks, that is what we are, each stuck to our own
side of the valley. We cannot stand like this all day.'

There was a brief release of tension beneath his skin. He
held me with his gaze and I noted the unrelenting kindness
in his eyes. Then—he could not help it—they slid away into
the distance as he caught the scent of mountain through the
mist.

Harry said that he would like to visit the Three Sisters
before we headed on to Medlow Bath. As we drove in a taxi
down Katoomba Street some of the older people recognised
him and raised their hats. Each time he smiled with surprise
and lifted his hand to wave, turning stiffly in his seat to watch
them out of the back window until they disappeared from
view. His broken fingers hesitated, unremembered, before his
chest, as if he meant to make some blessing, or a shadow
figure, in the air.

We passed the office of the *Echo* where my mother had
sent me in her place to collect her cheques from Mr Thornelow's eager hands; the church where Harry had looked up
from the doorway and seen the war massing darkly in the sky;
the pavements where, shortly after he had married, I spent
desperate evenings following Miss Moon's trails of broken
eggs just to see where they would end. A tar sprayer backed
and turned ahead of us, preparing the streets for the new
season. The taxi stopped and shook and grumbled on its tyres.

On the other side of the road, separated from us by a new expanse of pitch, was Harry's old studio, owned now by Mr Fowler's nephew.

'A fine young man,' Harry said. 'He wrote me once to ask me if he could purchase some of my old negatives to make fresh prints and display them in the windows.'

Harry had posted him the negatives, refusing to be paid. Now he bent and squinted in the effort to see his pictures through the mist. He did not know that they had been turned into postcards and put on sale to tourists with no mention of his name. None of the townspeople had remarked upon the theft. Used to thinking of the mountains through the frames of Harry Kitchings' sight, they had not even noticed it, for when they looked at his old photographs they merely recognised the landscape. They saw no art in them at all.

I was surprised to find I lacked the will to tell him. For when I received Harry's letter I had wished to find some way to hurt him. I had thought I would throw Les Curtain at him and make him read the knowledge of men's bodies in my face. I would force him to recognise the changes he had wrought: the careless way I had of brushing back my hair, the graceless postures of my hands and feet, the bitter summations which leapt quickly to my lips. I had planned to tell him that just outside the edges of his photographs there had always been spinsters and shadowed lungs and little deaths which issued from the failure to be seen. Now I was silent as I sat beside him in the car.

I had noticed things which drained the anger from my blood.

On the platform I had seen that Harry Kitchings no longer walked as if he had the light bones of a bird. Instead he placed each foot carefully before the other while his hands seemed to feel like a blind man's for some railing in the air. It was as if he stood once again with the keeper of Jenolan Caves upon a thin deck floating on the darkness and read the way with his fingers by the cording of the ropes. I had seen him start and wince as the young men swarmed and pressed around his body at the station like a waterfall of bats. Yet, at fifty, he had retained the firm set of his jaw. The skin, as thin as gold-leaf now, had drawn itself back around the symmetry of bone. I had thought, when he first looked towards me, that I saw a fleeting trace of love pass across his face. I wondered if I had been allowed a glimpse of his old feelings in the unveiled architecture of those nerves and muscles. At close range, however, his face refused a sense of definition. It seemed softer, more remote, as if a layer of cloud had slipped beneath the skin to take the place of flesh.

As we headed up the steps towards the car, Harry had seized the back of my hand, and squeezed it, his palm as swollen and tender as a bruise against my own tight skin. For a minute he had stopped and rested his whole weight upon my arm while his fingers twitched between my own in response to some internal shock. There was nothing sensual in this gesture. My mother and my eldest aunt, I remembered, had clutched me in this way. When I asked Harry what was wrong he had answered that he felt a twinge of indigestion. But he looked at me with an old man's eyes, from which the tears sprang easily, as if permanently irritated by the light. I could smell the fear upon his breath. I could not help regarding him with a nurse's gaze.

I had seen his expression many times in the faces of the dying.

He had come because he wanted me to give him back his life.

We took the road that had been put through the grounds of the old Harding estate. The house still stood among the drifts of needles from the radiata pines. But the door onto the verandah was no longer open, although once the corridor had showed as a polished triangle in the centre of the darkness and the rooms on either side seemed barely held together by a seam of light. Running beside us to the left a hawthorn hedge with pale new leaves had begun to grow where the road had cut the orchards off and would eventually rise to block the view. On the other side of us, the remaining stands of hazelnut trees grew thin and leafless to the tennis court where the tops of the net posts were barely visible above the weeds. The rectangle of wire around it gaped, red with rust at the edges of the hole, where someone had pushed the heavy grass roller out into the valley so that it crashed and tumbled like an elephant down the mountainside.

Around the corner, a new row of red brick houses, set high up from the ground, extended all the way to Echo Point.

There were several cars already in the cul-de-sac, when we pulled in at the lookout, filled with disappointed tourists who complained that because of the mist they could not see the view. A middle-aged couple drank tea out of a thermos. A little girl slid through the gravel like a skater on the outside edges of her shoes, until she fell and her mother picked her up and spanked the damp dust from her dress.

Sitting with his head cocked and his feet out of the car, Harry remarked that it was no longer possible to hear the Katoomba Falls, which were once so full that they had gushed like champagne down the distant cliff. He made no effort to walk to the railing of the lookout. However, when the driver asked if we wanted to move on, Harry said, 'Not yet.'

At last in the face of this blankness I began to speak to conjure up a version of the past before him. I recalled how he had stood, a thin black shadow, on the top of Orphan Rock, his hands in his back pockets to show his nonchalance, as he planned his photograph. I remembered the awkward angle of his camera; the way he placed his foot upon a step of rock and bent his knee, stretching the other leg behind him, until he was balanced in a fencer's lunge; the taut arc of his back; the press of his chest as he leant into the air; the jumping green and purple space beneath. The sharp click of the shutter echoing off sandstone.

'I put my camera there?' Harry had asked, incredulous, as if he could no longer recognise the place.

He sat, straight-backed, and stared into the void. His eyes seemed glazed, unfocused. It was a look I had seen on the faces of older patients, who told me later that they had experienced their own souls as a kind of dark penumbra muffling their faces and had found themselves peering, fascinated, in order to see through to the outer edge to find out where they disappeared. I wondered if I should offer him sal volatile or give an order to the driver.

'There is nothing but cloud,' Harry said at last, returning to himself.

Then, like a magician's handkerchief, the mist slowly lifted to reveal the dark bulk of the Three Sisters. Against that softness their stepped sides were rough with scrub and grass. The family in the Daimler crowded over to the valley's edge where they leaned on the railing and laughed and shouted at some raucous joke. I heard the dull snap of a Kodak shutter. When we reached them I thought for an odd moment that I saw one of the ribbons which my mother and I had thrown into the air many years before, limp and drained of colour, caught upon the smallest crest, as if it had been returned to me now by the complicated motions of the valley winds. Looking again, I realised someone had tied a pair of women's bloomers to a stick and climbed the sandstone cliff to plant it.

It was then that Harry turned and said that we could go.

The mist had begun to peel itself from the ground and we drove on through a band of thinner air beneath dank palms of cloud. At the Great Western Highway we had to wait for a line of cars which wound their way past the intersection towards the burned hotel. Many of the drivers had left their headlamps on. Beads of water ran across the glass, lengthening into clear threads which trembled like tears along the full length of each chassis.

Heading west, as the traffic crept and surged, the driver rode the brake, so that at one moment Harry and I were thrown forward and the next we were pressed back in our seats. Each time, Harry's damaged hand went up before my chest. It was the habitual movement of a man for whom space has contracted until it reveals itself only in its capacity to wound. Yet I was touched. It was my heart and not his own that he had covered.

To each side of us, on the edges of the road, Harry pointed out the pale scars where paths had once run steeply through sharp scrub and scribbly gum to forgotten streams and caves. When he looked at this landscape now, he said, from the window of the car, he saw only undistinguished bush. But back then he had judged the distances by burned tree stumps and the nests of bowerbirds and the different notes the water-falls made as they splashed upon the rocks. Sometimes the tracks split around great stones as smooth as river pebbles, where the feet of children had picked another way around a step, or they dropped through the bushes to lower paths, where young men had allowed their legs to run ahead of them like water, grabbing at tree roots as they skidded down a slope, seeking the quickest way to follow their desires. Often he would come upon still pools stained by lichen, where young girls held their skirts above their ankles in the tannin-coloured water and gasped and laughed as they took each icy step. At other times he would stand aside as groups of men and women marched up the mountain from some picnic, shouting shrill coo-ees and leaning on their staffs. Later, when tourists carrying guidebooks and photographs came only to see the major sights, the spiders, undisturbed, had filled these smaller cor-ridors with web. Harry remembered that even if he walked there in the coolness of late afternoons he had found his head netted in dead butterflies and silver thread, as if he wore a parody of the fancy dress women had once worn to balls.

He said he had noticed the Three Sisters fading after that, a little more each year, as if their surface had worn off. Meanwhile, the keeper of the Jenolan Caves had installed coloured lights behind the limestone arches, for the tourists complained that the jewel colours of the stalactites had dulled, from the continual use of magnesium flashlights, until they appeared to have the wan consistency of tallow. The great fans of water which once splayed over stone at Weeping Rock and the Cascades had dwindled to warm trickles. And all the time, the snapping of shutters could be heard like the distant crackle of a bushfire. Harry said he wondered if some things had been photographed too much.

At Medlow Bath, the sky was still dull and grainy with the haze of smoke; it seemed even the air wished to resemble its picture in the *Echo*. There were too many cars and carts abandoned at crooked angles along the edges of the road for us to park and walk the distance. Instead, we asked the driver to inch as close to the entrance as he could and meet us there again in half an hour. Ahead of us, a group of men pushed a car out of a ditch where it had become bogged in water which had seeped from the dousing of the fire, while other drivers jeered and honked their horns. Further up the road, I saw a horse rear when another driver, turning his head to stare at the ruins, veered across its path: a load of carrots scattered from the cart and rolled and squashed beneath the wheels of cars.

Driving from the east, there had been little sign of damage. Now, as we walked up the muddy path to the casino, we took full account of the devastation. In place of the west wing, there was a skeleton of bricks and pillars on a long charred piece of ground—as if a zeppelin had crashed and ignited as it tried to breach the cliff.

The firefighters' motor pumping engine had shattered the long white marble fence which ran along the road. Within the grounds, the lower limbs had been hacked off many of the pines and the lawn had been torn like the baize of a billiard table by boots and ladders. I could only recognise the wreck of the reception building by counting the three chimney stacks and noting the position of Les Curtain's iris beds where they had fallen. Hundreds of people moved about the ashes, stooping now and then to pick up forks and bed-knobs and coloured glass and the gilded corners of picture frames. Some of them posed for photographs on the charred remains of sweetheart sofas. A workman, recognising Harry, told him how the crowd had cheered when the last gable exploded and fell in.

'Half of the hotel,' Harry Kitchings said and shook his head. 'Half of the curved film in a panoramic camera. Gone.'

As we picked our way through the fallen bricks, I held his arm to steady him. I marvelled at its lightness.

At the farthest edge, behind a buckled wall, we came across an unburned shed. I recognised the man who stood before it, slightly bow-legged, using a jemmy to prise the rusted lock, as another, older man urged him to be quicker: he was one of the two Turkish boys, grown up now, whom I had glimpsed on my first visit playing in a bathtub full of mink. I do not know what the older man expected he might find there, but when the lock was broken he sneezed and ordered the Turkish workman to bring the objects out into the light. There was an old X-ray machine and three light boxes and some barrels of Baden-Baden water thick with dust. Then, entering again, the younger man had shouted out with fear, so that the three of us rushed in behind him. At the back of the shed I saw two shrivelled figures sitting in the darkness, naked, staring out at us with glassy eyes. I saw a crown and a trident lying beside them on the ground. We left the two men arguing and shouting, trying to make sense of these remains. For we had recognised them at once as the Medlow Mermaids, the stuffing spilling from the stitches in their skins.

We walked back along the valley rim, past the peeling signs which pointed to the Lover's Walk, the Sun Bath and the Colosseum. Beneath us the old mining tunnels extended through blackness to the valley floor. To the south, far out beyond the balustrade, the low band of stratus cloud kept the light too weak for the cliffs to cast their shadows. The mountains which encircled the Megalong Valley were a faded shade of blue. We stood beneath the wire of the flying fox. Harry did not even try to follow it with his eyes out into the sky. I thought I heard him say, 'All the love has gone,' beneath his breath, but I did not ask.

I preferred my own stories and illusions.

From behind us I could hear the sound of laughter as children made horse jumps out of charred planks and chased each other through them. I heard the rough exclamations of the city girls. No one else had joined us to look out to the sky. It was as if, for once, we all concentrated on the present without longing for some transformation to take place. Like Harry, I wanted to make the others see the memories which lingered: of members of the Russian ballet balanced on the edges of a fountain; of wet sheets and enemas and knee baths; of Potage du Roi, a scrambled poem on a hand, and the resemblance of an orchid to the human heart. On the other hand, I did not think, on the whole, that sadness was such a bad thing to give up.

'I am quite tired,' Harry Kitchings said.

He hunched over and grasped my hand, a desperate holding on to flesh.

The next day, when I came to meet Harry so that we could walk together to the station, the manageress of the guesthouse told me that he had been taken to the hospital during the night. She asked me who would take his luggage and pay his bill. She said the commotion had disturbed the other guests.

The ward was a dim room in a far corner of the building. I recognised the day nurse, a young Scottish girl, who had worked for a brief time at the sanatorium until she had been married. She said that Harry had been diagnosed with a perforated ulcer. He was receiving morphine for the pain, but he was febrile, his lips were cyanosed, and his pulse was rapid and weak. I knew from these details that he would not recover. She said she had some difficulty convincing him to let her call his wife until, an hour ago, he had at last consented.

We walked over to the bed where Harry lay, as thin as a mummy, beneath the tight white sheet.

His lips were slightly open, as if they waited to be kissed.

His broken hand lay outside the covers, palm up, the fingers pointing to the ceiling. I do not know if he reached for an imagined touch or if he thought he still held the shape of the wire as he rode the flying fox out across the valley.

That purple writing was still unreadable on the back of his hand, which did not flinch when the nurse put her fingers to his wrist.

T he *Niagara* is yawing. It rolls from side to side at the same time as it plunges up and down, and onward to the north. I have carried with me the negative which Harry Kitchings gave me, wrapped in old silk in the bottom of my trunk, out of cowardice perhaps, but also in the hope that one day, in a new place, I might look through those ghost trees without sadness and at last know that my heart has chosen its own home. Here, on the deck, as I hold it up to the clear sea light, I notice that one edge of the image has begun to lift up from the surface of the glass. If I found the courage I might pick at the gelatine with my nails until the whole picture flaked away and danced out across the ocean, darting and flashing on the wind like insects' tiny silver wings. The roughness brushes my fingertips and whispers. Then I remember. It is as brittle as those dried secretions which love leaves on the skin.

In my lap I also have the Ensign Carbine: the bronze weight of it, neatly closed upon itself. When Harry's effects were sold off at his wife's request, in a stuffy auction house in Camperdown, I pushed to the front of the crowd and bid for the camera without shame. I waved my hand and rapped the tip of my umbrella on the floorboards. I felt the young men nudge and smirk beside me. I did not care. I made sure that I was noticed. I had recently sold my aunts' house after their death and there were thick wads of pound notes curled and banded in my purse. I remembered the hazy blooms of dampness Harry's hands had left upon the metal, which dried up almost as soon as they appeared.

The waiters move around me and stack the other chairs, for the wind is brisk and I am the only passenger on deck. They have grown used to my daily presence here: this heavy journal, the camera, the little rectangle of glass I hold up to the light. I sense their contempt, when they notice me at all. They do not offer tea.

Lately, in the darkness of my room, I have taken to unfastening the catch at the back of Harry's camera and slipping a new dark slide like a magician's card into the snug space which is revealed. I have begun to stand with the camera open on my palm, peering down into the viewing crystal, at the edges of the groups who play flirtatious shuffleboard and quoits. I have even carried it beneath the hatches which hide secret stoves and boilers. I have attracted no attention. Between breaths, when the impulse takes me, I let my finger squeeze the shutter. So far these experiments have resulted in a collection of sly gestures caught upon the glass: the white hands of thieves gliding into pockets; forbidden morsels slipped beneath a waiter's tongue; the meeting of men's lips. Bodies are oddly cropped and framed by the edges of the glass.

Each night I move these rectangles about, as if they are pieces of a jigsaw, at once fragmented and suggestive. They hint at some compulsion which has remained unseen, even as it made its order felt. It has occurred to me that if I gather enough of these tiles and arrange them correctly I may assemble another ship, a ghost liner made heavy by history and yearning, which sails within the shape of the *Niagara*. Each night I dream of the bilge water, thick with weed and jellyfish, which slaps and shifts its weight within the hold.

There are brown stains in the sink in my cabin, left by the chemicals I decant and stir. The maid scrubs and curses in another language, although she does not complain or enquire to my face. Nor have I commented on the limp towels left hanging on the bath rail, or the gaping corners of the bed-spread which, once she has gone, I quietly retuck. I wash the negatives and imagine a silver trace, as thin and shiny as the mucous ribbon which a snail draws in its wake, unfurling in the sea, marking my passage through the different colours of the oceans.

At dinner I sit next to an ageing actress in a beaded hat who tells me, 'It is only now, too late, that I understand how to play young girls,' and I butter my roll and nod and listen to the cargo sliding far below. I have noticed that people often confide their sorrows to me in this way, drawn perhaps by some quality of watching, or recuperation, in my face; but the next morning on deck they regard me with blankness when I greet them.

I have thought of continuing in this way, drifting around the globe, slipping along gangplanks from one ship to another, until there is no more space for labels on my trunk. Yet when I hear talk of certain things—of hungry men and women pressing through the streets of London, slapping the chests of police horses with pale hands; of automobiles parked in certain alleys in New York with secret liquors fermenting in their tyres; of cases of British ribbons, uncrated, forming nests for rats on Indian docks—I begin to feel an itching in my fingers.

I remember how Harry Kitchings once taught me the rules of composition as he held his cool fingers in a frame around my face. Between his hands, at either end of a seesaw of light, I saw the black forms of the Three Sisters balancing dark storm clouds far out in the valley. He said, *This is the thing to aim for: to hold the gaze. The world the frame offers is complete.* Yet, perversely, my eyes were drawn to the creases in his thumbs. On the contrary, I think it may be useful to take photographs which act like hinges in the air. I have thought, if I find the right place, the right quality of light, I might take photographs so painful that they make people want to look away; that they will feel the urge to enter and put right the world they represent.

As I stand at the railing of the *Niagara* the wind whips my hair around my face so that it flies out in all directions of the compass. The air is so luminous it bulges. It is poised, on the horizon, like a great water drop, trembling on the sharp lip of a cliff. Or a blue lantern slide, shot through by light, aglow and waiting for an image.

—Eureka Jones, 1926.

ACKNOWLEDGEMENTS

S ome readers may have recognised much of the life of Harry
Phillips, the Blue Mountains photographer (1873–1944), in
the character of Harry Kitchings, especially if they have found
his superb viewbooks in second-hand dealers in the Mountains,
or read Phillip Kay's biography, *The Far-Famed Blue Mountains
of Harry Phillips* (Leura: Megalong, 1985). Yet, while Harry
Kitchings' career follows that of Harry Phillips very closely, this
is by no means meant as a portrait of the man or his life. The real
Harry Phillips was a popular man who had, by all accounts, a
happy and equal marriage to Isabel Jane Thompson. The couple
had a daughter, Isabel.

A number of real historical figures and institutions from
Katoomba during the period 1907–1922 walk through the
pages of this fiction. These people include Mr Medlicott,
Alderman Bronger, Nurse M. Coan the corsetiere, and Mr
Fowler. Among the actual institutions featured are the Fresh
Air League, the Katoomba Nigger Minstrels, the *Blue
Mountain Echo*, and the Katoomba Amusements Company.

Again, these are not intended as accurate portraits.

The motto and verse of dedication of the Fresh Air League in Chapter 3 are taken from the minutes of the League, which are lodged in the Mitchell Library. The lines of poetry which Eureka and Mr Medlicott laugh at in Chapter 5 are taken from one of Mr Fowler's advertisements which appeared frequently in the *Blue Mountain Echo*. The poem about germs which Mr Medlicott recites in Chapter 8 also appears, unattributed, in this newspaper. *Spes phthisica* is described in Lewis J. Moorman's *Tuberculosis and Genius* (Chicago: Chicago UP, 1940). Julia Horne's article, 'Travelling Through the Romantic Landscapes of the Blue Mountains' (*Australian Cultural History* 10, 1991), had a strong influence on my thinking about this landscape.

The following people have been very generous with their time and advice as I researched this book: Colin Slade and Kerry Leves, who gave me advice on gardening and Victorian domestic life in the Mountains, and who showed me the spirit drawings in 'Lilianfels'; Mary Shaw, who allowed me to look through the old Bath Books and clippings from the Hydro Majestic and talked to me about her grandfather Mark Foy while we fed the horses; and John Low, the local studies librarian at the Springwood Library, who helped me in numerous ways with research, and drew my attention, with a writer's eye, to a number of Blue Mountains oddities, including Dr Muskett's writings on Mountain Air and the Medlow Mermaids. I am also indebted to Michael Isaachsen from the Melbourne Museum of Printing, Footscray, who explained the printing processes Harry would have used at this time, and showed me a working linotype-machine; and Alan Elliott, from the Melbourne Camera Club, who shared his research materials, discussed photographic processes with me, and showed me how to use old reflex cameras. The following people also helped with research: Peter Otto, from the English Department at the University of Melbourne, Gwen Silvey from the Blue Mountains Historical Society, Davina Gibb at Scienceworks, and Liesl Bladin and Professor Harold Attwood, the Archivist and Curator respectively of the Medical History Unit at the University of Melbourne. Of course, the responsibility for how this information has been used is entirely my own.

The Service of Clouds was completed with the assistance of an Australia Council Special Projects Grant. I also wish gratefully to acknowledge a fellowship at Varuna Writers' Centre, Katoomba, from the Eleanor Dark Foundation, which enabled me to research and work on the novel at Varuna— in particular, I want to thank Peter Bishop for his advice, enthusiasm, and our discussions which were very important to the early shaping of this book. Thanks also to Beth Yahp, Paul Gillen, Bernard Cohen, Nicola Robinson, Judy Horacek, Tom Flood and Sharon Jones for making me feel so welcome in Katoomba. And to my agent Fran Bryson, Cassandra Pybus, Nikki Christer, Kerryn Goldsworthy, Brenda Walker, the English Department at the University of Melbourne, the Creative Media Department at RMIT, Mark Rubbo and the staff of Readings, Carlton—and my mother—for encouragement along the way.

I would like to thank Frank Moorhouse, Jonathan Carter,

Fran Bryson, Eleanor Hogan, Andrew Kaighin, and Alan Elliott for reading and commenting on early drafts—and Judith Lukin-Amundsen for her gentle and perceptive editorial advice.

Finally, thanks to Richard Harling, for his unfailing insight and support.